The Magnolia

League

KATIE CROUCH

poppy

LITTLE, BROWN AND COMPANY
NEW YORK   BOSTON

Also by Katie Crouch

Men and Dogs

Girls in Trucks

Poppy

Hachette Book Group
237 Park Avenue, New York, NY 10017
For more of your favorite series, visit our website at www.pickapoppy.com

Poppy is an imprint of Little, Brown Books for Young Readers
The Poppy name and logo are trademarks of Hachette Book Group, Inc.

The publisher is not responsible for websites (or their content) that are not owned by the publisher.

First Edition: May 2011

This is a work of fiction. Characters, places, and events are the products of the author's imagination and are not to be construed as real. Any resemblance to actual events or persons (living or dead) is purely coincidental. Although some names and real entities and places are mentioned, all are used fictitiously.

Library of Congress Cataloging-in-Publication Data

Crouch, Katie.
The Magnolia League / by Katie Crouch.— 1st ed.
    p. cm.
    Summary: After the death of her free-spirited mother, sixteen-year-old Alexandra Lee is forced to move from Northern California to Savannah, Georgia, to live with her wealthy grandmother, who expects Alex to join a long-standing debutante society, which, Alex learns, has made a pact with a legendary Hoodoo family.
    ISBN 978-0-316-07849-8
    [1. Debutantes—Fiction.   2. Grandmothers—Fiction.   3. Social classes—Fiction.   4. Voodooism—Fiction.   5. Savannah (Ga.)—Fiction.]   I. Title.
    PZ7.C88513Mag 2011
    [Fic]—dc22   2010042997

10 9 8 7 6 5 4 3 2 1

RRD-C

Printed in the United States of America

This book is for Phoebe.

AND UNDER THESE CONDITIONS
PROTECTED BY THESE SPELLS
THE WOMEN IN THIS LEAGUE
SHALL SERVE THE BUZZARDS WELL.

—Signed by the Founding Members of the Magnolia League,
May 12, 1957

1

You know what I hate? Sweet tea. Actually, I wouldn't call it tea; I'd say it's more of a syrup. Ninety-eight percent sugar, with a little water thrown in so you don't totally shrivel up and die in this torturous heat. It makes you fat just to pick up a glass, and then leaves your teeth rotten after one sip. Leave it to the crazy citizens of Georgia to flip out over a drink like that.

Other things that aren't so great? Georgia summers.

Georgia boys. My grandmother's rules. My entire new freakin' life in Georgia.

I know, I know. I have a bad attitude right now. Reggie would say I'm being a buzzkill. And if I had a buzz to kill, he'd be right. So, please, don't hate me— I mean, really, this sour, bitter Alex is a new thing. Back in California, I was always a *hey-the-grass-is-green-right-here* kind of girl. But I'm not in California. As you might have guessed from this pity party of mine, I'm in Georgia. Savannah, Georgia, to be exact.

I've been here for two weeks, living in my grand-mother's pre–Civil War, twenty-three-room mansion on Forsyth Park. She's tiny, but the ceilings and doorways seem designed for giants. As for practicality . . . well, six bedrooms, seven bathrooms, a gallery, a ballroom, and a carriage house—all for one lady. And the decor? It could be truly rad, but she's pretty much gone with the doily look. Think Southern fussiness meets the Addams Family. I've seen funeral parlors cozier than this place.

According to my grandmother and her lawyer, I'm doomed to call Gaston Street home until I'm eighteen. I'm sixteen now, so I guess that means I'm here for two more years. I'm pretty sure that's longer than a stiff jail sentence for dealing weed.

"Alexaaaaandria!"

I'm Alex. That's what everyone but my grand-mother calls me, so that's my real name. But I can't seem to get her to remember that.

"Alexaaaaandria! Are you up here?"

I *am* up here. Yup. I'm sitting on the railing of the upstairs porch, trying to get a little pot out of this pipe. It was the last present my boyfriend, Reggie, gave me, and I'm hoping that somehow it'll make it feel like he's here.

I hear her heels clicking around the rooms. I haven't seen her in any shoes other than heels. Always in a designer outfit, always in heels. Don't be fooled, though. My grandmother is a ninja with brass knuckles, dressed for a tea party.

"I'm out here," I call.

The footsteps slow for a moment as she homes in on her target. Then the pace quickens as she comes in for the kill.

Rap-rap-rap-rap-rap-rap-RAP.

Here she is: my grandmother, Mrs. Dorothy Lawson (first dead husband) Lee (second dead husband, and my mom's dad). By the way, Mr. Lee, I've just been informed, descended from the famous Confederate general. Not exactly a direct descendant, but a cousin's cousin or something. It's kind of crazy, because that's my last name too.

She just goes by Miss Lee now. Doesn't want me to call her Grandma, because it "ages" her. That's cool with me. And truthfully, she does look pretty young to be a grandmother. Her dark, shiny hair (no gray in sight) is tied back, with some perfectly placed tendrils escaping around her oval face. There are a few laugh lines (not that I ever see her laugh) around her dark green eyes, but other than that, her face is pretty much as smooth as mine. She is what Big Jon would call "doll pretty"—meaning she looks so delicate that it seems you might break her if you shook her hand too hard.

"Alexandria, it smells like a skunk daaaiiied up here." She has one of those Southern accents that manages, despite the region's reputation for hospitality, to be completely disapproving and unfriendly all the time.

"It's the herb," I say.

"The what?"

"It's pot. I'm smoking pot."

My grandmother puts one hand on her hip and points a surprisingly young-looking finger at me with the other. All available body parts seem to drip with jewels.

"Are you trying to per-tuuuuhhb me, Alexandria?"

"Sort of."

"Well, if you're goin' to smoke, at least smoke tobacco. I've got stock in Philip Morris, which means, since you are the sole heir to my estate, you do too. Anyway. Pahhh-lease dress. Your Magnolia sisters will be here this afternoon. I've arranged for two girls from your debutante class to come over shortly after my meeting."

"I *am* dressed."

"Alexandria, you are wearin' rags."

"I'm wearing shorts. And this is vintage. Look: the

4

Grateful Dead, Greek Theatre, 1985. Arguably the Dead's sickest show ever. This shirt's probably worth, like, fifty bucks."

"Please, Alexandria."

"Miss Lee, what they see is what they get."

My grandmother narrows her eyes. When she does that, they look black. It's a very frightening effect, as if the pupils have taken over.

"All right," she says. "If that's how you'd like to play this."

"Play what?"

"Oh, you'll see eventually, Alexandria. I'll call you when they're here."

Her footsteps click down the hall and, as if by magic, suddenly disappear.

2

Magnolia League Meeting, Number 417
Mrs. Lee presiding
Refreshments: Mrs. Buchanan

"So? What do we know about her?"

"Well, she looks just like her mother."

"That's a good start. Louisa was a lovely girl."

"But there's something wrong with her *hair*."

The Magnolia League meeting room is dark and cool, despite the scorching August heat outside. The League occupies a trim brick building on Habersham Street. It was built in 1826 by Isaiah Davenport, and in 1864—when General Sherman attempted to make it the headquarters of his godless occupation—he was met on the front steps by eighty-five-year-old Matilda "Marmy" Davenport, who said, "I just washed my floors, and no damn Yankee is going to scuff them up unless it's over my dead body." After that she took out a gun and shot herself. (Her pistol still hangs in the front hall as a testament to the decisiveness of Savannah women.)

As is the custom for the monthly meeting of the officers of the Magnolia League, the ladies, save Miss Lee, have arrived promptly at four o'clock. After handing their bags and parcels to the caretaker, Lucius, they gather around the long, carved mahogany table. A pitcher of sweet tea sits on the sideboard next to a large red velvet cake prepared by Mrs. Julie Buchanan. No one understands exactly why she attempted to make something as complicated as a red velvet cake, but a Magnolia Leaguer would rather die than bad-mouth a sister's cooking. There is plenty of tea to wash it down and, really, at least she didn't try to pass off store-bought as her own.

Lucius is as old as Methuselah. He can no longer cope with some of the heavier packages, and Lord help him if anything falls on the floor. But he is trusted, and that is worth its weight in gold, flexibility be damned. The monthly meeting of the Magnolia League is the tent-pole event around which Savannah's most influential women organize their calendars. All of Savannah's business and politics pass through there, whether officially or not, and while the *Savannah Morning News* would never dream of being so tacky as to ask after the meetings, that free weekly paper once tried to send a well-dressed spy to infiltrate. Lucius doused her with pepper spray that he kept on hand for vicious dogs, and to this day, six years later, he still brags proudly that the Savannah police hadn't dared to arrest him.

The League is tiny and exclusive, a fortress of etiquette and calm in the hectic modern world, and its ramparts are manned by the Senior Four: Dorothy Lee, the president and founder; Sybil McPhillips, the League vice president and wife of the Honorable Tom McPhillips, Georgia state senator; Mary Oglethorpe, treasurer; and Khaki Pettit, who, despite having a wide variety of opinions on all subjects, has never had any interest in an office and therefore does not hold one. These are the key members of the League, and their places at the table are marked with name cards. The other members— the daughters and granddaughters of the Senior Four who have already "come out" into society at debutante balls—sit wherever they can. Despite the fact that outside this building they are business owners, doctors, wives of bank presidents, and well-known philanthropists, on Habersham Street they are nothing more, or less, than Magnolias. Within that context, first there are the Senior Four, and then there is everyone else.

Before Mrs. Dorothy Lee arrives, the gossip is a free-for-all. Today's topic: Alexandria Lee.

"It's matted."

"No, it's locked."

"Her hair is locked?"

"Dreadlocked. That's what Hayes calls it."

"Deadlocked?"

"Lucy, darling, are you deaf?"

"Well, it does look like something died in there."

"And have you seen her clothes? All that girl's taste is in her mouth."

"Bless her heart, she's young."

"So is Hayes, and—"

"They can't all look like your granddaughter, Sybil."

Sybil's granddaughter, Hayes, was generally accepted as the very model of a modern junior Magnolia League member, and her grandmother couldn't help agreeing. Hayes is practically perfect in every way except for a slight overbite, and Sybil plans on having that fixed for the girl's graduation present, or maybe even her Sweet Seventeen. The only serious problem with Hayes, as far as Sybil is concerned, is her gratuitous boyfriend, whom Sybil refers to only as "That One."

"Bless her heart, she is chubby."

"That can be fixed. Is she on the up-and-up?"

"She smokes hashish."

"It's marijuana, honey."

"That's how they do in California."

"Well, it's not how we do down *hee-ah*."

"Not unless you're one of those scags on River Street, anyway."

Just then there is the sound of expensive heels pattering the hard oak floor. The ladies immediately hush as Miss Lee sweeps into the room. She regards them briefly, pours herself a large glass of sweet tea, and sits at the head of the table.

"Hello, Miss Lee," the ladies say in a chorus.

"Good afternoon, girls." Miss Lee regards them for a moment and smiles. She removes her purple silk jacket, stretches her thin, pale arm forward, and takes a tiny key off her charm bracelet. As the other Magnolia League members watch carefully, she uses it to open the ornate box in front of her, and then lifts from it a gold necklace with a dangling ivory pendant that is intricately carved in the shape of a magnolia. A sigh of envy fills the room as Dorothy grandly places it around her slender neck.

"Meeting to order."

"Order!" the ladies chorus enthusiastically.

"Now, what were y'all talking about in here?"

"Your granddaughter," Sybil says flatly.

Miss Lee raises her eyebrows. "Well, don't let me stop you."

"Dorothy, she is such a healthy, healthy girl, bless her heart, but do you really think we can get her ready in time for the Christmas Ball?" Mary Oglethorpe asks.

"Whatever do you mean, Mary?"

"We don't want to offend you, Dorothy," Sybil chimes in. "But the girl is a wild child, and we can't have her tarnishing the image that our young people, and my Hayes in particular, have worked so *hard* to main*tain*."

Miss Lee's eyes wrinkle at the corners as if she is about to laugh.

"Sybil, honey. Don't be daft, now. She's a little rough around the edges, but that's what sisterhood is all about. I'm sure Madison and Hayes will have her polished up in no time."

"This isn't a game, Dorothy. If she doesn't take, there are consequences."

"I'm well aware of the consequences," Miss Lee snaps. "I don't need you reminding me. My daughter was a victim *of* those consequences, and if you think I've forgotten what happened to her, then you're a damn fool."

Silence falls over the room.

"Does she even want to be a Magnolia?" Mary asks.

"Good Lord almighty, Mary, she is sixteen years old. She doesn't know what she wants," Miss Lee says. "But it's not a matter of *want*. She *is* a Magnolia, and she will sit next to me at this table come hell or high water."

As a practiced politician herself, Sybil is able to keep her expression as pleasant and serene as a day on the lake. But underneath the table, she clenches her fists so hard that her knuckles turn white and her nails dig into her palms.

"Believe you me," Miss Lee continues, "as her grandmother, I'd like nothing more than to let Alexandria go right on back to California. The girl rides a bicycle all over town, her hair is ugly enough to haunt a nine-room house, and she'd argue with a wall. But you know as well as I do, ladies, that Alexandria Lee doesn't have a choice. We all made our bed decades ago. And now, just like the rest of us, she's got to lie in it."

3

So, the obvious: I did *not* grow up in a mansion on Forsyth Park in Savannah, Georgia. My childhood was
more of an Allman Brothers song than a Southern prin-
cess storybook. I was born in Mendocino, California, in
the back of a VW bus, and my mom was a pretty Deadhead named Louisa Lee. She looked a lot like my grandmother, actually. Same high cheekbones, green eyes,
shiny brown hair, and tawny skin. But she was healthier-
looking than Miss Lee is. More exotic. The kind of

beautiful woman you see on a trail with a backpack on, hiking with her dog.

Me, I'm shorter and rounder than both of them. I have the same eyes, but my hair, when it's not dreaded, is a complete frizz fest, and my skin is nowhere near the creamy alabaster color of theirs. Plus, I put on ten pounds if I even look at a grilled cheese sandwich. My mom used to say that I'm "voluptuous." I'm just hoping it's prolonged baby fat.

Most likely I take after my dad, whom I've never met but who is someone—or something—called "Wolf Man." The only thing Mom ever said about him was that he was good with the herb and a real hit with the ladies—probably in the parking lots of Phish shows. Whatever.

I've never missed having a father. That's because I grew up on Rain Catcher Farms, a communal organic farm north of Mendocino, and that place is always crawling with people. Some of them come in for the harvest, but others, like my mom and me, stay for years. And I don't know why anyone wouldn't want to stay forever. It's awesome. I'm a big reader, and I don't use words lightly, so when I say *awesome*, I mean that the place, when seen, elicits true awe because of its beauty. The farm is in a small, lush valley, with gold-and-green mountains on one side and the Pacific Ocean on the other. Everyone eats and hangs out in the Main, a pretty, old carriage barn filled with books and plants and hammocks; beyond the gate, a mile-long white-gravel road leads to a stretch of pristine, wild beach.

Mom and I lived in a cabin in a grove of redwoods near the Sanctuary, the root garden she created. She was the RC's root doctor. People came from all around for Rain Catcher tinctures, and our products contributed a nice amount of money for the commune. Her garden, a lush, quiet, magical spot, was hidden from the world by a high wooden fence. It was the sweetest place anyone could imagine. The walls were covered with vines and flowers so thick they were woven together, like pretty knots of unkempt hair. Inside you were only allowed to talk in a whisper, as it was her theory that plants grow better in the quiet. She was always saying that the ground is alive—that one must work with Mother Earth and not just use what she has to offer. Sometimes Mom would simply sit under the trees, listening to the leaves rustle. "They're whispering to me," she'd say. To her, the life cycle of plants stood for the connection between the living and the dead.

As soon as I was old enough to crawl, I started working in the RC fields. Instead of *Sesame Street* songs, I learned the ins and outs of how to grow organic broccoli, kale, potatoes, beets, even bananas—basically anything that comes out of the ground. As I got older, Mom let me participate in what she called her "rituals." Mostly, these were homeopathic medicines and treatments. For instance, did you know that red-onion root is a sure cure for early colds? Or that gingerroot tea will make your period come if it's, as my mother would say, "stuck"? We'd make soaps and tinctures and tonics to heal anything from fevers to warts to depression. My mother's fingertips were always stained green. She smelled of grass and cloves.

She had other remedies, too, that seemed to require more than just herbs and berries. For instance, when I was seven I developed a terrible wheeze. We went all the way to a doctor in San Francisco, who said I had asthma and gave us a bag full of inhalers and pills. I remember that when we came back, my mother put the bag on the kitchen table in our cabin and looked at it a long time. Then she picked up a knife and led me outside by the hand and had me stand next to a young eucalyptus tree. She took the knife, put it over my head, and cut a hole in the tree that was even with my hairline. After that, she cut a lock of my hair and put it in the hole. She closed her eyes and began mumbling and singing, rubbing the rough stone she always wore around her neck. As soon as I grew taller than that hole, my asthma disappeared.

She kept many of the recipes secret. She wouldn't say why exactly, but I guess that some of the effects were too powerful for just any old person to be able to access. Nor would she ever tell anyone where she had learned these skills. All sorts of theories floated around the RC—that she'd studied in China and had a PhD in botany, for example. But whenever anyone asked how she knew so much, she would answer only with a dazzling, mysterious smile.

My mom died almost one year ago. When I found out about the accident, we were playing Hacky Sack—me, my friend Billy, and some college girl. The RC always has college kids who come for the summer, and they all kind of blend together, but this one I remember perfectly. She was a hippie, and she was trying to play the game with her shirt off.

"She's like her own personal volleyball court," Billy said. Billy could be really obnoxious. He loved to pinch my fat, and he made fun of anyone he could. Still, I'll always be grateful to him for making us all laugh just then, because that's about the best thing I can think of to be doing when you get news like I got that day.

I didn't know right away, of course. But I knew to stop laughing. Something was really, really wrong. Wendy, Big Jon's daughter, came up to us looking scared and interrupted our game.

"Alex," she said, "Big Jon needs you at the Main. The cops are here."

I thought someone had narced on us. See, the RC is known for its holistically grown organic produce and herbal tinctures. But to be straight, it's also a pot farm—just a few plants, but enough to make Big Jon, the owner, some money, and definitely enough to make everyone nervous when helicopters fly overhead.

My mom and I didn't have anything to do with that. Still, along with everyone else, I knew about the shady agriculture at the RC, and I was thoroughly trained in *just-in-case-the-feds-come* scenarios.

"Plants?" I was going to say. "What plants?" I'm pretty good at keeping a straight face, so as I walked into the Main behind Wendy, I was silently practicing what to tell the police. But it turned out that wasn't what they were there for at all.

Big Jon was crying. He's a big, jolly Santa Claus kind of guy, so this behavior was pretty alarming. When he saw me, he pointed to his favorite easy chair, which no one gets to sit in, ever.

"Alex," he said, "I'm afraid I got a bad trip for you. I'm so sorry. Go ahead, sweetheart. Sit on down."

Even thinking as hard as I can about that afternoon, I can't remember exactly what those policemen said. Instead, I have only little details and phrases. For instance, I remember that one officer had a birthmark on his forehead in the shape of a crescent moon and that the other had cheeks as shiny as waxed apples. I remember trying to make sense of the words themselves, because the whole story wasn't working for me. "Orr Springs Road." (*Ore?* I thought. *Like gold?*) "Hairpin turn." (*Mom uses barrettes, not hairpins.*) "Instant death."

(*Instant coffee?*) "Wouldn't have felt a thing." (*Huh, that's what I hear happens on a good LSD trip.*) It took a couple of days for me to fully comprehend that my mother's old VW bus went off Orr Springs Road while she was driving back from the hardware store in Ukiah. She had driven away and wasn't coming back.

My mom's dead. It's a pretty horrifying thing to have to tell people. And yet I have to say it all the time. When I do, reactions vary. Some people want to give me a hug, which I usually refuse. Other people simply change the subject.

I wish there were better words so that I could explain everything about her in a sentence. Because if I just say, "Yeah, she's dead," you won't get to hear about how cool her shiny brown braids were, or how all the guys stared at her even though she was a mom, or how she smelled like coconuts, or how she loved to sing but had the voice of a wounded badger. You'll never know how she planned secret meetings for us in the Sanctuary, with the eucalyptus trees bending in the wind and sighing overhead. How she would tell me ghost stories about the mysterious, unnamed town she came from, or how we'd sit for hours chatting at our daily teatime, or how she taught me to make a sleep potion from valerian root and chamomile. I say "accident" and you picture a bus flying off a cliff, and probably blood and broken bones, but what you don't know is that the accident wasn't the worst part. The most terrible thing about her death was the weeks after. The mornings when, instead of waking up to my mom's horrendous, out-of-tune singing and the smell of cinnamon-spiced coffee, all I heard and felt was silence.

Reggie walked into the RC on the two hundred fifty-seventh day of my fifteenth year, exactly four months after my mother died. I know that because I've been counting the days without her. It was a Thursday, and it was raining. I was in the kitchen, listening to the rap Cook likes to put on. My job on kitchen shift that day was to chop enough carrots for forty-five people. It gets old, prepping food for the RC. I like to do it in a rhythm. *Wash, peel, chop. Wash, peel, chop.* I go pretty fast, so when a hand looped in and grabbed a carrot coin, I almost took off my own finger.

"Watch it!" I said. I didn't look up. I was mad at having to chop, mad at freeloaders who came in and put their fingers in the food when we were clearly working to get the meal done.

When he didn't answer, I finally glanced at the culprit. There he was. Tall, lanky. About nineteen or twenty. Arms swinging like loose ropes.

"Sorry," he said, grinning. But obviously he wasn't sorry, because the next thing he did was reach in and grab another carrot. And my heart? It flipped out.

It would be a huge understatement to say that my

mother's absence had left a cavernous hole in my life. In fact, even on that day of the carrots, I'd awoken to a wet pillow. I cried so much I didn't even *know* when I was crying anymore. So Reggie, with his loose limbs and crooked eyes, came into my life at just exactly the right time to take me somewhere else.

"You want to get high?" he said, still munching.

I didn't, really. I've never been into pot, actually. Mom used to say it breeds perpetual laziness, and I've never liked the way it makes my mouth and my mind feel as though they've been stuffed with old cotton balls. But anything seemed better than crying into the carrots, so I said, "Okay, yeah. Sure."

Every couple days he'd come find me to get high. We'd talk about music, or I'd listen to his stories about the stuff he'd done. I mean, the kid had been everywhere. He'd run a hotel on some island off Thailand, fought fires in Switzerland, studied with Buddhists in Nepal. I never got tired of listening. He was just so . . . *cool.* Then one day about a week after he arrived, he put his arm around me. I remember that his body smelled strange and distinctly unfeminine — like onions, dirt, and beer.

"Listen, Pudge," he said. That was Billy's nickname for me. Much to my annoyance, Reggie had picked it up. "I heard about your mom. I'm really sorry."

"Thanks." I stared at the ground so he wouldn't see the tears starting to form.

"I totally know what you're going through," he said.

"What do you mean?" He had mentioned that his parents lived in San Diego. Were they dead?

Reggie looked away. "My girlfriend died last year. In a plane crash. So I know what it's like to lose someone."

"Oh, I'm sorry." God, here I was feeling sorry for myself all the time. But it wasn't like *other* people didn't have problems. "How? A big crash? Was it in the news?"

"Oh no. It was a small plane. No one heard about it. In fact, I never tell people because it makes me too bummed. But you're special, so..." He flipped his hair out of his eyes. "Anyway, I feel your pain. It's tough."

I nodded. The tears that before had been just a threat were now a mortifying reality.

"Oh, man. Sorry, Pudge," he said. "Here. Sit on my lap."

Pretty soon, a weird thing happened. I began thinking about Reggie so much that it was almost impossible to let anything else into my crowded brain—including how sad I was. I had never really cared about guys before. Some of the older ones were cool, but mostly what mattered to me was what kind of jokes they made or whether they were mean to me or not. But Reggie! He'd bring his guitar to the lawn and play us the most awesome songs about all of the places he had traveled.

He'd left home at twelve to circumnavigate the world on his friend's boat. He was an ordained minister, a trained chef—not to mention a thoroughly skilled pot farmer, which is most likely why Big Jon kept him around.

"You're the only person I can talk to, you know, Pudge," he'd say, making me feel as if I were a key member of some secret club. "You're really great, you know that?"

Of course, I hated it when he called me Pudge, but I knew he was just kidding. It was like our own private joke. He didn't *really* think I was pudgy. He couldn't, right? Because if he did, what was he doing hanging out with me all the time, taking me behind the Main for joints or down to the beach for long talks over Big Jon's horrible apple wine? And then there was the time, about a month after he showed up, that he took the tangy glass pipe from my lips and pushed me down roughly in the sand. I was confused, thinking it was a mud ball move, but then Reggie looked at me really strangely and leaned over and put his tongue in my mouth.

It was sort of weird, honestly. Almost a little gross. I'd had no idea a tongue would taste like that—an alien invading my mouth. But it was Reggie, so after a minute of being wigged out, I figured this was cool. I was kissing someone! *Yesss!* Truly, it was a great day. Which meant a lot after so many crappy ones.

Of course, I wanted to tell everyone right away. Gossip at the RC moves pretty fast. I knew everything would instantly change. "*Pudge?*" Wendy would say when Big Jon told her. "With String Bean Reggie? No way!" But Reggie said I couldn't tell anyone. At least, not at first.

"I'm still getting over the plane crash, Pudge," he'd say. "I'll get there. I promise. Just . . . not yet."

It was hard for me, of course. But everyone deals with grief in different ways. I definitely knew that. Besides, it wasn't like I wasn't seeing enough of him. Once we started hooking up, I could count on meeting him at least a couple of nights a week.

"Dunes, Pudge?" he'd say when no one else was around. I knew it wasn't straight up, but there was something exciting about it. And it wasn't like we were doing everything. I never let him go all the way. I could have, but somehow I knew my mom wouldn't have liked that. She'd always told me to wait for someone who loved me, and Reggie hadn't said that yet. I was still waiting.

But wherever Reggie was going, that was where everyone wanted to be. He was definitely the coolest guy at the RC, and everyone knew it. And now he was my boyfriend. Me, Alex Lee, the bookwormy, doughy hippie kid with the knockout mom. Only I didn't have my mom anymore. I had Reggie, and even though everything had fallen apart before, now it was okay.

Great, even. When he'd give me a secret wink at the Main during meals, or slip me a note that said *dunes at nine*, my heart would slam so hard that I'd seriously think my chest was about to explode. Nothing—not even having no parents, not even the new, crampy, incredible grossness of getting my period—could get me down. I missed my mom, but now everything was finally okay.

Which is, of course, exactly when something had to come along and ruin it all.

My grandmother's lawyer, Mr. Karr, came to Rain Catcher Farms on my sixteenth birthday. It was my first birthday with a boyfriend, and even though I missed my mom more than anything, Reggie made it pretty great. At breakfast, he gave me a big smile and even hugged me in front of everyone.

"Happy birthday, Pudge!" he yelled. "Kids, sing to her!"

Immediately, the whole place filled with a deafening serenade worthy of a drunken, tone-challenged glee club. Cook made my favorite tofu-sesame scramble, and Wendy gave me a dress she'd tie-dyed especially for me. I tried not to let them see that I was crying again, but I didn't fool anyone.

I cheered up a couple of seconds later, though. I was thinking about Reggie, who'd said he planned a surprise for my birthday. I was stoked. Would we finally be public now? I wondered. Was he ready? Or was he going to say what Wendy called the "L–bomb"? Anyway, what I'm trying to say is I was pretty preoccupied. So when Big Jon came into the schoolroom wearing an expression I couldn't read and said, "Alex, a lawyer's here to see you," I seriously thought it was a joke.

But it wasn't. No, there was nothing funny about it. Because Mr. Karr, in his perfectly pressed tan suit, wanted me to move somewhere in... *Georgia*.

We tried to fight him. Big Jon railed on for an hour about how we were common–law family. And as for me, I totally refused to go.

"No way am I going anywhere!" I cried. "I live here!"

But the lawyer just kept pointing to his papers. *Next of kin. Custody.*

"Listen here," Big Jon said. "We don't care about your laws. We love Alex, and we need her here."

The lawyer cleared his throat. His tan pants had mud on the cuffs from his walk around the farm. He was a little, round bald man with tiny, smart eyes.

"I helicoptered in, you know," he said carefully. "Alexandria's grandmother has many, many resources. And I know a lot of people. I can keep them away, or I can bring them in. One call to the DEA. That's all it'll take."

Big Jon put his hands in his pockets and was quiet for a moment. Then in a flash he pushed the books and cups off his desk onto the floor.

"You *suits!*" he yelled. "You don't care about anyone. Don't you see that's all we want? A place where people take care of each other?"

But Mr. Karr wasn't budging. "I can assure you," he said, "that Alexandria will be well looked after. Miss Lee is a very well connected woman. And Alexandria comes from a long line of debutantes. It's hard to understand outside of the South, but it's a very tight sisterhood. They look after one another."

"Debutantes?" Jon chortled. "Are you kidding me? What a crock of elitist crap."

"One call and the farm is passed over for ten years," said Karr. "Otherwise I'd put Alex on field-torching duty."

Jon gave a final roar. He hugged me so hard that he didn't even have to say he was sorry. Then he left the room.

"All right, then," Mr. Karr said. "I'm going to get a little spa time in Napa. I'll come back for you in three days."

And that's how my fate was sealed. No choices. No bargaining. Well, I guess there *was* bargaining. Because Big Jon managed to make himself a deal for ten more police-free years. And guess what? I was the price.

4

"Alexaaaaandria!" My grandmother's voice pierces my pleasant, thick blanket of sleep like a harpoon. "The guuuuurls are hee-ah!"

I sit up with a start. The pot put me under. Way, way under. This is why I'm not really into it. I feel like there's a brick tied to my face.

"Alexaaaaaaaandria!"

"All right!" I yell back. I look in the mirror. Okay, I *do* look disgusting. Maybe it's the weed, or falling asleep in the middle of the day, but suddenly my clothes look like rags. I can't face going downstairs dressed like this to be judged by people I haven't met and won't like. My grandmother bought me a bunch of stuff, all still in bags lined up against the wall. I've been trying to ignore the clothes, but now I look in the first bag and instantly regret it: There are hundreds of dollars' worth of things in there. Labels I've never heard of because I've never shopped anywhere other than the RC "mall," which is just a closet full of hand-me-downs in the Main. Anything I needed—flannel shirts, an old sweater for warmth—was there. I got everything but my underwear from that closet.

I pick up a tank top and realize it's probably the most expensive thing I've ever held in my life. I look through the bags and read the labels. Dolce & Gabbana—no clue. Marc by Marc Jacobs—even I know that one.

For the price of these clothes, my grandmother could have bought a cow for a village in Ghana. Ten cows! I should return all of these purchases right now and donate the money to Heifer International. Then I think about the people waiting for me, and I ditch my T-shirt for the Dolce sweater thing. With my cutoffs, it sends sort of an ironic mixed message, right? I fluff my dreads and jam my feet into flip-flops. Then, promising myself to return everything and donate the money first thing tomorrow, I head downstairs.

I have to say, every time I enter the main hall of the house, I get a bit breathless. My grandmother's foyer looks a lot like the one in the plantation house where Scarlett O'Hara went to the barbecue in *Gone with the Wind*. That was Mom's favorite movie. Actually, we never talked about it being her favorite; I just know that whenever she watched it, she'd get all misty-eyed. I like it because Scarlett is a badass, other than liking that d-bag Ashley Wilkes when Rhett Butler is so obviously superior. Anyway. In that last party they have before everything goes to hell because of the Civil War, they're in a house with a huge staircase that descends into the middle of an enormous hallway. My grandmother's house has a staircase like that, so when you walk downstairs, you feel like you should be wearing a hoopskirt. Cutoff jeans don't exactly fit the scene.

"We're in here, Alexandria," my grandmother calls from the parlor.

As I wander through the hallways, the sound of my flip-flops echoes off the ceiling. When I enter the room, three heads swivel to look at me: a blond one, a brown one, and my grandmother's perfectly arranged chignon.

Wow, I can't help thinking, *these girls are pretty.*

Not just made-up pretty, either. These are *seriously* pretty people. Like, people who seem to have their own personal lamp inside their skin. Scarlett O'Hara had it. Audrey Hepburn in *Breakfast at Tiffany's*, she had it. My mother had it. My grandmother, actually, has it. And now these girls—they definitely have it. It's like if it were dark out, they'd still be glowing.

"Alexandria," my grandmother says, "meet your Magnolia sisters."

"Hi," I say.

The blond one stands first. She has skin the color of milk, and her long, thick blond hair is arranged in little waves like that Botticelli painting of Venus that's super famous—the one in which she's standing naked in a big shell. The girl's wide-set eyes are the color of bottle glass. She is wearing a green-silk knit dress that looks as though it's been sewn just for her by her own personal elves, and tiny silver heels.

"I'm Hayes," she says, smiling. She has an accent like my mother's, but thicker. "Welcome to Savannah."

"Thank you."

And now the other girl steps forward. She is pale, too, with shiny, long dark hair and surprisingly blue eyes. She's wearing a very cool burgundy Chinese silk dress—vintage?—and wooden platform heels.

"Madison," she says in what I can't help feeling is an icy tone.

"Josie!" my grandmother calls out, prompting her housekeeper to appear a moment later. Josie walks with a limp and looks much too old to be keeping anyone's house. She's really nice but certainly gets no points in assisting me in my attempts to eat healthily. She puts bacon in all the vegetables and offers me pie whenever I turn around. I'm pretty sure I saw her feed lard to the cat.

"Sweet tea for the girls," my grandmother says. "And are y'all hungry?"

"Always," Madison says.

"Just bring out something light, Josie. Do we have any of those cheese straws left over from Sunday? And that cake Molly Stone made? And a little of that crab dip if we still have it." I wince, tallying up all the calories in my head.

"Yes, ma'am."

"I'll just leave you girls alone, and you can get to know one another."

"Sure," I say, although for once I'd rather she stayed. I don't particularly like my grandmother, but at least we always have a topic of conversation: *For the love of God, let me go back to California.*

Josie reappears and sets down a silver tray laden with a pitcher of tea and plates of food. I back off, expecting these tiny girls to do the same, but Hayes grabs the entire plate of ham biscuits and puts it in her lap. I pour myself a glass of tea and take a sip, nearly gagging. What does it take to get a glass of water in this house?

"We like our tea pretty sweet down here," Hayes says, watching with a smile.

I nod, trying to neutralize the sweetness with a

cheese straw so intense it could double as a cat-sized salt lick. I lean back into the sofa—then, noticing their ramrod posture, sit up again.

"So," Hayes says, "how's the transition going?"

"Horribly," I admit. "Not to be a whiner, but it's hot as hell, and I miss my boyfriend."

"A boyfriend?" Hayes says, her eyes lighting up. "Madison, she has a boyfriend."

Madison bites into a cheese straw.

"I have a boyfriend too," Hayes says. "Madison prefers to play the field."

I look at Madison. She chews at me.

"Huh," I say.

The conversation lies down and dies.

"A boyfriend in . . . California?" Hayes tries.

"Yup."

"We were wondering what you think of the guys here."

"I *don't* think of the guys here. I'm going back as soon as I can."

"Ha!" Madison contributes.

"Well, I think you'll like Savannah after you give it a little time," Hayes says patiently. "It's always good to be where you belong."

"No, see, I belong in Mendocino. I was born there, so . . . basically, I'll be going back ASAP."

Madison sneers. "Us country cousins'll try to survive without you."

"I'd love to hear more about California," Hayes says, cutting her off. "Tell me about it."

"Well," I say, trying to ignore Madison, "it's beautiful. Kind of foggy. It's never hot or humid on the coast. Also, I didn't have to go to regular school. I basically lived on a commune and read great books and smoked pot and had awesome friends and a great boyfriend. What else could I want?"

"A shower?" Madison says under her breath.

"Madison..." Hayes says.

"Gee," I say sarcastically, "for Southern girls, you're kind of rude."

"Gee," Madison shoots back, "for a California girl, you're kind of a cliché."

"Listen, this is sort of an awkward way to get to know one another," Hayes says. "But what we want you to know is just that we're so glad that you're here. The Magnolia League is a real sisterhood, and if you just give it a chance, I know you'll fit right in."

"Thanks, but—"

"Hey, some of my brother's friends are partying out at the Field tomorrow night. Why don't you come?"

"That's okay," I say. "I'm busy."

"Doing what?"

"Well..." I rack my brain. "I've never read any Flannery O'Connor, and I figure now's probably an appropriate time."

"Alex," Hayes says, "I know you think your situation is bleak, but, please, don't sit home reading a book on Saturday night. It doesn't have to be that bad."

"It's really nice of you girls to ask me. I appreciate all of this sisterhood and whatever. Seriously. Very cool. But no, I don't want to get to know this place. Honestly, I plan on vacating as soon as possible."

"Don't let your mouth write checks your ass can't cash," Madison says.

"What do you mean?"

"She doesn't mean anything," Hayes says. "Think about it. I know the Field's not a particularly glamorous proposition, but I think you'll have a better time there than you'll have sitting alone in your room."

"Thanks very much. But I'm pretty sure I'll pass."

"All right," Hayes says. She and Madison exchange glances and rise at exactly the same time. "Well, I suppose we'll see you later."

"Right. At school or whatever." I walk them to the entrance and stand in the doorway as they drift prettily down the steps toward Hayes's Mercedes SUV.

"Hasn't anyone told your parents there's a global-warming crisis? Not to mention a recession."

"Magnolias are a bit impervious to economic hard times," Hayes says with a chuckle. "But you're certainly right about Mother Earth."

Mother Earth. Weird. That's what my mom used to call it too.

"'Impervious to hard times'?" I say, incredulous. "*All*

of you? Well, eventually that sweet Southern luck is going to run out, and you'll have to deal with reality."

Hayes hesitates thoughtfully and then waves, as if she hasn't heard me. The girls climb into the SUV and, with a great V-8 roar, peel out onto Savannah's dark, slow streets.

5

"So," Hayes says, checking out her lovely image in the rearview mirror. "What do you think?"

"I don't like her," Madison replies.

"You don't like anyone."

"She's obnoxious, judgmental, and ungrateful. A self-righteous know-it-all with roadkill on her head."

"But she *is* an MG," Hayes says, using their shorthand for a young Magnolia Leaguer — a Magnolia girl.

"She's not an MG. She's a punishment. Clearly we

committed a crime in a previous life. Anyway, what's the plan?"

"If you checked your e-mail, you'd know," Hayes says as she stops at a light. Picking up her BlackBerry Curve, she IMs a to-do list to Madison. Again. Madison picks up her phone, reads the screen, and frowns.

"Bonaventure Cemetery? Twice in one week? Jesus, Hayes, these midnight crawls are making my eyes puffy."

"I underestimated how much Sybil needed for next week, and she flipped, which means my mom flipped, which means I need more goofer dirt, which means you're coming with me to Bonaventure," Hayes says.

"Your family drama is prematurely aging me."

Hayes drums her fingers on the wheel.

"Even with that awful hair," she says absently, "you know . . . she *has* it."

"That doesn't mean we have to be soul sisters."

"But don't you think she's got it?"

"Yes, yes," Madison says impatiently. "All nature, no nurture. She's so wonderful."

"You're just jealous of how hot she is," Hayes says, at which they both burst out laughing—Madison so hard she ends up spraying the dash with Vitaminwater.

"No, but seriously, what a little ingrate," Madison says, wiping the dash with a sock. "Dropping into that crash pad? Not to mention her future position."

Hayes blasts the air conditioner to ward off the brutal August heat and weaves her car through the streets like a pro. It's not easy. Savannah is a beautiful old city, but the cramped downtown has twenty-two public squares, which means almost all of the streets are one-way. The canopy of live oaks stretched over the winding streets casts ghostly shadows in the late-afternoon sun. Madison watches neighbors chatting in the squares, walking their dogs, sitting on benches and fanning themselves. In Savannah, no one's going anywhere fast.

"So, is your brother going tomorrow night?" Madison asks nonchalantly.

Hayes ignores her and turns up the Taylor Swift song that's playing.

"Hayes," Madison says. "Hayes?"

Hayes starts singing along to "Fearless."

Madison turns the music down. "I don't mean to get all Kanye, but you need to hear me."

"The last time you got near my brother," Hayes says, "you put him in the hospital."

"Not on purpose. I'd never hurt him on purpose."

Nothing from Hayes.

"I'm sorry," Madison says. "You know how sorry I am."

Hayes's face softens. Madison bumps her fist against Hayes's where it clutches the wheel, and Hayes's knuckles start to unclench.

"Come on, Hayes-ee. MGs for life. Yo?"

Hayes smiles.

"There's my li'l gangsta," Madison says. "MGs got respect. We don't stab each other in the back—"

"We stab each other in the front," Hayes finishes. "Holla."

Madison sits back, satisfied. Hayes turns the music up again.

After a bit, Madison says, "I wish *I* could go to California."

"Probably overrated."

"It's just that we're so *trapped*."

"If you want to see it that way," Hayes says. "But you know how I see it? I'd rather be a big fish in a small pond than a nobody in California."

"Savannah isn't a pond. It's a puddle."

"We can do anything we want here. You heard Alex, and she's right. There are people struggling out there right now. They have to shop at, like, Urban *Outfitters*, Madison. But as long as we play by the rules, we never have to worry."

"I'd trade," Madison says. "I would. I'd go live on that hippie dirt pile in a second just to be free."

"But she's not free," Hayes says. "Out of all of us, she's the least free. You wouldn't want to be in her shoes."

"That's because I don't wear flip-flops."

"Just give her some time. She'll be good for us. We'll be better as a threesome."

"I hear threesomes are overrated," Madison says.

"Gross. Anyway, we need to get her to the Field on Friday."

"Because it's a mega-happy roller coaster of fun," Madison trills. "You'll let Jason feel you up in his dad's Suburban, and I'll watch the idiots swill Coors and blast Black Tusk. If we're lucky, maybe some freshman will manage to set his car on fire again."

"Madison," Hayes says, "you have a very limited imagination. Let's use this as an opportunity. We're in charge of making her a Magnolia, and there's no time like the present. She'll be our little back-to-school project."

Madison snorts. "That dirty hippie is no little project. She's a Gulf of Mexico cleanup mission."

"You *love* a challenge. Besides, think of who she is."

"She *is* her mother's daughter," Madison says thoughtfully. "And everything she hears about the Magnolias will be spoon-fed to her by us. It actually has possibilities in an evil kind of way."

"That's my li'l gangsta," Hayes says. "Now, let's get manis at See Jane and then stop by 700 Drayton to see if that hot bartender you like is working. At midnight we'll head out to Bonaventure Cemetery for some goofer, and then tomorrow we'll be *totally ready* to start showing our little hippie just how fun being a Magnolia can be."

6

Once the girls leave, the house is deathly quiet.

Fine, okay. I have no friends here, I know no one, and I really should have probably said yes to that party thing. Still, if there's one thing Mom taught me, it was to be true to myself.

"Pick a path and stick to it," she'd always say. She hated it when people flaked on things, or when I'd leave something unfinished. She wasn't brought up that way, she said. Although she'd never talk about exactly how or where she *was* brought up. Whenever I asked about it, she'd just say, "The past is past."

Mom. I can't even imagine her here. Every time I talk to Miss Lee, I just want to say, *Seriously? This is your mother?*

"Miss Lee?" I call. My voice echoes down the hallway. No answer. "Josie? Helloooo?" I do a lap of the mansion (no small feat) from the top floor to the basement. Safe for now—no one's home but Jezebel, the cat, one of those super-fluffy Persians that would disappear if it rained on her. She stares at me with disgust.

"What, you're a snob too?" I ask.

She gives one petulant meow and slinks away.

So the house is empty—meaning that right now is the perfect time for trying to find out more about my grandmother and this hellacious place. Not that I haven't already searched the entire house. My grandmother, though, must have known that as a curious teenager with bad manners I would do exactly that, because the most incriminating things I could find were some photos of her as a debutante. No pictures of Mom, no family photos. Just a lot of group shots of the original four Magnolias. Oh, and bank statements. Hayes was right. My grandmother doesn't have to worry about this recession thing. She's certifiably rich.

There's one room, though—at the very end of the second-floor hall at the back of the house—that's always locked. Strangely, there's a large framed Escher

43

puzzle on the door. The room must have been my mom's; none of the other bedrooms contain any of her things. I've never tried the full-on break-in, because Josie's always here. But must be grocery shopping at the moment, so now seems as good a time as any.

I tiptoe down the hall to the door in question. I've tried the knob at least fifty times, but I do it again anyway. It's still locked. Why would my grandmother lock it? Okay, she was hurt when Mom left, but is locking away all her things in her room really necessary? This house is a fortress—I have no idea where a key might be. Although I have noticed that one of the room's windows has its own little decorative iron balcony. It's about eight feet to the left of the main second-floor porch. That's too far to jump, of course, but there's a drainpipe between the two porches that might—if I grow some major cojones—serve as enough of a foothold to enable me to hop from one balcony to the other.

"Miss Lee?" I call again. "You want to ask the Magnolia sisters over for dinner tonight? Maybe I'll make my famous California wheat gluten veggie balls?"

Nothing. She must really be gone. I flip my legs over the porch railing and, taking a wide step over two stories of free fall, place my foot onto the drainpipe and then hop onto the ledge of the balcony next to the locked room's window. No one's on the street below except a curious dog, which stares at me with unmistakable boredom. Okay, I haven't killed myself—yet.

I peer through the window. Bummer. The view is blocked by thick drapes. I press my nose against the glass, but there's not even a crack in the curtains to peek through. Reaching into my pocket, I pull out the nail file I swiped from my grandmother's bathroom. Reggie taught all the kids this trick: To break in through a window that's not bolted, just slip something flat and long in the opening. (He told me he learned that while doing a stint as a cat burglar in Paris.)

"Alexandria, *what* do you think you are doing?"

I swear, the woman's voice could freeze boiling tar. My grandmother, looking immaculately groomed, is leaning over the porch railing, peering at me from my left.

Having grown up in an environment where there are about 6,748 ways to get into real trouble daily (the feds discovering the farm's illegal crop, being attacked by a wildcat or a shark, getting lost in the woods), I've long thought it best to just say what I'm doing—legit or not—when asked.

"I'm trying to break into Mom's room," I say evenly. "I don't think it's fair that you've locked up all of her stuff. I am her daughter, after all."

Awesome line—too bad my voice is trembling. Sometimes it really sucks being a girl. Tears always seem to come at the *worst* time.

"That's not her room anymore," my grandmother says, her voice softening very, very slightly. Have I managed to bring a little radiation to the polar ice caps? Is it possible?

"I don't believe you."

"Believe what you want. But you'd better come off that balcony. It's decorative, at least one hundred forty years old, and most certainly not up to code. I know you're anxious to leave the house, but not in a hearse, I expect."

"Well, I'm just about in here, so —"

"Sugar, I have a few things of your mother's for you, but you're going to have to come off there first."

"Okay," I grumble. I raise my leg over the railing.

"Good God! I can't watch." She clasps her jeweled hands over her eyes.

"Don't sweat it. I know I seem hefty to you, but I'm actually not bad at this." I bound from the balcony to the drainpipe to the porch. "We had a climbing wall at the R.C. Okay. You can open your eyes. I'm here now."

"Mercy." She takes her hands from her face. "All right, good. Follow me." She turns around abruptly, her dress swishing behind her, and walks back into the house. I follow her down the cavernous hall into the carpeted sanctuary of her bedroom. Actually, it's less a bedroom than a luxury suite, complete with a dressing room, an ornate, silk-draped canopy bed, and a sitting room with a pretty little white desk. Almost everything is silver, including the wallpaper, the brocade fabric on the bed, and the chandelier cascading from the ceiling. Of course, there's also a small, fully stocked silver bar with two silver stools. The bar is lined with crystal decanters. My grandmother pauses before leading me to her closet, opening it grandly, and pulling out a long cream-colored dress.

"Here," she says. "This was your mother's."

I shake my head, not understanding. "Wait, she was *married*? I thought—"

"No, dear, this was her debutante dress," my grandmother says patiently. "Magnolia League Ball, 1989."

"Huh." It's hard to believe we're talking about the same woman. My mother lived in hemp skirts and jeans and tank tops. She'd take one look at this thing and use it for curtains or something. As dresses go, though, it's pretty rad. The material is silvery white, covered with a sheath of gossamer lace and embroidered with intricate beading.

"Wow. Are those real pearls?"

"Of course. Here. Take it."

Cautiously, I take the dress in my hands. "Miss Lee, this is really awesome of you. But you do know there's no way I'm doing this whole ballroom thing."

"Alexandria, you have not yet been invited to do the 'ballroom thing.'" She smiles coolly. "So perhaps you should rein in your haste to reject an invitation, hmm?"

My grandmother takes a key off her charm bracelet, drifts over to her large walnut jewelry box, and opens it.

Even from here, I can tell it's seriously stacked in there; the jewels wink in the soft light of the lamp. She reaches in and draws out a surprisingly modest bracelet made of dimes.

"This is for you," she says. "Your mother made it."

"For art class?"

"Something like that," she says. "It's supposed to bring good luck."

"Too bad she wasn't wearing it the day she drove off a cliff."

My grandmother inhales sharply, looking at me in horror.

"I'm sorry. That was a terrible thing to say. I don't know what's wrong with me." Miserably, I put the bracelet on my wrist. Weird—it's way too big.

"It's an anklet, actually," Miss Lee grumbles. "Well. That's all I wanted to show you." She looks in the gilded mirror, composing herself. It's so odd—in this light, she could be as young as my mother was when she died. "And please bathe before dinner. It appears to have been a while."

"Fine." I turn to go.

"And one more thing, Alexandria..."

"Yeah?" I hesitate by the door.

"This is your home and I want you to be comfortable here, but the rules are to be followed."

"Meaning?"

"If a door is locked, my dear, *you are not welcome there.*"

7

When I wake up in my new room thousands of miles away from my old life, I'm feeling more than a little negative. Let's face it—I miss Reggie. So, to cheer up, I drag myself out of bed and go to the kitchen to brew a bath tincture Mom would have made: some orange slices, cinnamon bark, pine straw, rosebuds, cloves, and nutmeg. See, Mom taught me that taking a bath is about more than just washing off dirt. "It's a time for spiritual renewal," she said. "Purifying and strengthening your soul." Before every bath, she'd mix up a batch of ritual herbs and salts. Salt, she said, is derived from the passion of God—it comes from his tears. Mix it with water and you'll clear all forms of negativity. Then by blending the mixture with herbs and oils, you can anoint your aura in order to shape your fate.

Today, I ponder as I blend my mixture over the stove. There's no question what part of my fate I'm trying to shape. Obviously, I'm seriously jonesing in the love department. Josie, who is sitting at the table with her coffee (she doesn't drink sweet tea either), shoots me a questioning look but doesn't bother to ask why I'm cooking up a pot of straw first thing. I take my batch of brewed herbs upstairs, put it in the bathwater with a cup of salt, and soak, chanting the mantra Mom taught me:

> *Salt and rose and spirits,*
> *listen to what I say.*
> *Bring me my lover*
> *by the end of the day.*

I lie in there for about half an hour. Then, down below, the doorbell rings. Actually, it's more of a grand, old-timey gong sound.

"Alex!" Josie calls up the stairs now. "Visitors!"

My eyes fly open. Could the salts have worked that fast?

I shoot out of the tub and, leaving a trail of puddles

on the floor, pull on my cutoffs and favorite Phish shirt. (No way am I letting the RC-ers see me in that Dolce thing.) I run down the stairs so fast that I almost slip. But it's not Reggie. It's just Hayes and Madison again, looking irritatingly beautiful in outfits even more glamorous than yesterday's.

"Gosh," Madison says, studying my crestfallen face, "we're not *that* bad."

"Sorry. I was just expecting someone else."

"Zac Efron? Taken."

"Who?"

"Listen, we're here to insist that you come shopping with us," Hayes says.

"Thanks, but if you haven't noticed, I'm not really into mindless consumerism."

"OMG," Madison says. "*Mindless* is the last word you could apply to shopping. Clearly, you have no idea."

"Alex," Hayes says, "I know you think your situation really blows right now, but for the time being you're stuck here. You might as well make the most of it."

"Also, if we're taking you to the Field tonight, you are not going dressed like that," Madison says. "It's disrespectful to God and yourself and us and the whole concept of clothing."

"Why can't I wear this?" I look down in confusion. "The kids at the RC would have killed for this shirt.

And what's disrespectful to the world is spending so much money on clothes."

Madison bursts out laughing. Hayes kicks her.

"I really respect that you're so thoughtful about spending money," Hayes says. "But your grandmother wants us to help you pick some new things for school, and she gave us this."

She pulls a gold credit card out of her wallet. It's so new, it glitters.

"It's not even really money," Madison says. "It's plastic."

"My grandmother already bought me a ton of stuff."

"Can we see it?" Hayes asks, and before I can stop them, they're both halfway up the grand staircase. I follow. As they enter my room, Hayes nods with approval. "Your grandmother has such great taste. I love this wallpaper."

"Really?" I say. "I think it looks like Marie Antoinette threw up in here."

"Slightly gross, but that's the first joke I've heard you make that normal people might understand." Madison smiles, dumping the shopping bags on the bed.

"She's got some nice pieces," Hayes says, like a jeweler appraising diamonds. "The Marc Jacobs military jacket—that's a good start."

Madison nods. "She could wear it with those trashy T-shirts if we added some decent skinny jeans. I'll put it together for you. I'm studying to be a designer."

"See?" says Hayes. "We've got you covered. You

won't even have to buy that much. Plus, it's a way out of the house."

"Fine." I *do* need to get out of this tomb before I find myself in more trouble with my grandmother. "I'll come, but I'm warning you both: If you think this is going to be some kind of shopping spree, then you're going to be disappointed."

"If you weren't disappointing," Madison says, "you wouldn't be you."

On a whim, I hold up an old necklace of my mother's. It's a small pointed rock woven into a tiny, crude straw basket. The pendant hangs from a piece of hemp twine. Even *I* know it's a horribly ugly piece of jewelry, but my mother used to love it. In fact, I don't ever remember her without it. I found it in the Sanctuary after she died.

"And I don't care if you hate this," I say defiantly. "I'm wearing it anyway."

Madison's eyebrows shoot up. Hayes leans in as if she's going to touch it, but she stops with her fingertips an inch away from the rock.

"Where did you get it?" she asks in a hushed tone.

"It was my mom's."

"It's eco-chic," Madison says quickly. "Barely. But WTF, is that Bubble Yum on your dresser? Alex, bubble gum is very WT."

"WT?"

"White trash. I'm not being un-PC here, just

accurate. Gross. Okay, put that thing around your neck, flush that gum down the commode, and let's go."

Together, we march down the stairs into the scorching afternoon. Hayes's SUV is missing. Instead, there's a brand-new gold Prius waiting in the driveway. I look at her incredulously.

"You switched cars?"

Hayes smiles. "Sure. You made some very good points about how fuel-inefficient my truck was."

"That was . . . fast."

"I take your advice very seriously, Alex."

"Well, if you were really serious about going green, we'd bike."

"Don't push it," Madison snarls. "For God's sake—I already have to cram myself into this hippie pellet."

"It's a little hot for biking, Alex, don't you think?" Hayes says. "Just look at this as a glass that's half full. Come on. Hop in."

I climb in the backseat. As soon as she turns on the engine, the music starts blasting. It's all drum machines and processed vocals and keyboards—not an ounce of soul, really—but I have to admit I kind of like it. I stare out the window at the vine-covered houses and lush squares, taking in this new place. For about three minutes. Then our tour of Savannah comes to an abrupt end. The store, it turns out, is all of six blocks away.

"We should have walked," I say as we pull up in front of a string of boutiques on Broughton Street. The street is crowded with cars, their drivers circling as they look for parking, but Hayes parks about four feet from the curb in a handicapped spot.

"Hey, you can't park here."

"Don't worry," Hayes says. "I'm an MG. They know me."

"Who knows you? The old lady with rheumatism who's out of a parking place?"

Madison puts her finger over my lips.

"Shh," she whispers. "You're being annoying."

They lead me into BleuBelle Boutique, obviously the chicest shop on the street. As soon as we walk in, there's a sudden hush; everyone seems to be waiting to hear what these chicks are going to say. The air is cool and fragrant, as if we've dived into a very pleasant, lavender-scented swimming pool.

"Miss *Madisonnnnn!*" a man coos as he comes out of the back room. He wears a shiny pink button-down shirt, dress pants, and—if I'm not mistaken—a bit of eyeliner. "Oh! And Miss *Haaaaaaaaaayes!*" A girl brings out a tray of champagne, and the MGs swoop up glasses. Reluctantly, I take the last one, feeling suddenly unable to abstain from this preposterous ritual.

"We're here to save our friend from herself," Madison announces. "Damien, this is Alex. What do you think? Is she too far gone?"

"Hmm," Damien says, clearly perplexed. "She hasn't missed many meals, has she?"

"She's a Magnolia," Hayes says flatly. "*The* Magnolia, sort of. She's Miss Lee's granddaughter."

Damien's eyes grow wide with understanding. "Oh," he says. "Louisa's daughter."

I nod uncomfortably. How does this guy know my mom? Her favorite outfit was a sundress she made herself out of denim patches. No way she ever would have shopped here.

"What a beautiful, beautiful girl she was." He sighs sadly. "Her mother used to bring her to the old store all the time. Well. What sort of things are you looking for, Alex?"

"I'm not, really."

"The girl came from a pot farm," Madison says. "So we're pretty much starting from ground zero."

"Hey, I told you. These T-shirts I wear are *vintage*. Like this one? It's super old and belongs to my boyfriend."

"I can see why he deaccessioned it," Madison says.

"It happens to be very rare. Reggie says it's a collector's item. Surely Damien can appreciate that."

"Oh, Damien does, honey," he says soothingly. He leads us across the floor. "Alex, is it? I actually like this hippie-punk thing you have going. Very Patti Smith, but maybe too much of a good thing? Let's maybe hone that wicked little fashion weapon of yours to a razor's edge and then balance it with some pieces that'll make it sing. Rock and Republic is going to be key."

*

"One item," I say. "Tops. The fashion industry is a conspiracy to make women hate their bodies, and no matter how much I buy, it's not going to solve the real problems of the world."

"She grew up on a commune," Hayes explains gently.

"But you're helping the economy, sweetie," Damien says. "We're all in trouble, haven't you heard? Consider this your way of pitching in."

We spend a total of an hour at BleuBelle's, during which, despite my protests, Damien manages to completely outfit me for my first semester at school in Savannah. Two pairs of jeans with fancy designs on the butt, velvet and tweed blazers (to go over my T-shirts, which I refuse to give up), fitted beaded tank tops, sweaters made of something really soft. Every time I say it's enough and I don't want any more, Madison and Hayes sneak more things into the bag.

They try to hide the receipt from me, but on the way out of the store I wait until they're air-kissing Damien good-bye and I grab it. The total is staggering. They come out on the sidewalk and see me fuming.

"This is . . . this is bullshit," I say, about to cry. "We can't spend money like this! Don't you know what's going on in the world? People are dying in Sudan, and we're doing *this*?"

Hayes pulls out her cell phone and, using my grand-mother's credit card, proceeds to donate the exact same amount to Doctors Without Borders.

"Is that all right?" Madison says. "Or do you have a problem with them too?"

"How do you girls have such a cavalier attitude about money?" I ask. "If you *are* that loaded, let's do something worthwhile! Start a community garden, maybe."

"Good luck getting *my* sister to grub around in the dirt," a voice says. We turn around, and there's a movie star in front of us. Or I'm pretty sure he's a movie star. I haven't seen that many movies, but this guy definitely looks like he's straight out of Hollywood. Tall. Blond hair that slips down his forehead. White shirt tucked into khaki pants. Converse tennis shoes. Tortoiseshell glasses framing a pair of very green eyes.

Despite myself, I can't help hearing my mother's love chant in my head:

> *Salt and rose and spirits,*
> *listen to what I say.*
> *Bring me my lover*
> *by the end of the day.*

"Alex," Hayes says, "meet my brother, Thaddeus. He's a year ahead of us at school."

Oh, God. A male MG. Well, never mind *that* little crush...I guess.

"Are you shopping?" Hayes asks.

"SCAD library," he says.

"Checking out the fresh art-student meat, no doubt," Madison purrs.

"Hayes," Thaddeus says, ignoring Madison, "I'm going out to the beach house this afternoon. Mom said you might need me to pick up something from the doctor?"

"No," Hayes says quickly. "Thanks, though."

"Going all alone?" Madison says to Thaddeus, tipping forward ever so slightly so as to offer up a prize view down her shirt. "You really ought to practice the buddy system if you're going swimming."

"I'm not swimming," Thaddeus says coldly. "I've got reading to do for school."

"Oh, *school*," Madison says with distaste. "What is up with everyone and *school*? It's like you all think this crap is actually going to be useful later in life."

"I know it's gauche, Mad, but some of us actually feel we should apply ourselves."

"Maybe I'd apply myself if it mattered. But since I'm stuck in this town forev—"

"What book are you reading?" Hayes interrupts.

"A Farewell to Arms."

"That's not such a bad one," I say. "Except for all the castration anxiety."

"What?" Thaddeus says sharply, as if my talking to him is some sort of affront.

"No, don't get me wrong—the book's really good," I say. "I've read it. Awesome war scenes and a bitchin' romance. It's just pretty sexist because of when it was written and all, and the main guy's a little messed up, but you still side with him somehow. But, like I say, it's where you can see the roots of Hemingway's infamous castration anxiety. Everyone's always losing fingers and legs and arms...you know, working our way toward *The Sun Also Rises*, where he loses the full—"

"Anyway," Hayes says, cutting me off.

Thaddeus looks me up and down and then turns back to his sister. I feel my face turning red. I gather it's "uncool" to talk about books to your basic country-club-belonging, golf-playing, yacht-sailing, magazine-layout-looking snob. Well, screw everyone, then. I feel tears sting my eyes as I think for the thousandth time today about how much I miss my imperfect Reggie and the shaggy, genuine RC.

"See you," he says to his sister. He looks at Madison and me but doesn't say anything to us before striding away.

"Wow," I say. "Is he always that friendly?"

"He's just having his period," Madison says.

"God, I'm burning up," Hayes says, gracefully changing the subject yet again. "Wanna go swim in Madison's pool? Tan a little?"

"Sorry, I'm not really into skin cancer."

"MGs don't get skin cancer." Madison laughs. "Or wrinkles or age spots. Didn't you know that?"

Hayes coughs loudly.

"It's in our genes," Madison adds, winking at her.

"You know, I've got to get back," I say, and my voice trails off. Because, in reality, I've got nothing to do. "Guess I need some 'me' time."

"Sure," Hayes says. "You should get some rest before the party."

"I told you, I'm not going to—"

"Just *come*," Hayes says. "I want to see how you look in your new clothes."

"And what else do you have to do, anyway?" Madison asks.

She has a point. Besides bonding with Miss Lee's neurotic cat, all I can think of doing is reading a book. Which is great, of course, but I've been doing that a lot lately.

"All right," I say. "But strictly for sociological reasons. Not, you know, to get drunk and stuff."

"Of course not," Madison says. "God forbid you actually have fun like normal people."

"We'll drive you back," Hayes says.

"No, it's cool. I'll walk."

"With those bags?"

"I'll be fine," I say, bending over to stuff the new clothes into my backpack.

"Oh my God," Madison says, turning away. "I feel sick. Please tell me Damien's not seeing this."

"It's okay. See? All gone," I say.

The sun has moved behind a cloud, and the city lies before me. Ever since my mom died, I get like this sometimes—overcome with the desire to be alone. "Hey, thanks again. That wasn't so bad, and Doctors Without Borders is probably really grateful."

"You should have let us spend more money, then," Madison says, almost merrily. Hard to tell.

"We'll pick you up at eight thirty," Hayes calls. I wave, then fade into Savannah's beckoning maze of one-way streets.

8

Savannah was founded in 1733 by James Oglethorpe, a dashing young colonist from England. According to the book my grandmother gave me, he chose this particular site because it was a little bit inland, on high ground, and it could be easily defended. Basically, that means we're far enough from the ocean to be mind-blowingly hot but close enough to the coast to be humid enough to suck all the water from your body after a two-block walk. Oh, and then there are the swarms of mosquitoes that come up from the swamp. Smooth move, Ogles.

Still, no matter how grumpy and homesick I may be, I gotta say it's a pretty freakin' charming place. The city is laid out in a grid of pretty squares that start at the river and end at Forsyth Park. Each one has its own style and is graced by huge trees and benches where people sit and do nothing. It's not that people here are lazy, exactly; it's just literally too hot to move. Unless, that is, it's early in the morning or late at night. Once I got up super early, and all sorts of people were in the park running around and doing jumping jacks. Trust me, Savannah's also got its share of crazies. That particular morning I spotted a man in a purple ball gown on roller skates. There's also a Willie Nelson look-alike who cruises around town with a big radio on his bike. I've been here for two and a half weeks, so by now I have my favorite spots: the best place to watch tourists get hustled is Chippewa Square; Whitefield Square has a really nice gazebo; and the back of Colonial Park Cemetery is a safe place to smoke pot, because it's usually pretty empty.

On days this blazing hot, the best way home is not always the shortest but the route that provides the deepest and most consistent tree coverage. Weaving back and forth between Bull, Barnard, and Whitaker, I pause on Jones, noticing a narrow opening between two old, decrepit houses. I slip down the alley and find a high-walled, untended garden next to what looks to be an abandoned house covered in flowering vines. Weeds and ivy run wild over the ground, and at the end of a path paved with cool old bluestone sit two wrought-iron benches by a weathered brick wall.

I settle on one of the benches and take out my book. This week it's *Jane Eyre*, the one novel on the school summer reading list I haven't already read. Thoughts so far: Edward is hot, but a total nightmare. And what is with this banshee in the attic?

"Alexandria?"

Jumping so high I almost fall off my bench, I turn to see a seriously hot African-American man standing in the entranceway wearing blue sunglasses, Levi's, Converse All-Stars, and a soft, formfitting T-shirt.

"Yeah?" I say.

When he takes off his glasses, I note that this guy is one of the best-looking people I've ever seen. Maybe even topping Hayes and Madison. Snobby Thaddeus too.

"Well, hey there. I've heard a lot about you." He steps into the garden.

"L-listen," I stutter, standing up. "I'm really sorry if I'm on your property. I thought it was public—"

"Don't worry about it. I don't live here. This is actually Mary Oglethorpe's garden, but she won't care. She knows who you are."

"I'm sorry, have we met? I'm not that great at names, but I really think I'd remember you."

"Oh no. We haven't met yet. We *will* know each other, though." He thrusts his hand forward. "Samuel Buzzard."

"Hi."

"May I?" he says, motioning to the bench across from me.

"Sure. As long as you think Miss Oglethorpe wouldn't mind."

"Oh, I think she'll allow it." He brushes the bench off a tiny bit prissily and sits. I notice that he doesn't look overheated in the slightest, while I'm shvitzing like I'm in Big Jon's sweat lodge.

"So, you know my grandmother?"

"Of course. Everyone knows your grandmother. She's been excited for your arrival for a long time."

"Huh."

"So, how do you like it here?"

"Well, Mr. Buzzard..."

"Sam."

"Okay, cool. I mean, I don't want to offend you, Sam, but it's kind of a drag."

"Oh?" He looks over my shoulder at something and then puts his sunglasses on again. But when I turn to look, no one's there. "'A drag.' That's an interesting way to put it. How so?"

"I don't know. Well...it's super formal, for one thing. See, I'm supposed to be in this weird sort of stupid debutante thing."

"The Magnolia League."

"Right." I look at him with surprise. "You know about that?"

He nods.

"All they care about are clothes and how to act and who says what and whatever." The floodgates seem to have opened. I don't know what it is about this guy, but he's very easy to talk to. "I mean, it's cool that they're trying to get me situated. It's awesome, actually. I just... I don't know."

"You feel like you have nothing in common."

"Totally. I'm from a communal farm. I mean, I'm happiest on my knees in the dirt. These girls grew up in huge mansions. Their mothers probably nursed them with champagne bottles."

"Or something like that." Sam takes out a beautiful pipe inlaid with iridescent mother-of-pearl. As he lights it, the air fills with the sweet smell of tobacco. "You know what you need to do?"

"What?"

"Show them what you have to offer."

"What I have to offer?" I look at him, confused. "What do you mean? Like, how to grow an awesome organic tomato?"

"Hmm. Well, not exactly. What I'm saying is, you've had a lot of experiences they *haven't* had. Madison and Hayes probably want to know what it's like in California. They're just Savannah girls, remember, and they'd probably think it would be cool to learn from you."

"How do you know their names?" I ask.

He continues as if he didn't hear me. "So, I'd say you should beat them at their own game. Sure, they're the princesses of Savannah, but you've got something different. And that's cool."

"I guess." I play with the fray on my cutoffs. "I sort of just want to go home, though. You know? I don't belong here."

"You might find that you do, eventually," he says. He reaches inside his jacket and produces an engraved card on ivory card stock. *Samuel Buzzard, PhD.* The paper feels heavy in my hand.

"What's your degree in?"

"I studied ethnography at Yale," he says offhandedly. "All right, you call me anytime, okay? I've heard you've had a lot on your mind."

"Who told you—?"

Sam's face suddenly freezes. He leans forward, intently staring at my necklace. *"Where did you get that?"*

"This?" I back away slightly, frightened of his tone. I rub the stone between my fingers. "It was my mother's. I found it in her garden—"

"What? She wasn't wearing it?"

I shake my head.

"Why?"

"It fell off, I guess. I found it in the dirt a couple of days after she died."

He straightens, composing himself with obvious effort. "Well, that's a very precious thing, isn't it? If it was your mother's."

"Yeah. It's kind of heinous, but I wore it today just to annoy the girls."

"Oh, I'd wear it all the time if I were you," he says forcefully. "It's an heirloom."

"I guess. I have a lot of things of hers. Like this ankle bracelet. See? It's supposed to be good luck. The dimes or something."

Sam is obviously upset. Why does he care so much about my necklace?

"Well, take care," he says hastily.

"Thanks." I have to admit, I do feel better. Sam's the most real person I've met in this place. "Maybe I'll give you a call sometime."

"I look forward to it, Alexandria," he says, giving me a small salute. "By the way, it's true what they say about the dimes around the ankle. It's definitely good luck—especially if you rub the dimes on a frog's back by the light of a full moon."

"What?" I cry, confused. Is that some kind of Southern witticism? But I never get my answer. My new friend has already disappeared around the block.

9

The Magnolia League's "Wine Time," which takes place every Thursday afternoon, has one rule: no business. Actually, the event has hundreds of rules governing everything from what kind of wine is served to how many glasses each individual is allowed to drink without appearing tacky and who can wear what outfit and when. But those rules are bred right into the genes and hardly need to be explicated. "No business" is the one rule the members do have to remind themselves of,

and it's something they all take very seriously. Therefore, during Wine Time the ladies set aside their personal agendas, their business maneuverings, the
advancement of their husbands' careers, the betterment
of their children, and their handshake real-estate deals
in order to kick back, relax, and traffic in the kind of
back-alley gossip that would make a harbor pilot blush.
During the rest of the week, the Magnolia League ladies
do things the nice way. But on Thursday afternoons,
there's nothin' "nice lady" to be found at Magnolia
Hall.

"You know, her daddy shot his daddy back in '74.
He only wounded him, but still. So after they got married, I was just on pins and needles for thirty years waiting for the other shoe to drop. When he finally ran her
over with that Volvo, I was just so relieved."

"Not everyone knows, but she's as mean as a snake,
and when her husband doesn't do right, she beats him
like a rented mule."

"Well, sure, he's a preacher, but he's a Presbyterian,
and that's almost like having no religion at *all*."

Miss Lee is the last to arrive. As the president, that is
her right. One of the unwritten rules is that no one
may follow her. Wine Time starts at five, and people
can come whenever they want. But Miss Lee arrives at
five fifteen, and if you come after that, somebody's
going to cut your tail.

"Hello, girls," Miss Lee says. A chorus of greetings

71

wafts into the air. Miss Lee looks as perfect as ever, in a blue shift that shows off her firm figure. "What's the word?"

"Mary is catting around with a twenty-four-year-old," Ellie, Sybil's daughter, blurts.

"Mary!"

Mary Oglethorpe shrugs. "He thinks I'm thirty."

"The only thirty-year-old on the earth born in 1942," Miss Lee says. "Be careful, honey. There are some things no root doctor can fix."

Sybil intercepts Dorothy and offers her a glass of white zin.

"Dorothy," she says sweetly, "you look good enough to eat. Have you been doing that Pilates?"

"Now, I know you're not about to ask me for something on a Thursday afternoon, Sybil."

"I wouldn't if it wasn't urgent, Dorothy," Sybil says, lowering her voice into her serious register.

"Out with it," Dorothy snaps. *It's hardly a surprise,* she thinks. *The girls always want something—every last one of them. And they always want it now, now, now. They are worse than a bunch of teenagers.*

"I need more Love Charm," Sybil says. "Tom is not...fulfilling his duties as a husband, and I'm worried that he might...his eye might...."

"You're worried that the senator will get hungry for another run across the Mexican border."

You could cut the silence with a butter knife.

"She was Argentinian," Sybil mumbles.

"Sybil, you've dosed that man six times already this summer. The Buzzards are going to run out of dragon's blood altogether, and he's still not going to stop chasing South American heinie."

"But I don't think they're mixing it right," Sybil says. "He's been calling that home wrecker every night. If the reporters find out..."

"The spell can only spark love that's already there," Dorothy says. "It can't make a stallion out of a fish. You need to think of a different angle."

"But I can't—"

"Can't never could, now could it?" Miss Lee snaps. "We have limited resources here, and you are wasting them. You need to work harder to keep him in line, Sybil. Wear a low-cut dress, show a little leg, shorten his leash. Good Lord, girl. Can't you control your man without outside assistance? I've kept bigger men than Tom McPhillips in line with nothing more than my sunny disposition, and it's about time you did the same."

Sybil flushes red with humiliation. The other Magnolias exchange glances. No one is happy when Miss Lee gets stingy with the Buzzards' spells. *Who is she saving them for, anyway?*

"So," Khaki says, trying to change the subject, "I hear Alexandria is settling in?"

"She is," Miss Lee replies, taking a long sip. "Gradually."

"My granddaughter, Madison, says she has a lot of...spunk."

"She's like her mother that way," Dorothy says. "Although it's up to those girls to start instructing her in some social graces."

"They're taking it slow," Khaki says. "They don't want to scare her."

"Of course not," Miss Lee answers. "It's a lot to take in. The dances, the walk. She's starting at nothing."

"Has she met the Buzzards yet?"

"Absolutely not. She doesn't need to be acquainted with Sam Buzzard just now. She needs time to adjust."

There is a flicker of disapproval in the room. No other Magnolia has been kept from the Buzzards this long. *What makes Alexandria so special?*

"That's funny," Mary Oglethorpe says. "I could have sworn I saw Alexandria and Sam Buzzard together in my garden today."

Miss Lee looks over at Mary, startled. "I'll have to look into that," Miss Lee says abruptly. "But the most important thing is for the Juniors to have that girl ready for the ball by Christmas. As we know, she is lagging far behind—but it would be so embarrassing if she didn't come out with the girls in her class. So, Sybil, please talk with Hayes about getting my granddaughter caught up. Mary, you'll take care of the dance lessons, yes? All right." Miss Lee smiles wickedly. "Y'all know that we don't do business during Wine Time. What else can we possibly talk about?"

There's a long silence, and then Julie Buchanan says, "I promised I wouldn't say anything to anyone, but yesterday morning at the crack of dawn I ran into Jeanette Witherspoon's ex-husband coming out of the Morning Roast with a little bitty thing who could not have been more than seventeen. I don't want to be ugly, but I think she is one of the checkout girls at Kroger. I like to have died."

Other voices join in, elaborating all of Tim Witherspoon's character flaws and laying out his various failings in graphic detail, including the likelihood that he was if not actually robbing the cradle then at least casing the cradle for a future heist. As the Magnolias move on — strands of gossip merging, voices rising and falling, harsh laughter ringing out, wine glasses being refilled — no one notices as Sybil McPhillips quietly slips out the door.

10

During my walk home from the secret garden, I end up literally sopping. Northern California has a nice, cool climate, so I've never experienced weather like Savannah's. Just walking outside is like diving into a bowl of thick, gardenia-flavored soup. I never knew that a bra could get sweaty, but apparently boobs perspire when heated to 102 degrees. It's so bad that eventually I duck into a driveway, take off my bra altogether, and stuff it into my bag. When I dart out again, I spot a lady watching me from her porch across the street. I just wave and give her my best Magnolia League smile.

My grandmother's mansion appears to be empty as I walk in. "Miss Lee?" I yell. Nothing. Thank you, sweet Jesus. I run upstairs, unzip my backpack, and dump all the new clothes onto the bed. Blazers by Theory, pants by Joe's Jeans, a sweater by something called Inhabit. Inhabit what? Am I supposed to live in this thing? Who's Joe? Rock *what* Republic? I shake my head. Guess I'm not quite getting this fashion thing yet.

I shuffle to the pretty little antique desk that overlooks the garden and sit down in front of the MacBook that Miss Lee got for me as a welcome present.

"You'll need it for your studies," she said. "I expect good grades out of you. Also, you can talk to your friends on the screen. I'm not privy to how it works, but I'm told all the children do it. Khaki's granddaughter apparently chats with her friend in *Japan*."

Madison confirmed this today on our shopping trip. "Oh yeah. Mokiko. She's awesome. We trade sex tips. They have a whole different way of doing things over there."

"Huh," I said, changing the subject. Because you know what? I don't need sex tips. I may *never* need sex tips. Reggie and I didn't have time to go all the way. And honestly, I'm in no hurry.

Not that there wasn't a ton of sex going on at the RC. It's a very open place, where people are — as Big

77

Jon would say—"free with their bodies." But Mom kept things in our cabin pretty strict.

"I manage to keep *my* clothes on all the time," she'd say, referring to the nude sunbathers who often populated the RC beach. "So should you."

Still, we'd talk about it at teatime. Sometimes she'd add stronger herbs if something was wrong; then she called the drink Swamp Brew. The brew smelled like an old horse's tail and tasted worse, but it instantly made everything better. During those hours, no topic was off limits, including going "all the way."

"Make sure they say it," she would stress. "Trust me. It won't feel all that great, but if you're with someone you love and who loves you, it will be good and worth remembering."

"Who was *your* first time with?"

"It was someone wonderful," she said. "A good friend, a good person. And that's the kind of experience I want you to have."

I always thought that was pretty awesome advice. I never worried about getting to be sixteen or even twenty and still being a virgin. Sure, I have hormones, so I *get* why kids do it earlier. There are times when all I can think about is rolling around naked in the sand with Reggie. In my fantasy he kisses me, tells me that I'm beautiful and rad and that he loves me and…you know. I always just figured we'd get around to it. No rush.

But now the person I finally found to do it with, maybe — my "someone wonderful" — is more than two thousand miles away. And at this point, it doesn't look likely that I'll ever see him again.

Grimly, I open my e-mail, the only reason I ever use the MacBook. I know it sounds weird — *Crap! Why does everything I say always sound weird?* — but I haven't really gotten into this Internet thing yet. It just seems like a time suck. At the RC, we had one computer for the whole place, and it might as well have been powered by a sick hamster. It took five minutes just to get a home page up. Plus, all the people I wanted to talk to were around me, anyway, so I didn't need e-mail or IM or texting or Skype.

But now that I'm stranded away from them all, I'm trying to get into it. Mostly I'm finding, though, that it's just another way to realize that Reggie's not missing me nearly as much as I miss him. He's called only once and e-mailed just twice in three weeks. It's hard to blame him; the RC has only one pay phone, and then there's that moon-landing-era community computer. Still, it would be nice if he'd borrow someone's cell once in a while . . . or something.

But hang on! An e-mail, finally! Holding my breath, I click on the message and open it:

to: RC_Alex@gmail.com
from: reggieveggie@yahoo.com

Hey Alex! What's up? Life on the RC is exactly the same.

(Even though I'm not there?)

We played mud ball today

(Wait. Mud ball is my favorite game. And they're playing it without me?)

with some new kids. They're in from Oregon, five girls and guys

(Girls? What girls?)

and they're pretty cool. Katrina is especially funny.

(Katrina?)

Anyway, hope all's cool in Florida.

(Florida???????)

Bet there are some weird parties down there. By the way, we all might go to the Bluegrass Festival in San Francisco. You know I'm not into that hippie stuff, but I'll try and nab you a bootleg.
Good times,
Reggie

I close the laptop, feeling completely miserable. Good times? *Good times?* That's all he can come up with? I mean, I think about this guy every second. Like, he is constantly taking up valuable space in my brain. And all he can say is "good times"?

Downstairs, I hear the door open and shut. Miss Lee must be home. I spend the next hour hiding in my room, thinking about Reggie playing mud ball with sexy girls and how I'll be an ostracized, out-of-place virgin for the rest of my days.

Oh my God, I hate my life.

"Alexaaaandria..." My grandmother is just outside the door.

"Hi, Grandmo—I mean, Miss Lee."

"How are you, dear?"

"Okay."

She sounds a little suspicious. "What were you doing today?"

For once, I've got the right answer. "Shopping with Hayes and Madison. We're going to a party later."

"Excellent!" she says. "Darling, do you mind freshening up and then meeting me in my bedroom? I have a couple of items to discuss with you."

And with that, I hear her footsteps grow fainter. It really is the creepiest thing, how you can just fade away in this place. I pull on my fancy new jeans and one of the black tops Madison picked out, and then I join my grandmother in her silver-walled chambers. Always the perfect, slightly inebriated lady, she's sitting at her writing desk, sipping a cocktail with Jezebel in her lap.

"What's up?"

"Well, first of all, Alexandria, I was wondering if Hayes and Madison have prepared you at all for the fact that this Christmas you may be allowed to come out?"

I look at her, stumped. Then it hits me. Oh my God, does my grandmother think I'm gay? That thought—especially after the hours I've spent obsessing over Reggie—is so funny that I can't stop the snort that comes out of my nose.

"You want me to come out?"

"Yes, of course. Have the girls mentioned this to you?"

"Uh...no. I don't think it's occurred to them, really. I mean, they know I have...that I had...whatever. They know about Reggie, and he's a guy. So...you know..."

My grandmother gives me a long, perturbed look and takes a healthy sip of her cocktail. "Would you please get a hold of yourself, dear," she says, setting the glass carefully on a lacy coaster. "I am talking about your debut. As in the Magnolia League Debutante Ball. Or the Christmas Ball, as we call it around town."

"Oh! Right. See, I thought you meant—"

"Yes, I understand. Not that I *would* mind if you were gay, honey. I'm Christ Church *Episcopal*, you know. Been driven from my house of worship simply because I support those light in the loafers."

"Light in the—"

"The gay Episcopalian bishops. I fully support them. We all deserve the same chance to serve God, don't we? I don't care what you've got going on in the sheets. Anyhow, a nice, well-mannered girlfriend would have been just fine for you. However, given your preoccupation with that young man in California, I hadn't had any thoughts of the kind."

"Oh."

Wait—how on earth does she know about Reggie?

"All eyes will be upon you, especially since you are new to this. So what we need to discuss is how to get you up to speed on this training."

"Training? For a party?"

She sighs impatiently, then continues. "You have the genes, of course, but there are certain codes that you need to learn. Mannerisms, dance steps. That sort of thing."

"Dance steps? Mannerisms?"

"Please, stop repeating everything I say, dear. You sound like a broken answering machine. I've arranged a few sessions in the coming weeks. It's hardly rocket science—you're a smart girl, so you'll pick it up."

I shake my head, trying to figure out how to let her down easy.

"Listen, Miss Lee. I know you're coming from the right place. It sounds...really nice, this ball thing. But it's cool, okay? I don't really need it. I'll just go to school and be low-key until graduation, and then, you know, be on my way."

Miss Lee listens to me, thoughtfully playing with the bling on her bracelet. I make a mental note to get her some literature on blood diamonds. Big Jon used to say for every diamond ring, some kid in Sierra Leone had to lose a finger.

"Alexandria," my grandmother says sternly, interrupting my thoughts. "Have you ever considered the term *destiny*?"

"Um...not really. At least, not in this case."

"Well, believe it or not, it is your *destiny* to be a Magnolia League debutante. You were born into this extremely privileged group of people. We are leaders in the community. People look up to Magnolia League members. If you don't act a bit more ladylike, you may not be allowed to come out at the ball with your sisters. And not participating...erodes the custom."

"I don't want to erode anything," I say as politely as I can. "But I'm just not into it."

She smiles coolly. "Let me put it another way: This is how you earn your keep here."

"What do you mean?" I say, a bit angrily. "My *keep*? I never wanted to come here. I was earning my keep just fine at the commune. Remember? I already have a skill."

"Well, while it is true that you were reported to be good at gardening—a highly valued talent, both there and *here*, as a matter of fact — I'll have you know that the head of the place, Jon, was concerned about affording to keep you at the farm. He was actually the one who first contacted me."

I shake my head at her obvious lie. "I don't believe you. He didn't want me to go."

My grandmother sighs. "Fine. Ask him if you'd like. He really does love you, I think. He just had an inkling that your mother came from money, and I suppose he wanted some."

"Big Jon doesn't give a crap about money," I retort. "The guy runs a communal farm."

"Even communal farms need to pay their taxes, dear. Nevertheless, the fact remains that you are here, and as a guest in this house, you need to adhere to my rules. I feel I've been extraordinarily lenient about most things, but I will not have you disrespecting my organization. I was a debutante, and so was your mother. You are next in line."

"I'm sorry, I just can't believe that Mom was —"

My grandmother opens the drawer of her desk with a loud snap, fishes out a picture, and hands it to me. It's my mother in the white dress I saw the other day. She's standing on a large marble stairway, surrounded by a group of similarly frocked girls. She looks so pretty, it's hard for me to tear my eyes away.

"Wow."

"Yes," my grandmother says. "She looked exquisite.

She *was* exquisite. Though she wasn't born that way, Alexandria. Being a Magnolia shaped her. What I'm hoping is that by following in her footsteps, you'll learn something. Don't you want to be like her?"

I look away, trying to control my emotions. "She's the only person in the world I want to be like."

"Well, then, start your training. It's a very important step to being part of Savannah's social circle."

"Fine. I'll try to do better. You know, fall in line with this manners thing." *How bad can it be, anyway?* "Can I keep this picture?"

"Certainly."

"Okay, I'd better get ready. Hayes is probably on her way."

"All right," my grandmother says. "Oh, and one more thing, Alexandria. I was told you made a new friend today."

I cock my head. "Damien, the fashion guy?"

"No. Sam Buzzard."

"Oh yeah. He was cool. I was reading in this strange little garden and—"

"Doc Buzzard, his father, has been our personal health-care provider for some time," my grandmother says.

"Whose? The family's?"

"The Magnolia League's."

I shake my head. I swear, this town is getting weirder and weirder.

"In this day and age, it's best to secure one's health care, dear. But . . . his family is a bit eccentric. Did Sam say anything strange today?"

"No," I say. "He was a nice dude. Although I do think it's kind of odd that he didn't tell me his father was the Magnolia League's doctor. I mean, he said he knew the Magnolia League, but . . . that kind of information would stand out."

"That is precisely what I'm saying. The Buzzards can be secretive. A bit strange. I would limit my time around them, if I were you."

"I guess."

"I would prefer it if you did. Avoid speaking with Sam alone, I mean."

See, this is where we run into trouble. Because of course the minute my grandmother tells me to do something, what I really want to do is exactly the opposite.

"We'll see," I say. "I mean, I'll certainly try."

My grandmother stares at me coldly a moment and then drains her martini glass. It really is the oddest thing. Seriously—she must be at least sixty, but she has barely *any* wrinkles on her face.

"Excellent. Well. Run along and get ready for your social engagement, why don't you."

"Okay." But for a couple seconds, I remain right where I am. For the briefest moment, I feel a little sorry for her. It must be lonely living in this big house with no one but Josie and me. And she lost her daughter, after all, just as I lost my mom.

But if my grandmother is suffering, she doesn't show it. She's already picked up the receiver of her fancy phone, which has all her Magnolia League friends conveniently on speed dial. No doubt she's anxious to line up some fabulous evening plans.

"All right, then, darling," she says. "Run along." And with a swipe of her hand, she waves me away.

11

Early Saturday evening, the sky over Buzzard's Roost shimmers in the late-summer heat. Sina presses a wet cloth to the back of her neck. Some of the houses out here have air-conditioning, but she's never liked the feel of recycled air. No, she lives with the windows open, in winter, summer, even hurricane season. The air is filled with the buzzing of crickets and the smells of wood smoke, cloves, and bacon. On the table, the edge of the newspaper lifts and falls to the rhythm of the ceiling fan. A bee, trapped between the window screen and the shade, ricochets feverishly back and forth.

Sina opens the doors of her floor-to-ceiling apothecary's cabinet. She taps the side of her face as she thinks a moment; finally, she extracts a large cloth and several jars. She lays a heavy green cape on the ironing board and plugs in the iron. Bloo, the Buzzards' dog, whimpers at the hiss as Sina runs it over the cloth. He was bitten by a snake the previous year, and though Sam got to him in time to treat the bite, the dog has never forgotten it. The Buzzards all know, of course, that the incident was a hex put out by their rivals on St. Catherines Island. Sina had wanted to take revenge on their two cats, but her brother, Sam—ever the peace seeker—wouldn't allow it.

While Sam is the most knowledgeable of Doc's children about the history and intricacies of hoodoo, Sina is the practitioner with the most natural talent. No one can mix a mojo bag like she can. She takes great pleasure in preparing for a ritual, loves the meditative feel of it. Yet she is aware of voices invading her peaceful bubble this afternoon. Her little cousins are fighting in the courtyard. For hours, they've been playing on an old twin-size mattress that Sam has rigged up with ropes to hang from the branch of a large oak tree. It's the only spot of shade in the common garden, so everyone in the family spends hours there reading, gossiping, or sneaking naps. The swing is in high demand in the summer, but out of fear that the old branch may snap, Sam has limited the weight load to two hundred pounds. Presently there are three boys and four girls jumping on and off it, trying to negotiate swing time.

"You've been on it for an hour!"

"No I haven't!"

"You have!"

"Haven't!"

"*Ow!*" screams Little Callie, the next-to-youngest and the brattiest by far.

Sina sighs, puts down the iron, and walks to the window to investigate.

"Ahh!" Little Callie cries. "Plat-eye! Plat-eye!" She begins to convulse uncontrollably.

Sina shakes her head. When she was growing up, Buzzard kids were kept from practicing hoodoo until they were at least fifteen. Lately, Doc's been starting them a lot earlier. Sina's not sure why this is, but it's definitely a bad idea in her book.

"L.S.! You *know* Doc didn't ordain that. Fix her! Now!"

She doesn't have to wonder who pulled the plat-eye root. Little Snake, Doc Buzzard's single direct grandson, is the only one with the brains and finesse to conjure it so quickly. She looks at the poor girl, who is shaking uncontrollably at the vision only she can see—most likely a large gray shapeless form hovering five feet above the ground, snarling and reeking of the dead.

"But I—"

Sina thrusts a flask through the window. "Get that plat-eye some whiskey and dispel it. Then give her a turn on that swing. *Now.*"

After throwing a pebble defiantly at Sina's cottage, Little Snake reluctantly turns to his cousin.

> *"Powers, powers, powers,*
> *let her be.*
> *Oh John the Conqueror,*
> *the trouble was only me."*

He pours the whiskey on the ground near where Little Callie is lying. Immediately, the girl stops twitching. She hops up and scuttles to the mattress. L.S. cuts an evil look at his aunt and slips down the path to the woods.

"Off to do no good," Sina says aloud. Humming to herself, she meticulously measures out exact portions from the glass jars of frankincense, clove powder, archangel herb, bayberry root chips, goofer dirt, cinnamon powder, and a special white powder in a bottle-green jar.

The goofer dirt—gathered from new graves—is especially precious. The fresher it is, the more effective. Often she asks the Magnolias to pay for their side spells in goofer. They're often at funerals of the most influential people in town, so it's close to no effort for the ladies to slip a bit of cemetery dirt into their fancy little purses.

Sina takes three cones of incense from a plastic container labeled *Money Draw* and lights it. Then she blends her ingredients in a coffee grinder and puts half the mixture in a green flannel bag. She sews the bag shut and then carefully sprinkles it with nine drops from a vial labeled *Prosperity*.

"Hey," Sam says, coming in the door. Sina nods but doesn't answer. She puts some of the powder into a green saucer and lights it on fire with a long match.

"Prosperity Oil?"

Sina nods.

"Who for?"

"That Mary Oglethorpe." Sina snorts. "Guess she's broke again."

"Man. The treasurer, no less."

"Woman has a problem. *Serious.*"

"I was just in her garden. House looks pretty run-down. She must be in a bad way."

"Well, this should help. If not, I'll cook up a lottery charm."

"Maybe some Irish moss tea?"

"Oh, smart. If I only knew where it was..." Sina goes back to her cabinet and begins to rifle through the hundreds of bottles and vials.

"Well, I thought I'd tell you—I saw her today."

Sina doesn't answer.

"The new holder of the mantle."

"I *get* who you mean."

"She's funny," he says. "Smart. Though she has no idea what's going on. Miss Lee's still got her in the dark."

"Big surprise," Sina mutters. "Damn! Maybe I'm out of moss."

"Callie!" Sam yells into the courtyard. The little girl rolls off the swinging mattress and comes to the window. "Go'n down to Grandaddy's house and get some Irish moss."

Callie nods and runs down the path.

"I think you'll like her," Sam continues.

"I don't like any of them," Sina says. "Waste of time—half century's worth. Look at me. I'm cooking up a ritual for an idiot who can't control her credit card. You think this is what our ancestors had in mind?"

Sam sighs and helps himself to some fresh chamomile flower tea. Sina's tea is always better than anyone else's; his sister is wildly talented at ferreting out the best herbs and roots. As usual, Sam skips the sweetener. Like the rest of his family, he has a powerful reaction to sugar because of his father's doings. The Buzzards draw their power from their conjure bird—known locally as the turkey vulture—and Doc fully expects to come back as one. A few years earlier, it was a trend in the Low Country to kill the birds with traps set with poisoned sugar. The buzzards began dying in droves, so to protect his family and himself, Doc Buzzard put a root on everyone at the Roost. So far it's shielded them from harm, but now everyone in the clan becomes violently ill at the taste of anything sweet.

"Can I ask you a question?" Sam says.

"Not if it has to do with the Magnolias. I'm done with that topic for the day."

"Come on."

"What?"

"How powerful is a buzzard's rock?"

Just then, through the window, another, older voice drifts in. It's their cousin, singing a hymn: *"Oh Lord, oh do Lord, oh do remember me . . ."*

"Lucretia!" Sina yells. "Ain't nowhere *near* Sunday yet! Put my iPod on! Alicia Keys!"

The singing stops and is replaced by Sina's favorite music. With her long limbs, queenly cheekbones, and light brown—almost golden—eyes, Sina is the most beautiful woman in the Buzzard family, if not in all of Georgia. "Lord Jesus, I *am* sorry, but can we have *one* church-free day around here?" Sina—whose name is short for the Yoruba name Adasina—plops down in her carved wooden rocking chair and crosses her slender ankles.

"Well? The buzzard's rock?" Sam asks again.

"Nothing more powerful," she says of the stone. "You know what they call it. A Fear Not to Walk Over

Evil. 'Course, I've never managed to get a good one. Almost paralyzed myself trying once."

No charm, of course, is easy to create, but the buzzard's rock is particularly difficult—and cruel—to procure. You must find a female buzzard who has laid eggs, and then wait until she leaves her nest. Once the nest is empty, you climb to the roost—usually about sixty feet up a dead pine tree—and steal the egg. Then comes the grisly part: killing the embryo with a long pin and returning the egg to the nest. When the buzzard comes back, she will sit on her egg for a day or so. But since buzzards can intuit death before any other creature, the bird soon realizes that the embryo is dead. Being attracted to death, she finds a sharp rock to crack the egg and look at the corpse. It is this rock, charged with anger and sorrow, that all root doctors seek—but almost never find.

"That buzzard's rock you had worked better than any root I've ever made," Sina says.

"Well, Alex has it now," Sam says. "She's got the one I gave Louisa."

Sina stops rocking.

"How'd *that* li'l chigger get it?" she cries. "She steal it?"

"Alex said it fell off her mother's neck."

"What kind of fool would lose something that valuable? It must have been right before she—" Seeing the look on Sam's face, Sina bites her tongue. "I don't trust this story. With that rock, she can do pretty much

96

anything. How well you know this Alex? You know she's not a cheat?"

Sam shrugs. "I like her. But I'm not sure of anything."

"Uncle! Here you go!" Callie tosses the packet of moss through the window. Sina rises to pick up the package. She inspects the gooey, moldy leaves in the light.

"All right. This ought to keep Miss Mary out of debtors' prison," she says, gently putting the moss into a small tin container.

"Let's hope so. It's the last Miss Lee is allowing her. Guess she wants to teach a lesson."

Sina whistles. "That woman best be careful she don't cause an insurrection."

"Long as they pay their bills, it's not our problem."

"True." Sina gathers her purse, the new green mojo bag, and the jar of moss. She pauses and then smiles craftily at her brother. "Well, I've got to go to town now, anyway. You know what? I think I might just check in on Miss Alex and her new friends."

Sam frowns, puzzled. "I thought you didn't care about her."

"I don't," Sina says, heading for the door. "But I care a hell of a lot about that buzzard's rock." Waggling her fingers at her brother, she leaves, tossing a handful of salt at the children as she passes. They roll over on the mattress swing, laughing, to thank her for the good luck.

12

I know it's lame and this night doesn't mean anything, anyway, but by the time the girls show up to take me to the party, I'm seriously nervous. I'm sitting on the bed wearing this dumb shirt they told me to put on, looking at my dreads in the mirror, and I'm ashamed to say I'm tempted to take them out.

This hair wasn't totally my idea, anyway. Reggie and I were hanging on the picnic tables one day watching the college kids, and he kept staring at this one girl with long blond dreads.

"She is so hot," he said.

"She is?"

"Yeah. I really dig her hair."

"You do?"

"Totally."

"Because," I lied, "I was, um, thinking of dreading *my* hair."

"That's an awesome idea," Reggie said.

And so: dreads. Not that Reggie noticed, but then again, he's never said much about how I look. *And* he thinks I'm in Florida.

Suddenly, the doorbell rings.

"Alexandria!" Josie calls. "Your friends are here!"

Friends. *Suuuuure.* I give myself one last look in the mirror. Hayes was right; the red shirt I bought today does look good. It manages to cover my fat and taste-fully makes the most of my boobs—the only parts of my body that look sort of okay. I walk to the bottom of the stairs, where Hayes is waiting. She's wearing jeans, too, and a halter shirt that looks like it's made of liquid silver.

"Oh, you look darling," Hayes says. "I knew the red would play up your tan. Here, I got you something." She hands me a black thing that looks like a claw, carved with tiny magnolias.

"What is that?"

"It's a mahogany hair clip. One hundred percent vintage and the answer to your hair crisis."

"What hair crisis?" Hayes gives me a patient smile. "And harvesting mahogany is an unsustainable practice that's destroying the rain forest."

"Hush," she says, and takes me by the shoulders, firmly turning me around. The gesture reminds me so much of something my mother would have done, I get tears in my eyes. I can't even protest when she pulls my dreads back and clips them. She turns me around again and looks me over, then tucks a stray one behind my ear.

"Perfection," she says, and she squeezes my shoulders, letting her hands linger for a minute. Suddenly, I feel a strange, electric tingle all over. It must be a new form of sadness I haven't experienced yet.

"Oh—I almost forgot—one last touch," she says, opening her enormous leather purse. She takes out lip gloss, glittery powder, and some kind of herbal perfume. It smells familiar, but I can't quite place it. Finding myself at a loss for words, I just stand submissively as she adorns me. When she finally steps back and looks at me, her expression is filled with pride. "Oh, I like you much better this way!"

"I'm so glad," I grumble.

"Okay, Madison's in the car, and she's not getting any happier. Let's go."

We walk out to the Prius. Hayes doesn't stop talking. "I'm really into this thing," she says. "Although I can never tell if it's on or not, because it's so quiet. I sort of miss the roar of the SUV."

As I slide into the backseat, I remember Sam's words: *Show them what you know.*

"Trust me, Hayes, no one *cool* would drive an SUV," I say, trying to imitate Madison's haughty tone. "Every tank of gas sinks us deeper into a pointless conflict in Iraq and puts us in greater danger of oil spills."

"This is the South, Lady Greenpeace," Madison says. "Down here, guzzling gas is a matter of national pride."

"C'mon, be serious," I say. But then, after the half-hour ride down a series of dark, oak-canopied roads, I see that she *was* serious. The parking lot of this party is filled with trucks—and not just any trucks, but the kind of trucks that burn a tank of gas just backing out of the driveway. Every single vehicle looks like a contestant in a redneck truck parody pageant: roll bars, gun racks, jacked-up bodies, oversize tires, fog lights, camo paint jobs, truck nuts. Their rear windows are plastered with stickers: Deadhead bears dancing, odes to hunting and fishing, and dozens of stickers of a flag that I don't recognize. It has two big horizontal red stripes—one at the top and one at the bottom—one horizontal white stripe in the middle, and seven white stars in a blue square in the corner.

"What's up with the Texas state flag?" I ask.

"It's the first flag of the Confederacy," Madison says.

"In Savannah, we're too status-conscious to put an actual rebel flag on our trucks, but not many people know what the Confederacy's first flag looks like, so it's a socially acceptable, slightly chickenshit way of giving the bird to all you Yankees."

"I didn't know people down here were still so racist."

"Oh, don't be stupid," Madison snaps.

"What she means to say," Hayes steps in, "is that not all Southerners are imbeciles. Most of them don't even know what that flag stands for; they just think it looks cool. Trust me, as Magnolia Leaguers, we're quite embarrassed that our state is most famous for slavery, peanuts, and the Allman Brothers."

"Oh, but the Allmans *rock*," I say.

"If you're seventy." Madison has clearly had enough of my whole grains for the evening.

"We're the New South," Hayes says. "Like Justin Timberlake."

"Ugh, Hayes. Eeee-nough," Madison drawls. "Justin Timberlake lives in LA. He abandoned Memphis at, like, thirteen. And don't let her fool you, Alex. Savannah's still Savannah, and for a lot of people down here, being Southern is a full-time job."

I follow them past the trucks, and there everyone is: a massive, milling, laughing, dancing, jostling, drinking, shouting, smoking, spitting crowd of kids. The Field is basically a landing next to the river, shaded by huge old trees dripping with really thick moss that looks like ghost fingers. The crowd fills the landing as far as I can see. A thick blue cloud of cigarette smoke hovers over everything.

Kids are everywhere. Despite the redneck trucks in the parking lot, it's a mixed crowd, I'm relieved to see. Black, white, Asian. Three chunky Hispanic boys are running the keg next to an idiotic bonfire that's way too close to the trees—one of them keeping it confusing by wearing a Confederate flag belt buckle and a *Don't Mess with Texas* baseball cap.

The guys all wear a uniform: khaki shorts, a polo shirt, and a baseball cap. The girls, on the other hand, look like exotic birds, bright, colorful, dressed to the nines, even though they're out here in this dusty field. The boys bob their heads solemnly to the music and drink seriously out of their red plastic cups; the girls laugh loudly and manage to text nonstop while juggling cigarettes, plastic cups, lighters, and purses and still never missing a beat in their conversations. All of them are slapping at the mosquitoes that swarm their faces. All of them, that is, except Hayes, Madison, and me. I can hear the insects whining in my ears, but for some reason, they aren't biting.

"It's our perfume," Hayes explains, spraying more on me. "Magnolia herbal secret."

"Herbal?"

"The Magnolia League was into herbal medicine

way before anyone else was," Madison says. "Why do you think they all look so forever twenty-one?"

"My mom knew a lot about herbs," I say. "Maybe that's where it came from."

Madison looks at me oddly.

"Come on," Hayes says. "Let's see who's here."

As we plunge into the crowd, my heart beats so hard it hurts. I've never felt this out of place in my life. Everyone is staring at me, and I realize that Hayes really was trying to help. She wasn't giving me a makeover; she was offering me protective camouflage. Too bad I didn't let her go all the way, because right now I feel like a fat frump.

She and Madison stop to chat with a big, good-looking boy, and I step back, trying to avoid the moment when he looks at me and the disappointment registers in his eyes.

"Hey, Piggy!" someone says. It takes me a minute to realize a girl is talking to me.

My face turns scarlet. *God, can't I just go home?* I hate them. I hate them all.

"Unbunch your underpants," she says, suddenly smiling. "I'm Carson; this is Natalie. We're just playin'."

"Oh," I say, trying to smile. "Sorry. That's cool."

"Yeah," the little rat-faced one called Natalie says. "It is cool. We're very cool people."

I notice that they're flanking me. I look around

desperately for Hayes or Madison, but all I see are polo-covered backs. I'm on my own.

"You're not from Georgia, are you?" Carson asks.

"I'm from Mendocino."

"Oh, wow. So you must smoke a lot of pot. Are you a stoner?"

"I like a little weed every now and then," I say, trying to sound worldly.

"I bet you do," Carson says. "We both love your hair."

"Yeah," Natalie says. "What a statement. You're such a unique individual. So different."

The sarcasm drips off her tongue like poison. My face burns. I mumble something.

"And those flip-flops," Carson says. "Piggy baby, you shouldn't wear your nice shoes to the Field. Save them for all the special places you have to go, like the welfare office."

I will not let these girls get to me, but my eyes burn, and I feel something wet slide down one of my cheeks. Carson notices, and I see a mean little smile sneak across her lips.

"What's it like to be a burner?" Natalie asks. "Are you high right now? Are you flying?"

And then a pair of hands are on Carson's shoulders, and Madison is kissing her on both cheeks, leaving lipstick smudges. Carson's mouth becomes an O, and then

Madison has me by the arm and is pulling me away into the crowd. Her lips are moving, but I can't make out what she's saying. Behind me, Carson shrieks.

"Something bit me!"

Beside me, I hear Madison muttering fast, "*Jon-ta-conku-er. Jon-ta-conku-er.*" I stop and look back to where a crowd of people are gathering around Carson.

"Is that girl okay?" I ask. Because she definitely does not seem okay. If she were okay, she wouldn't be lying on the ground. If she were okay, she wouldn't be starting to convulse.

"Snake!" someone yells helpfully.

"Call nine-one-one!" someone else shouts.

"Fuck you!" a third voice shouts back.

From the ground, Carson is making wet, gagging noises.

And then Hayes is there.

"Madison!" she whispers, and pinches her arm. Madison snaps out of it. Hayes turns to me and flashes her million-dollar smile.

"Alex, come on over here. I want to introduce you to some people," she says, beaming.

"But that girl..."

"She'll be fine," Hayes says. Sure enough, Carson is suddenly standing. Someone hands her a beer, and just as quickly as the illness seemed to arrive, it's gone, and she begins to dance.

"Wow," I say, trying to act as if this scene were normal. "Who are they?"

"Regular cotillion debs. They'll be at the Christmas Ball too. But they're not in the Magnolia subset."

"They seem really . . . special. Awesome first impression of the scene here. So, who do you want me to meet?"

Hayes points to a group of girls. I can't believe it. They're standing at attention, as if they're soldiers. She curls her finger inward once, and four of them scuttle over.

"What's up, y'all?" one of them says. She's a platinum blond, with spray-on-tan-gone-wrong orange skin.

"This is Alex," Hayes says. "She's from California."

The girls are looking at me the same way Carson and Natalie did. Clearly, they have as much interest in talking to me as they do in, say, eating dirt. I can feel my heart starting to wallop inside my chest again.

"Her grandmother is the president of the Magnolia League," Hayes adds.

Now, I've seen a lot of things: a seventy-year-old woman on an acid trip, a pod of whales playing off the beach. But I've never, and I mean *never*, seen people's expressions change as quickly and as thoroughly as when Hayes said those words.

Magnolia League. Can that really be all it takes to earn respect in this town?

"Do you play tennis?" one of the girls asks.

"No."

"I'll teach you," says a redheaded girl quickly. Freckled, and seriously stacked. "I'm Mary. I've been dying to teach someone to play tennis."

"Sure," I say. I'm feeling uncomfortable.

"Do y'all want me to get you beers?" the orange girl asks.

"Do we look like Canadians, Anna?" Madison snaps. "Go get us three Manhattans from Johnny Vader's car bar."

Anna smiles obligingly and trots off.

Suddenly I see Hayes's and Madison's expressions change. I turn and see yet another girl approaching—a tall, truly stunning girl with eyes just like Sam Buzzard's. She wears long dangly earrings, a silver headband, and a top that sparkles in the bonfire light. Put her on the side of a highway, and she would literally stop traffic.

"Sina," Madison says quietly. "Hello."

"Hi, girls," Sina says, and then, without shame, she checks me out. Even though I seriously could care less about this teen politics crap, she makes me nervous. Madison and Hayes are snobby and a little silly, but this girl is on a different level. There's something unsettling about her.

"So's this the prodigal grandbaby?"

"Sina," Hayes says, smiling weakly, "this is Alexandria Lee. Louisa Lee's daughter. She's living downtown with her grandmother."

"Huh," Sina says. "Your mama was a beautiful lady but, must say, don't see the resemblance. And what's goin' on with your hair? You tryin' to be black or something?"

"It's just a style," I mumble. "I don't know."

I look at Hayes and Madison, but they won't meet my eye. For once, even Madison seems to have nothing to say.

"Are you a Magnolia?" I ask.

Sina tips her head back and laughs wildly.

"Magnolia League's a bunch of withered-up old white ladies, sippin' wine and plannin' garden parties," she says. "I swim in deeper waters than that, trustafarian."

I wait for Madison's barbed retort, but it doesn't come.

"Look," I say. "It's not the coolest pastime, this debutante thing, but it's no better or worse than whatever it is you do that you think is so great. They're just ladies with some old-timey traditions. What's wrong with that? You don't have to be a . . . a friggin' racist about it."

"Sounds like you've fallen right in line," Sina says. "Do anything to maintain that certain lifestyle you all like."

"Hey, don't try to lump us all in as rich socialites. Some of us are really involved in working-class issues."

Right on cue, Anna shows up with the drinks.

"Madison," she simpers, "he didn't have any cherries for the Manhattans. Can you believe that?"

"Oh, lookee." Sina laughs. "Your cocktails are here, missus."

"Those aren't for me. I'm getting a beer," I say. I don't even like beer, but I have to prove a point. "It wasn't very nice to meet you."

"Be careful, sweetie," Hayes calls as I storm off.

Ugh. *Sweetie?* These chicks are so girlie they make my teeth hurt.

I work my way through the crowd, stewing. What was *up* with that girl? Madison and Hayes aren't exactly my best friends in the world, but it kills me that Sina was picking on them. And even worse, they acted so...helpless. I'm so pissed that I forget about everything else, and before I know it I'm trapped in the mob by the bonfire. The keg is on the other side of an impenetrable wall of sweaty bodies, and the fire is so hot that I feel like I'm going to pass out.

There's a gap next to a boy in a T-shirt and a sweat-marked cap. He looks earthy, exactly the kind of guy who would be working for the summer at the RC.

"Hey, can I get in there?"

"I don't think so, Fatso," he says. "Yo, Roger! This girl's got that possum we run over last week on her head. This is Georgia, girl! We like our women big-tittied and blond!"

"Screw you, Gilroy," says a dark-haired girl with a flat chest.

Defeated, I retreat to the parking lot. All right. Fine. I don't like beer, anyway. But...oh God. Apparently,

I'm crying again. Savannah has turned me into a leaky faucet. I can't help it. I've never felt so alone in my life. I'll never fit in here, ever.

"Ugh. Reggie," I whisper. "Where *are* you?"

"Hello." Furiously, I wipe my face with the back of my hand. A figure emerges from the shadows. It's Thaddeus, Hayes's brother. Even though we're all hanging out in a dirt field, even though it's the middle of August and there's an enormous bonfire raging, he looks perfect walking around in his spotless white shirt and khakis—as if he has his own personal air-conditioning unit. "What are you doing back here?"

"Oh," I say, straightening up. "Hi. I'm just...checking out this license plate. Huh. *Georgia...on my mind.* Cool."

"You should be careful," Thaddeus says. "Carson Moore was just bitten by a snake."

"I know. Although with all of this ironweed around, I'd probably be okay."

"Excuse me?"

"Ironweed. If you apply it to a fresh snakebite, it absorbs the poison. I should have said something."

"She recovered on her own, actually," Thaddeus says, looking at me with a flicker of interest. He still doesn't smile, though. I don't get it. Is he a narc?

"I'm not drinking or smoking or anything," I say. "I'm just hanging out."

"Fine," he says distractedly. Why is he being so standoffish? After all, he's the one who came to talk to me.

"Are you looking for a beer?" I say finally. "Because the keg's back by the bonfire."

"God, no," he says with what sounds like disdain. "I don't drink."

"Well, no offense, but then why are you at this party?"

"It's a lacrosse party."

"Oh," I say, confused.

"I'm the captain of the lacrosse team," he says.

"Cool."

"Not really. I hate these things."

"Me too. But that's because I don't know anyone here."

"You know my sister."

"Yeah, she's cool."

Why do I keep saying "cool"? I sound like an idiot.

"She's very loyal," he says. "So is Madison."

"I guess."

"We used to go out. Madison and I."

"Fascinating," I say. At least it's not "cool." And it's not really fascinating at all. It's boring—the hot blond jock, the snobby brunette. They were made for each other. "So, what happened?"

"I don't kiss and tell," he says dismissively.

"You were the one who brought it up," I say, annoyed. Because he actually *did* bring it up.

"Well... it was sudden and passionate. I just fell for her one day, as if I was possessed. And then just as suddenly—wham!—it was over."

"Man..." I don't know what to say. *What if Reggie does that to me?* "So you must still like her?"

"Not in the slightest. Some relationships are just, like—I don't know—temporary insanity."

I don't reply. All I *want* is a relationship that's insane. Isn't that what being in love is all about?

"Anyway," I say, changing the subject. "That Sina's a piece of work."

"Oh, Sina. Yes, all the Magnolias are terrified of her. Madison rules the school, but only because Sina doesn't go there."

"Sina goes somewhere else?"

"She lives out past Pin Point, toward Skidaway Island somewhere," Thaddeus says. "No one knows where she comes from. But everyone certainly knows her. She's at all the parties."

"She sort of sucks."

"Maybe, but everyone wants her to like them."

"Not me. If I want to be abused, there are plenty of other people here to pick from."

Thaddeus looks at me thoughtfully. "You don't really look like a Magnolia."

"Why?" I say defensively.

"Your hair, for one thing," he says. "It's pretty out there."

"Where I'm from, it's normal," I say. *Whatever. Why should I care what this guy thinks about my hair?*

Behind him, some guys are tapping a second keg, and the party is getting nutty. Three jocks throw a wooden chair on the bonfire, and sparks flare up, getting dangerously close to the overhanging canopy of Spanish moss. A flock of boys has settled down around Hayes and Madison. A completely gorgeous black guy has his arm draped around Hayes's shoulder.

"That must be Jason," I say.

"They've been dating forever. Jason's family is major Georgia new money. Golf courses, I think."

"Huh," I answer, thinking about what Reggie would do at this scene. He'd probably be rolling joints and doing keg stands, well on his way to being everyone's best friend.

"So, you grew up on some kind of commune?"

"A collective farm."

"And now you're here for good."

"No way! I'm moving back as soon as I turn eighteen. Or college."

"That'll be a first."

"You think women don't go to college?"

"No, Magnolias don't leave Savannah."

"What?" I look at him uncertainly. "I'm sorry, but

there is no way that someone like your sister won't end up at Princeton or something. She's an admissions officer's wet dream."

"That may be," he says. "But she'll go to Armstrong Atlantic or Savannah State. Not Princeton, not even Georgia Tech. Because she's a Magnolia, and Magnolias don't leave. Ever."

"Now I know why Sina thinks you're all so lame."

"I promise you, sweetheart, I have much better reasons than that," Sina says, suddenly appearing. "What are you doing back here, Thaddeus? Molesting children is still a crime, even in Georgia."

Thaddeus doesn't answer.

"We're just hanging," I say. "And I'm probably the same age as you."

"I doubt that," Sina says, and she takes a breath in preparation for saying something really mean that'll totally humiliate me in front of Thaddeus and—oh God—I know I won't be able to help it. I'm going to cry again. But then we all hear yelling.

A pretty serious fistfight has erupted next to the keg. The kid who said I had roadkill on my head—Gilroy—is currently being pounded into the dirt. The crowd has moved back to a respectful distance, happy for the entertainment.

"Faggot!" Gilroy screams at the other boy as they roll around on the ground, arms wrapped around each other's necks.

"If that's true, then I think Gilroy's definitely the bottom," I say, and I detect a tiny smile flitting across Thaddeus's face. It's not like me to be so bitchy, but what the hey? I finally got him to smile.

Then things go bad. Sparks from the bonfire ignite a clump of Spanish moss dangling from the canopy. It smolders, bursts into flame, and drops like a rock into a bunch of scrub at the base of the trees. The scrub is bone-dry from the August heat.

"Those idiots are going to get killed," Thaddeus says. Without a backward glance, he runs toward them.

"Jimmy! Roy!" he yells. "Look around you!"

They continue to roll on the ground—doing themselves no favors in proving they're not attracted to each other. I look over to where Hayes and Madison are standing, and they're staring at the bonfire. The crowd is jostling and people are running into each other as they back away. No one's in a panic yet, but it's only a matter of minutes. The scrub at the base of the live oaks is blazing, and the flames are creeping across the ground. Thaddeus tries to break up the fight, but a flying leg from the man tangle on the ground sends him back on his ass, right into the burning scrub.

Hayes starts toward him, but she can't get there through this river of people. I'm closer, and no one else is nearby except Sina. I don't know what I'm going to do, but someone has to do something.

"Thaddeus!" I yell. "Watch—"

And then something seriously strange happens.

As I come near him, the flames shrink away from me, and then the fire dies down, as if someone has blown out an enormous candle.

I step back, stupefied. Did that really happen? Maybe I imagined it. It *is* hot out here. I look down at Thaddeus on the ground. I reach out my hand to help him, but he stands up on his own.

"Are you okay?" I ask.

"Perfectly fine," he says, his face red, his clothes covered in ash.

"Did you see that?"

"No."

"But—"

"Just watch out for snakes, Alex," Thaddeus says curtly, walking away. As I watch, mouth agape, Sina sidles up to me.

"Nice work," Sina says. She leans in close and then brushes my necklace with her fingers. "I see you've learned to use your protection."

"What?" Some idiot has already started another fire in the pit behind us. Sina's eyes glitter in the new flames.

"I'm onto you, Alexandria," she says. "Remember that."

I watch as she sashays away into the darkness, leaving me to fend for myself next to the fire.

13

Okay, so, I'm sixteen years old. Yes, sixteen . . . and this is my first day of school. *Ever.*

What do you even wear to real school? At the RC, we wore overalls or old shirts and work pants. Whatever we were planning on wearing later while we worked the soil. When I mentioned that to Madison, she turned pale.

"Overalls?" she whispered. "Sure, they're great if you haven't turned four yet, but after that they're a big no-no. Maybe—*maybe*—if you worked in a traveling circus, like in the sideshow, and you shaved your eyebrows and bit the heads off live chickens for money— maybe then you could pull off overalls. Anyway, I'm sorry, were we talking about overalls? I'm going to have to go wash my brain now."

So...no overalls. Instead, for my first day as a student at the River School for College Preparation, I'm going with a pair of Rock & Republic jeans, my String Cheese Incident T-shirt (it's not vintage, but I still think it's pretty awesome), and a blazer. It doesn't look too bad. I consider putting my hair up the way Hayes showed me, but then I decide against it. The dreads are my look. I'm not going to change myself just for these snobby, judgmental girls.

Still, I have to admit I'm totally nervous. Even more nervous than before that stupid party, because now, instead of just having to deal with a bunch of new kids, I have to meet with teachers, coaches, a principal...all of whom will no doubt spend a long time telling me how unusual my upbringing has been and how wrong all my mom's ideas about education were.

What's important is that *I* know my education wasn't weird. After all, do weirdos know that the secret to growing really great kale is old coffee grounds? Or that Dostoyevsky wrote *Crime and Punishment* in six weeks because he needed the money? Or that John Wilkes Booth was actually a hot, famous theater star before he shot Lincoln? Actually, these are probably *exactly* the things weirdos know.

I decide to ride my bike—another miscalculation on my part. MapQuest said the distance to the River School was eight miles. I was down with that; after all, back at the RC I used to ride twenty miles all the time. But after the first pretty stretch, the rest of the route is malls and Quiznos places. Plus, of course, the temperature is scorching, even at seven forty-five. By the time I show up, my fancy blazer is stuffed into my backpack, my shirt (and bra) are soaked, and I have car soot all over my face. Maybe I should have taken Miss Lee up on being chauffeured to school by Josie, but it bugged her so much when I insisted on biking that I had to do it.

"Bicycle?" she said two weeks ago when I told her that was my preferred mode of transportation. "That is just hogwash, Alexandria. No, no. No, no, no. And again, no. Magnolias should travel the way God intended—in an automobile."

"Um…"

"It would be so much fun to buy you a car. How about a cute little Saab, or—"

"Nah. Just a Bianchi," I said.

"Is that an Italian coupe?"

"It's a bike."

She grimaced, unimpressed. I didn't get my Bianchi, but she managed to meet me halfway—the next day a truly rad Public M8 in chartreuse showed up in the garage. I'll say this for my forever-twenty-one-looking grandma: She's not cheap.

Although now I'm sort of wishing I *did* have an Italian coupe. Because here I am, drenched, locking my bike to a light pole in front of the River School's compound of swank brick buildings, and who should walk up looking at me like I'm a salamander that just crawled out of the primordial ooze but Thaddeus, completely camera-worthy in a cranberry-colored shirt and chinos.

"Hey," I say. "I couldn't find the bike racks."

"No," he says. "No one bikes to school."

"Huh." I stand up, rolling down my right cuff to cover the bike grease on my ankle. "How's the reading?"

"You were right," he says. "That was an excellent book. Not the easiest to get through, but quite good. Especially the war part."

"Yeah. And how about those love scenes with Frederic and Catherine? Totally orgasmic."

"Right," Thaddeus says, looking at me oddly.

Crap. I can't believe I just said that.

"Not that I even know what an orgasm is!" I say. "I mean, I do know. I do it all the time! Or sometimes. Whatever."

Stop talking! my inner voice screams. *Stop talking now!*

Thaddeus smiles. I finally made him smile! So what if I made an ass out of myself?

"So, were you okay the other night?" I say, trying to

121

steer the conversation away from this infinitely awkward territory.

"What do you mean?" he asks, his voice snapping back to its usual distant tone.

"After the fire."

"Of course."

"It was weird how it was burning and then just went out like that," I press, determined to get some answers about the other night. "Is that some kind of special Southern fire-making? Because I get the feeling you didn't find it at all weird that it just sort of extinguished itself when I came close."

"Thad!" someone yells. A group of people at a picnic table out on the sun-beaten lawn are waving to him.

"I don't know what you're talking about," he says hurriedly. "Just remember, Savannah's not like California. Especially if you're a Magnolia."

"What do you—"

"Dude!" A ruddy boy in a rugby shirt joins us and slaps Thaddeus on the back. "How was your summer? Did you make it up to Rockville for the regatta? I heard the chicas were bangin'."

Wow. I am invisible to these people.

Without another word, Thaddeus and Rugby Shirt walk toward the picnic tables. Not even a backward glance.

"Thanks for introducing me to your friends," I say to his retreating back. I take a deep breath, trying to slow the frantic thumping in my chest. School is swarming with kids, and they all either ignore me or give me the stink eye. A couple of younger boys pretend to hold their noses as they walk past.

"It's called soap, hippie!" one of them says.

"Look!" someone else yells. "Whoopi Goldberg and a marshmallow had a baby."

The bell rings. Everyone begins rushing inside as if gathered up by the world's largest vacuum cleaner. They all seem to know exactly where to go, but I hang back, clueless. For once I sort of wish Hayes and Madison were with me.

"Lost?"

A tanned, tough-looking woman in her mid-thirties stands before me. She's wearing a khaki shirt and matching pants, and she holds a carved wooden cane. She looks like she's about to go on safari—all that's missing is the pith helmet. It takes a moment before I realize what else is different about her: She's not wearing even an ounce of makeup. After the glamourama look everyone else sports around here, I have to say I'm sort of digging it.

"Not lost," I say. "New."

"Name?"

"Alex Lee."

"Oh, well, I'm Constance Taylor, and you're assigned to my English class."

"Cool." I'm actually looking forward to English class.

It'll be fun to hear what someone other than RC hippies has to say about American literature. At the RC, everything always seemed to come down to the fight against "the system" and—I don't know—composting.

"Stand here. I'll get your assigned homeroom." She disappears into the building, leaving me to wait outside. I wander over to the doors and peer into the hall. Even though this is clearly a fancy school, it still smells a little like disinfectant. The walls are painted a pearl gray. Shiny brushed-steel lockers line the sides of the passageway. It's all very pleasant and very…sterile.

All of a sudden, the smell and the silver lockers take me back to a vivid memory of my trip to the morgue.

I'm so sorry, honey, but as next of kin you need to identify—

As if bitten, I jump back from the door into the sunlight, bumping into a fat kid dressed in droopy hipster jeans, Buddy Holly glasses, and a completely rad black *Save CBGB* T-shirt. Sure, it's a little too tight and, yes, there are man-boobs present, but it looks authentic.

"Easy there, Grace Slick," he says with no trace of a Southern accent as he bends down to pick up his sketch pad. His skin is refreshingly pale compared to everyone else's perfect golden tan.

"Sorry," I mumble.

He looks at me curiously. "You're new, aren't you? I'd definitely remember that hair."

"Yeah. I'm Alex."

"From?"

"Mendocino."

"Nice. I'm Dex," he says. "As in Dexter. Like the show."

"The show?"

"Yeah. But my parents named me years before the show even came on, so I'm pretty sure I'm the result of hate sex. *Dexter* is my parents' expression of verbal regret."

"Um...ha-ha?"

"Or it was really *good* sex, and this was their way of expressing their guilt at enjoying it. Which would make sense, because they're Jewish."

I'm starting to like this guy. He's more embarrassing than I am.

"That's a cool T-shirt."

"Yeah? I've got one in every color."

"They only made the *Save CBGB* shirts in black," I say.

"Yeah, well, I've got black, black, black, black, and black too. Not many people would have that particular factoid on file, by the way."

"I like to keep things old school."

"No diggity. We'll have to break out my turntable sometime. I've been buying all this vinyl from Daptone, and listening to it is like pouring honey into your ears, only without the ants, and the mess, and any of the hor- ribleness of actually pouring actual honey into your ears.

Digital reproduction is like listening to twenty percent of a song played on instruments made of scrap metal. It's a copy of a copy of a copy. There's no soul."

I smile.

"Anyway, I have to go, because I'm late. But I'll find you at lunch. You'll need me then. This place is like the sequel to *Mean Girls*. As in *Mean Girls 2: Even Meaner and More Hateful Girls Who Will Burn Your Soul to Death with Their Eye Rays*."

"It can't be *that* bad," I say.

"Oh, really? There's this one pack of debutantes who will tear off your face and eat it just for fun. They're like rabid dogs. Their moms are all in this reactionary right-wing group called the Magnolia League. Ask yourself: Who joins something called a league besides supervillains?"

"I'll be careful," I say, my cheeks flushing.

Just then Constance approaches, carrying a sheaf of papers. "Hello, Dexter," she says pleasantly. "The first day, and already—"

"Late," he says. "I know. Would you expect anything less?" He grins and dashes down the hall.

"You're due for a placement exam, I understand," Constance says to me. "Because of your lack of traditional schooling."

Here it comes.

"I don't know, it *felt* pretty traditional," I say. "I mean, we read Shakespeare. And Bob Dylan's autobiography.

There was a breadth to our learning that I might not have *had* in a more traditional environment."

Constance raises one eyebrow. "Then I'm sure this exam will be a breeze for you. You'll take it in my homeroom."

I follow her into the dreadful hallway, keeping my head down. She leads me to a classroom and closes the door. Someone's gone crazy with a bunch of bright turquoise-blue paint, and the walls are lined with huge *National Geographic*–worthy photos of families all over the world—Australian bush people, what look like Eskimos on the tundra, Tibetans in traditional dress.

"Did you take all of these yourself?" I ask.

"I did," she says. "When I'm not teaching I travel."

"Cool."

I look around some more. There's a quote painted in black near the ceiling:

> *I confess I do not believe in time.*
> *—Vladimir Nabokov*

"He wrote *Lolita*, right?" I ask. She nods. "That's a pretty creepy book."

"Particularly for a teenage girl," she says, handing me my test. "So, you've read *Lolita*? That's either a good sign or a bad one—I'm not sure which."

I nod. And then shake my head. I have no idea why it would be a bad sign.

She looks at me curiously. "You came here from California?"

"Yeah. I came to Savannah because my mother died. I live with my grandmother."

"Oh," she says, frowning. "I'm sorry for your loss." She looks down at my file, and her face tightens. "Your grandmother is Dorothy Lee?"

"Yes."

"So your mother was—"

"Louisa," I say. "Louisa Lee."

Constance looks stricken. "I knew your mother," she says finally. "I knew her in high school. I wasn't aware that..."

"Car accident," I say quickly, to get us off the topic.

"I see," she says again, recovering her composure. "Are you ready for the test, then?"

I sit down and fill out answers. It's not too bad, and I must do okay, because the next thing I know it's third period, and I'm being shuttled to junior history.

"This is Mr. Roberts's class," she says before opening the door. "If you do well, he'll let you take the AP exam."

"Cool," I say, wondering what the hell an AP exam is. "Thanks, Constance."

She hesitates, looking at me strangely. "We're pretty formal here at the River School. Let's stick to Miss Taylor, okay?"

"Oh," I say. "Right."

She opens the door. Inside, class is already under way. I spot Madison near the back of the room.

Mr. Roberts, an extremely square-looking teacher with a salt-and-pepper bowl cut and a short-sleeved yellow button-down shirt stained with sweat around the armpits, looks over, obviously annoyed by the interruption.

"Hello," Constance—I mean, Miss Taylor—says. "This is Alex Lee. She'll be joining class this year. I'm sure you'll all make her welcome."

Everyone stares. I feel like I'm in a zoo.

"There's an empty desk next to me," Madison says.

I scuttle over and plop down. Maybe I'm wrong after all. Maybe she's actually pretty cool.

Um...not so cool, though? This *class*. Mr. Roberts drones on and on about the syllabus—mainly reading out of a heinous-looking textbook. I'm so bored that finally I raise my hand.

"Yes?" he says tersely. The other kids turn and stare.

"Will we be reading Lincoln's letters?" I ask. "Like, when we get to the Civil War?"

"Is the syllabus not sufficient for you, Miss Lee?"

I look around at the increasingly hostile room. "No, I just thought...well, if we're learning about that time, we'd want to...uh...read what he wrote about it. I mean, that's what we did where I used to—"

"Primary sources?" Mr. Roberts barks. "Is that your suggestion?"

"This girl's a runaway truck," Jason—Hayes's boyfriend—blurts. The class bursts out laughing.

"I guess..."

"Then I'll add that to the reading list."

From my new peers, a collective groan.

"By Monday, I want everyone to have read the first eighty pages of *The Collected Works of Abraham Lincoln*. Volume Two. I'll put copies on reserve in the library. And while you're reading, I encourage you to think hard about Miss Lee and her hunger for knowledge."

No one looks at me for the rest of the class. But when the bell rings, a hand reaches out and slides my papers and books onto the floor.

"Way to go, hippie," Gilroy, the boy from the party, mutters.

Jason gives my shoulder a reassuring, pitying pat as he passes.

"Gilroy," Madison says smoothly, putting her hand on his arm, "leave Alex alone, please. She's one of our best friends."

Gilroy squints his beady eyes at me.

"So what?"

"So, you mess with her and you're messing with all of us, knuckle dragger," Madison says curtly.

Gilroy shakes his head and stomps off.

"Are you *completely* suicidal?" Madison demands, ushering me out of the classroom and dragging me toward the lawn. "That hair is bad enough, your dirty clothes aren't much better, and then you make us do more mind-numbing reading? Even *I* hate you, and I like you."

I shrug my shoulders defiantly. "I don't know."

Just then I feel a presence at my other shoulder. It's Anna, the radioactive blond girl from the party. She seems to have gotten a fresh coat of orange fake tan for her first day of school. Mary, the busty redhead, is trailing after her.

"Y'all eating on the lawn?" she asks.

"The lawn is for sophomores, Mary," Madison says impatiently. "Juniors eat at the benches. What are we? We're juniors. Now, go clean off the bench in the shade."

"But kids are already sitting—"

"That's what I mean. Clean it *off*." Mary frowns uncertainly and trots away. Madison rolls her eyes and turns to me.

"Alex, as Magnolias, we are respected at this school. People look to us for guidance on what is and isn't the proper way to do things. We are paragons of virtue because everything we do is always appropriate. This will not work if you insist on acting like a total spaz."

"I'm not a spaz, okay? And that's a really inappropriate word to use. Think of all those kids with cerebral palsy."

"How about *bonehead*?"

"I come from a place where kids don't judge each

other," I say. "Sure, I didn't go to a traditional school, and that's weird. I get that. But from what I can tell so far, real school sucks."

Madison laughs. "'School sucks'?'" she says. "How original. What's your next brilliant academic observation? Cheerleading uniforms objectify women? *Of course* school sucks. It's a rigid hierarchical pyramid with the losers on the bottom, an enormous mass of irrelevant people in the middle, and the important people at the pinnacle. The trick is to be at the pinnacle."

"What about the idea of revolution? Changing the system? Instead of being part of the problem, you could be part of the solution."

"Alex," Madison says through clenched teeth, "if you keep talking in bumper stickers, I am going to stab you in the face."

"You don't have to hang with me. It's not like we're the Three Musketeers or something."

"Actually, I do have to 'hang' with you," she mutters.

Hayes joins us with Jason in tow. "Hey, girls. What's happening?"

"Damage control," Madison says. "Alex is trying to completely sabotage her River School career within the first three hours."

"That *was* pretty ugly in there," Jason says.

"Well, I brought bacon mac-and-cheese for everybody," Hayes says brightly. "Mom made it last night."

"Cool," Madison says. "I had Mary order Reubens."

I grin, in spite of myself. At least these girls aren't anorexic.

Out of the corner of my eye, I see a commotion at one of the benches on the edge of the lawn. Dex, my new friend, is working on his sketch pad under a tree. Or he's trying to, but Mary is frantically pulling on his arm.

"Looks like Mary's about to burst something," Madison says. "Hope she chose saline over silicone."

"What's she doing?" I ask.

"That *dweeb* is on our bench. Mary's explaining the rules to him. It's killing two birds with one stone, really. She's proving her loyalty to us, and he's learning about our territory."

"He's not a dweeb—he's my friend."

"Alex," Hayes says sweetly, "I don't think you've been here long enough to have friends besides us."

I stand up and march over to the bench where Mary is having a meltdown. Her face is red and sweaty, and her eye makeup is smudged.

"Dexter, you have to move, you fat fag!" she screams. "They're coming! They are! Look!" It takes me a minute to realize she's pointing at me.

Dexter looks up coolly and smiles. "Hey, Slick," he says to me. "This is what I was telling you about. Crazy debutantes."

"Don't talk to her directly," Mary screeches. "She's a *Magnolia*."

Dexter looks at me, confused. "What?"

"Well, not really," I stammer. "I mean, my grandmother's making me do it. It's a family thing. But—"

"Oh," he says. "Well. Sorry I bashed them. I mean, you seem all right, but..." He looks at Madison and Hayes, who have now appeared behind me.

"Good-*bye*," Madison says to the staring kids. As if possessed, they gather their books and lunches and shuffle off. "Dexter. *Off.*"

"This is stupid," I say. "There are, like, twenty benches. Or we can just cop a squat on the lawn."

"Yes, but this is the junior Magnolias' bench," Hayes says patiently. "It always has been."

"I'm done, anyway," Dexter says, throwing his sketch pad and pencils into his messenger bag. "Alex, you want to eat in the art studio? It's air-conditioned."

"Sweet. Thanks."

"Alex," Madison says, "it's really not cool to abandon us on your first day."

"I'm not abandoning you," I say. "I'm just expanding my horizons."

"Just remember, we're your real friends," Madison snaps. I look to Hayes for a token bit of reason, but to my surprise, her face looks oddly dark.

I shoot Dex an apologetic look. "Guys, it's not a cult. It's a social club. That our mothers and grandmothers belong to. It's not a lifestyle. I'll see you later, okay?"

I turn and follow Dex across the lawn. The one

time I glance back, Madison is huddled with the other girls around her, whispering. Hayes is still staring at me as if she expects that at any minute I'll come back.

During lunch in the art studio, Dex gives me the dirt on the politics of the River School. "Madison and Hayes run the school," he says between bites of a microwaved Krispy Kreme. (Dex has the same appetite as Madison and Hayes but seems to lack the metabolism.) "You know the type. They're the queens, and all the other girls are their subjects."

"What makes them so special?"

"Come to think of it, I don't know, really. I mean, they're pretty, but there are a lot of pretty girls here. I don't know—the kids just...follow them around. It's like they have some special social power or something."

"What about that Sina person? Do you know her?"

"Of course. She's notorious. A total fox."

"Where does she come from?"

Dex narrows his eyes while wiping frosting from his mouth with a napkin. "I don't know. The boonies somewhere." He eyes the lunch Josie made me—deviled eggs, fried chicken, some kind of "salad" consisting mainly of bacon and mayonnaise. Not an organic veggie or fruit in sight. "You gonna eat all that?"

"No way," I say, sliding the bag toward him.

"Thanks." He pops a deviled egg into his mouth, rolling his eyes to the ceiling with pleasure. "I'll tell you what, though. Those Maggots really don't like her."

"Maggots?"

"No offense, but that's what we underlings call you Magnolias. At least until now."

"None taken." I try not to look bothered. *Oh God. What has my grandmother gotten me into?*

"Sina's the only one who holds a candle to them socially. She's at every big party, and they just shrink from her. Personally, I'm glad she's around. She's totally hot, and interesting. Although she might be even worse than they are."

"In what way?"

"Oh, she can be really mean. She plays tricks on people just for fun. Like, this one guy who said Madison was better looking than Sina? Sina slipped him some kind of drink that made really weird things happen. He sprouted hair on the back of his hands, man. Instantly. Like, we were all watching."

"What? How?"

"I don't know. Maybe it was Propecia or something. Or some kind of antidote to Nair."

"That's the trippiest thing I've ever heard."

"That's nothing, friend. Savannah is a weird, weird place. I'm telling you. The city was founded by pirates and runaway slaves straight from African tribes and shit. There's black magic everywhere."

"Come on."

"I just moved from Iowa two years ago. Things are normal there. You don't like someone, you don't like them. Girls are mean to one another, but it's normal mean. They just hate-text or videophone each other buck naked in the locker room and throw it up on Facebook."

"People do that?"

"Welcome to high school, Alex. It's the land of the mean-girl tricks. Only in Savannah, the hoaxes are weirder."

"Like what?"

"Well, there was that hand hair thing. Oh, and last year, that Orang-Anna girl tried to start her own posse. Then she got, like, majorly spooked. She said a gray man was following her everywhere."

"Gray like *old*?"

"Like the color. He was transparent or something. I don't know. She told the police and everything. But no one could ever figure out what she was talking about."

"Was she high?" Plenty of people saw weird stuff at the RC, but it was always with the help of organic mushrooms.

"No way. That girl is as squeaky clean as they come. She won't even drink soft drinks. She goes to parties only because Madison makes her, to pad her group."

"So, you're saying Madison and Hayes hired a henchman to follow her around or something?"

"I'm just telling you what I heard. I don't have

concrete theories. All I'm saying is, we're not in Kansas anymore. Or California or Iowa. These rules are different. Like once at a bonfire, I ran into Sina. I don't ever talk to her. I mean, she's way too hot for normal dorky conversation. But I was taking a leak in the woods, and I bumped into her by accident. She looked... weird. Like *old*. Really old. Then she kind of hissed at me, and I blinked, and she was totally gone."

"You sure it wasn't just something you ate?" I say, watching him pop another egg into his mouth.

"Fine, it's true. I'm a human garbage disposal," he says, still chewing. "But this is a weird, weird place, dude. I'm telling you—beware. Almost nothing in Savannah is what it seems."

14

The sun's been cooking the town all day, so the ride home from the River School is even more miserable than the trip there. I pedal my way through the thick, hot air, thankful when I finally reach the shaded inner sanctum of the downtown streets of Savannah.

As I coast up Abercorn, I mull over my bizarre day. My first experience with school, at sixteen (is that a record?), actually wasn't that terrible. Sure, the classes were all boring except Constance's, and I accidentally gave a girl a black eye during gym class (I thought capture the flag had more or less the same rules as mud ball), but at least I made a friend. That Dex, he's pretty cool.

I stop my bike and look around Forsyth Park.

"Well, if it isn't Alexandria Lee," someone calls from the direction of the fountain. I whip my head around and spot Sam Buzzard, who is leaning against a wrought-iron lamppost and smiling at me.

"Hey," I say, stopping next to him. I wipe the sweat off my forehead with the back of my hand. Just like the other day, Sam's not perspiring at all.

"How is everything?"

"First day of school," I reply.

"Oh, man. That can be brutal."

"It was okay, actually. Weird, but okay."

"You know, I was thinking about you the other day. Wondering if you wanted to come out to my house. There's a great dock for swimming, and—you're into gardening and herbs, right?"

"I try," I admit. "It's something I learned from my mother. Just your basic root stuff. I'm kind of scared I'll get rusty."

He nods. "Well, why don't you come out and see what I've got? Begonia tess, for starters."

"Begonia tess? The kind those botanists just found in India?"

"Turns out they could have looked right here in the States."

I shake my head in disbelief. Begonia tess is a notoriously powerful leaf, but no one has reported seeing it here for more than one hundred years. It can be used for all sorts of things, from clotting blood to getting rid of colds. Some people even say it can be used as an aphrodisiac. Every summer, my mom tried to create a hybrid like it, but she would always end up cursing the shriveled, dead seedlings.

"Want to go check it out now?"

"Okay."

"Throw your bike in the back." He points to a gorgeous robin's-egg blue vintage Chevy truck, perfectly restored.

"Nice ride," I say, loading my M8 and climbing up to the passenger's seat. Sam turns on the radio, and we weave through the green downtown streets, quickly reaching the suburbs and the highway dotted with strip malls and tanning parlors. Eventually even those thin out, and we're in the country, driving along the Savannah River. I look out at the thick, junglelike forest and the miles of marsh grass. The din of crickets drifts through the open window.

"That marsh grass is so pretty," I say. "The more I stare at it, the less I can tell what color it is. Green? Yellow?"

"It changes every day. That's what's so gorgeous about it. See? We'll make a Georgia girl of you yet."

I look up at the sky, which is milky white in the shimmering afternoon heat. Every once in a while Sam takes a turn; the roads are getting wilder and thinner. The land is dotted with little houses and trailers. We pass a group of men gathered around some fighting roosters. Many of the men grip liquor bottles in their hands, and there are guns attached to the back of several of the trucks.

It's at this point that I realize a few things:

1. I might have agreed to this trip a bit too quickly.
2. I really don't know Sam Buzzard at all.
   a. He might be a psycho killer.
   b. He might be kidnapping me.
3. If he *is* kidnapping me, I have no phone and no idea where I am, so I'm seriously screwed.

"We almost there?" I ask, trying to sound casual.

"Just about," he says reassuringly. "I know it seems like a long ride, but you'll get used to it."

I will? I wonder. *Why?*

"Have you lived out here long?"

"Oh, a real long time. My entire life."

"Seriously?" It doesn't compute. Sam Buzzard seems too urban and cool to live out here in the boonies.

"I travel, of course," he says. "But I like it here. My father lives here, and my grandfather before him, and my grandfather's grandfather before that. My family was given this land after the Civil War."

My jaw drops. "Your family has lived here on the same land since 1865?"

"Eighteen sixty-eight, actually. Forty acres and a mule, baby. Although Sherman didn't actually give anyone forty acres, and my family never did get that mule, but we got three parcels on the river. During the war, the federal government seized a lot of the land down here and redistributed it. White folks tried to take it back by any means necessary, but my ancestors were smart—they not only held on to their own but bought more."

"So, your ancestors were slaves?"

"Of course. When my great-great grandfather was freed, he'd been a slave for three years, and he couldn't speak a word of English. There was a whole population of Africans here who were exactly like him, just off the boat. A lot of families out here still speak Gullah—a mix of English and West African dialects, a little Krio, a little Vai, a little Mende."

A huge water oak rises up in the middle of the highway. One of its broken branches is painted like a smiling alligator. Sam follows it to the left. Oak branches form a canopy over the road, and as we drive they droop lower and lower until they're brushing the top of the truck. Then, after half a mile, we reach a shady stretch of land completely covered by live oaks that rolls gently all the way to the river. The oak trunks rise up like twisted pillars, and their branches burst like fireworks and form a green roof over the entire area.

Close to the river is a cluster of one-story wooden houses. They look like white boxes, with bright turquoise shutters and doors, and the dirt in front of them is carefully swept. To one side is a larger building with a big screened porch and a sign that reads *Buzzard Social Club—Members Only*, and next to it is an enormous satellite dish.

"Welcome to Buzzard's Roost," Sam says.

"I like that turquoise."

"We call that haint blue. People believe it keeps the devil away from the house."

"Maybe not such a fan of the satellite dish," I add.

"Just because we live in the country doesn't mean we don't like football," he says. "This *is* still Georgia, after all."

He gets out of the truck. I open the door, letting my feet dangle below me. The air is cool and salty from the marsh and the river. The only sounds are the wind rustling in the trees and the soft call of wind chimes made of stained glass and old forks.

"If you can bear to look past the dish, you might see something of more interest to you," Sam says.

I look again, and there it is: a greenhouse, long and low, flanked by smaller buildings that look like work sheds. Behind them I see a gate—also painted haint blue—and beyond that there's a garden. Everything is crafted of naked wood, long gone silvery gray in the sun. Even from here, I can smell cloves, cinnamon, lemongrass, and an intoxicating mix of herbs. It smells almost like home.

"And this is my humble abode," he says, walking up onto the plank porch of a clapboard cube by the river.

He slides back two huge iron bolts — they're meant to lock out the weather, I guess. The house is one long, low room, with windows that open out on the river. It looks like a weird archaeological museum — every surface is stacked with artifacts. I recognize a lot of them; the RC was a hotbed of people who were "searching," running from one religion to another. There are Tibetan prayer wheels, dozens of Sacred Heart milagros made of tin from South America, a set of O-kee-pa hooks, and some Brazilian smudge pots. Just about every kind of folk art is represented somewhere on Sam's walls, but after that, I'm lost. There are handwoven blankets and rugs draped across his furniture, crystal skulls lining the shelves, crosses covered with icons snipped from tin hanging from the rafters, beadwork dangling from leather headdresses, bottles and vials stoppered with cork and melted wax. And books. There are bookshelves on every wall, bookshelves hiding his bed, bookshelves framing the kitchen, bookshelves attached to the bathroom door, bookshelves in the bathroom.

It's such a cool place. Why didn't my grandmother want me to come?

"Man," I say, looking at Sam. His urban-chic outfit of linen pants and an expensive silk shirt is utterly incongruous with this house. "It's not exactly what I pictured. I sort of thought you'd live in some slick, modern McMansion."

"Never judge a man by his clothes," Sam says. We

stand in silence, taking in the chaotic, overwhelming beauty of this place.

"Is all this stuff from when you studied at Yale?"

"Most of it."

Suddenly, the enchanted air is pierced by the sound of the phone ringing.

"Excuse me, Alex," he says. "I need to get that."

He heads for the kitchen, and I walk to one of the bookshelves, which is jammed with all kinds of titles— medical books, Russian novels, cookbooks. A red leather-bound volume is set slightly apart from the rest. I look at the title: *Lady Brown's Book of Conjure and Spells. Copyright, 1943.* An overwhelming fragrance drifts up. It's not the old-book smell I was expecting, but something different. Some sort of exotic herb. I flip through the pages. The margins are filled with handwritten notes.

"What are you doing?" Sam says sharply as he comes back into the room.

"Oh, sorry. I was just—"

He strides briskly toward me and whips the book out of my hand. "You should not be touching that."

"Sorry," I say again, backing away. His eyes, usually so kind, are frighteningly cold. But maybe I'm just imagining it. Because when he turns to me after replacing the book on the shelf, his pleasant expression is back. "Let's go to the garden, shall we?"

"Sure," I say, following him outside. He leads me down a path lined with a low fence made from driftwood, old bottles, and parts from bicycles and junk cars. The wind is getting stronger, bending the branches above. In front of us there is a high gate with a large, formidable padlock, which Sam opens with a key. When the gate swings open, I can't help gasping.

The garden is bigger than it looks from the outside—almost a full acre. And it's exquisite. The ground is crowded with pots that overflow with rich green plants and neon-colored blossoms. Thick flowering vines climb the walls. The garden is like a jungle, but meticulously ordered and maintained. And at the far end stands the most spectacular feature: a screened-in aviary, teeming with brightly colored, unusually plump birds.

I take it in quietly. At the RC, my mom and I built the Sanctuary with our bare hands, planting every herb, every creeper, every shrub and weed and vine ourselves. We weeded and watered it every day, and it was as unique and private as my mother's soul. And now, at the opposite side of the country, I've walked into the other half of the Sanctuary. It's as if I'd walked into a Barnes & Noble and found her diary for sale on a shelf. For the second time today, I feel an acute, stabbing pang.

"What's wrong?" Sam asks.

"It's just that my mom... really would have loved this place."

Sam smiles sadly. "Your mom *did* love this place," he says quietly.

"She was here?"

"Of course. Your mother and I were close friends."

I shake my head.

"It's so crazy," I say. "She had this whole...life before me."

"Most people who have children do," Sam says, smiling. He picks a few leaves from a plant I don't recognize. "I'm going to mix you a batch of Swamp Brew. To help chill you out when your day-to-day becomes overwhelming."

"Swamp Brew?" I ask. "The same as my mom—"

"Who do you think taught her?" he says. "I'll be back."

He disappears into the vines. While he's gone, I continue to wander around, fingering the plants, the flowers, the pots. The ones I recognize, I name aloud: "Lemongrass. Verbena. Clove. Valerian."

Yet there are so many more: in one pot, a sticky fern that smells like cotton candy; in a flower bed, a vine that looks exactly like a snake. When I lean over to touch the vine, I can swear I hear a hissing sound. I jump back, scuttling down the path, to what looks like the end of the garden wall. But it's not just a wall. There's a small door, ajar. Through the opening, I can see a dim green light.

I look back but see no sign of Sam. Slowly, I approach the opening.

"Hello?" I call.

Hearing nothing, I push the door open wider. Inside is a small, windowless room with a stone floor. There's nothing in it but a table laid carefully with several objects: a black candle, a white candle, a glass of salt, nails, a mortar and pestle, and an old fountain pen and ink. Out of the corner of my eye, I think I see something move in the corner. An animal, maybe. Perhaps a large bird.

"Hello?" I whisper.

No one answers. I creep closer to get a better look. Suddenly, the oldest man I've ever seen steps forward out of the shadows. His limbs are as gnarled as cypress roots, and his hair is snow-white. He's wearing the same blue sunglasses Sam wears, despite the serious darkness in the room.

"Oh, hi! Where did you —"

"Doc Buzzard," he says, extending his hand. "How are you?"

"Fine, thank you." His palm is cool and dry. "I'm here with Sam."

"I know," he says.

"What is this place?"

"My garden shed. And meditation center. That's where I pray." He nods at the altar.

"Cool." I squint at the candles. "Are you Catholic or something?"

He smiles. "Or something."

"Alex." Sam is calling from outside.

"Say hello to your grandmother for me."

"Okay." *This guy knows my grandmother?* "See you

later." I can feel him watching me from behind his sunglasses. I step out into the garden, relieved to be in the sunshine again.

"My dad in there?" Sam asks.

"Yeah. He was praying, I think."

"He's a very religious guy," Sam comments vaguely, clearly unwilling to say more. "Here's your tea. Remember to flash boil it for ten seconds, tops, and then serve it. Boil it longer than that and it won't work."

I put my nose inside. Yes, it's exactly the same mixture my mother made: dried blueberries, chamomile, and that horsey secret ingredient she would never reveal.

"Will you give me the recipe?" I ask.

"Not likely," he says, smiling. "All right, it's getting late. You still want that swim?"

"That's okay," I say. Usually I wouldn't pass up the chance; after all, that's a beautiful river out there. Plus, I love a good swim, and I'm no wimp, even in the bone-chilling water of the Pacific Ocean. But something feels . . . not right about being at Sam's house now.

"Next time."

He nods. "Okay, then." We head back to the truck. On the way down the path, I think I see something dart from one tree to another. But when I turn around, only the long early-evening shadows are visible. The lone sound is the wind in the leaves, whispering as if they have a secret.

15

It's only when we come blazing down Drayton Street in Sam's awesome blue truck, obvious as a Mardi Gras parade float, that I remember my grandmother's warning to stay away from the Buzzards altogether. And because I am, and always have been, a somewhat inherently unlucky person, there she is—naturally!—standing on the porch, staring us down.

"Hello, Miss Lee," Sam sings out from the window.

"Sam," Miss Lee answers, smiling sternly as her eyes travel from him to me.

"Thanks for the ride," I say hastily, hopping to the ground and lifting out my bike to head inside and face my grandmother's wrath—and when I tell her where I've been all afternoon, wrath is exactly what I receive.

"To his *home*?" she sputters. "Are you joking?"

I shrug. I'm not a liar; even though I know that making up stories or avoiding the truth could make things a lot easier for me sometimes, I've never been into it. It's too confusing. How are you supposed to remember what's true and what's not? But now that she's going so nuts over this, I seriously wish I had just said he'd stopped to offer me a ride home from school.

"You *deliberately* disobeyed me," she hisses.

"I didn't, actually. I just forgot what you'd said. It was my first day of school, which was seriously over-whelming. I mean, those Magnolia girls? They are *nuts*. So I saw Sam Buzzard, and he was nice to me, and I just forgot you said not to hang out with him. Okay?"

"Okay?" Miss Lee spits. "Okay? No, this is most certainly *not* okay. You went to a strange man's house. What egregiously irresponsible behavior! Is this the way people act in California?"

"Well, I can't speak for the whole state, but, yes, I'd say I'm a pretty open person."

Miss Lee purses her lips. "All right. Well. I'm sorry, Alexandria. I have no choice but to ground you."

I stare at her in disbelief. She's okay with me getting into a car full of teenagers with bad driving skills and spending all night at a keg party, but she's grounding me for checking out a friend's garden?

"Are you serious?"

"Yes. For the time being, you're not to leave the house. And you may never go to Sam Buzzard's again."

"But that's just crazy," I say. "You can't imprison a young person like that. It's . . . un-American."

"I can't talk about it any further, Alexandria. I'm late for dinner out. I'll have Josie make you something." She looks at me hopelessly, gives one last dramatic sigh, and leaves.

I slink up to my room and plop on the bed, shaking my head in disbelief. Grounded? I never got grounded at the RC, even when I sneaked off with some kids to San Francisco for three days to see a concert without telling anyone. What am I supposed to do in this house? Learn ballroom dancing? Listen politely while my grandmother explains the correct way to sip friggin' sweet tea?

Suddenly, I have an idea. I flip on the computer, waiting impatiently for the Internet to come up. No new e-mails from Reggie . . . big surprise. But that's okay. After tonight, we won't need this stupid e-mail system anymore. I bring up Delta.com and grab that brilliant new credit card out of my backpack.

Okay. I know the Visa was meant for new clothes, not a plane ticket back to California. But I promise you one thing, Grandma. As soon as I get there, I'll get out some scissors and cut it up for good.

16

Magnolia League Meeting: The Senior Four

September is the height of hurricane season in Savannah, and this morning, though the weatherman has issued no warning, it's raining hard enough to feel like one might actually be on the way. Miss Lee struts from the car to Magnolia Hall, holding her trench coat tight around her. When she steps into the hallway, she sees that Mary Oglethorpe has forgone the sweet tea (and the pink wine, for that matter) for a strong, hot pot of Swamp Brew.

"Hello, Dorothy," Sybil says.

"Hi, girls," Miss Lee says. "Thank you for coming on such short notice."

Miss Lee phoned the other Seniors last night after returning from her dinner date. When Mary, Khaki, and Sybil got the call, naturally they dropped everything to come. The Seniors are rarely summoned, but when they are, it's important.

"I probably should have called a full meeting, but I didn't want to alarm the whole damned world." Mary and Sybil exchange glances at their leader's candor. Though they have known her since they were toddlers, as president of the League, "Miss Lee" usually separates herself from her friends with a veil of formality.

"Here," Mary says. "Have some brew." She pours the thick, pungent liquid into a cup. Miss Lee gratefully takes a sip, looking at Mary's rumpled dress and bird's-nest hair with an amused eye. "Mary, you're looking a little disheveled this morning."

Mary smiles sheepishly. "It's this new kid I'm dating."

Sybil shakes her head. "I keep telling you. You conjured yourself too *young*."

"Sybil, you've been lecturing me for thirty years about that."

"And now look. Where were you last night? Doing karaoke on River Street? Jell-O shots with high school students? How is a sixty-five-year-old woman supposed to keep up with that?"

"*I'm* not the one who can't keep her senator husband out of the news for skinny-dipping in Rio," Mary snaps. "Maybe if you'd chosen a better age, you wouldn't have such problems keeping Tom in check."

"I told you, she was Argentinian, not Brazilian."

"Girls, please." Miss Lee sighs.

"Well, we're here for Miss Lee," Sybil says, trying to focus the meeting. She turns to the president, who, despite her evident distress, is resplendent in a silk jersey wrap dress. "What is the issue at hand?"

"Alex is missing," Miss Lee says.

"Hmm." The Senior Four are not alarmed. Magnolias, protected as they are, have more freedom than normal teenage girls. "Did you call Sam to investigate?"

"No. Certainly not. Not with our history."

"Ah," Sybil says, nodding. After what happened to Louisa, that certainly makes sense.

"Anyway, I don't need his insight on this matter. I'm certain she went back to that...zoo where she was raised."

"On her own?" The women are more concerned now. Things are different outside the safe boundaries of Savannah.

"I believe so. Her backpack is gone, and she bought a one-way airline ticket to California with the credit card I gave her."

"Are you going to get her?" Sybil asks. "You can use Tom's plane.... We'll just lump it in with the other non-state-business flying he's in trouble for."

"That's the question," Miss Lee says, obviously frazzled. She takes a sip and closes her eyes. Sybil and Mary wait for the brew to take effect. After a moment, a visible sense of calm comes over their leader's lovely face. "I'm thinking of just letting her go."

Sybil puts her hand over her face, but it's impossible not to see that she is pleased.

"Why are you so smiley about this?" Miss Lee snarls. "Anxious to get the heir out of the way?"

"Don't be ridiculous," Sybil replies. "I simply know that it will make her happy. Hayes is concerned about Alex's happiness."

Miss Lee gives Sybil a long, distrustful stare.

"Why does *she* get to go?" Khaki asks. "What about the Blue Root?"

"She's got a buzzard's rock," Miss Lee says. "She can do anything she wants."

"How did she get *that*?" Sybil demands.

"It fell off my daughter's neck," Miss Lee says quietly.

"You mean before..."

"Yes."

A hush falls over the room.

"I'm so very sorry, Dorothy," Mary says.

"I'm not!" Khaki shouts, suddenly rabidly furious. "This is what you get for ruining my life!"

"Khaki," Miss Lee says, "you were in danger of ruining us all. *Everything*. I couldn't just let you tell all of New York society our secrets. I had to do something."

Sybil remains cautiously silent. Miss Lee looks at her friends coldly and purses her lips for a moment. "I made all the wrong choices with Louisa," she says finally. "So this time I'm letting Alexandria do what she wants."

"Then who gets the mantle?" Sybil asks.

"Careful, Sybil," Miss Lee says. "Your eagerness is not entirely ladylike."

Khaki and Mary giggle as Sybil's face turns red.

"The truth is, honey, I still believe she's the one," Miss Lee says. "This will be the test, I suppose. If Alex is a real Magnolia, she'll be back."

17

So, the bus ride from San Francisco to Mendocino? Totally brutal. The scenery is breathtaking, of course, especially if you choose to take the coastal route, as I did. It adds a few hours, but I figure I have the time. Still, I forgot how gut-churning those hairpin curves on Route 1 can be. I press my nose against the glass, staring at the ocean thousands of feet below, trying to concentrate on not throwing up.

I haven't told anyone yet that I'm coming. For one

thing, it's impossible to get a hold of anyone at the RC. If you call the pay phone, usually no one answers it, and if someone does pick up, good luck getting that person to find the one you're trying to reach.

The other reason is my grandmother. I'm sure the RC is the first place she'll contact when she finds out I'm gone. (In fact, she probably already *has* checked.) If she gets on the phone with Big Jon and he doesn't know I'm coming, well...there's nothing to lie about, is there? Besides, I'm kind of liking this element of surprise. I mean, if Reggie showed up suddenly on the steps of my grandmother's spooky Gothic mansion, I'd be so totally stoked.

I look at my watch. Eleven a.m., California time. Yup, she must definitely know by now. Yesterday, after buying my ticket, I grabbed my backpack, sneaked out of the house, and rode the seven miles to the airport on my bike. I didn't take my phone; I'd never had one before I got to Savannah, so why bring it now? I boarded my $1,029, last-minute flight to California, and now I've spent five hours on this Willy Wonka joyride bus. When the driver pulls into Bodega Bay for a pit stop, I'm so thankful that I'm ready to hug him.

The other passengers file out into the parking lot, some lighting up cigarettes, others taking pictures of the coast and the elephant seals. Most of the people on the bus are retirees on vacation. We're used to them in this part of California. They come in white-haired, plastic-visored herds, emerging from the cars and tour buses to get the views and spend money on post-cards and T-shirts for their beloved grandkids. No rules, no ultimatums, no weird debutante societies. Just good intentions and tacky gifts. Watching them now, I feel a pang. I wish *my* grandmother were like that— proud of me, buying me a California snow-globe paperweight.

"All aboard!" the red-faced bus driver yells. "Leaving in two minutes!"

I get in line, determined to be the last one on this stinky gas-guzzler. Out of the corner of my eye, I see another girl approaching—a skinny hippie girl wearing what Billy always called "eco-hottie rags": a tattered patchwork skirt, a tiny tank top with no bra, a tattoo around her ankle, and bracelets that jangle on her arms. I smile politely and shift a little. I don't want to be rude, but she smells a little funny. She doesn't smile back but instead pushes past me and hands the driver a handful of crumpled bills.

"Mendo," she says.

He nods, not looking at her.

"You know Rain Catcher Farms?" she demands.

The driver shakes his head.

"Well, that's where I'm paying you to take me. Can you handle it?"

"I'm sorry," he says, not unkindly. "I just don't know where that—"

"Isn't this, like, your route? Rain Catcher, okay? It's a pretty major landmark." She puts her hands on her hips. I'd forgotten that a lot of the kids who come to the RC are really rude and forward. My mom always taught me to be polite, no matter what. She was super into manners. I guess that makes sense, now that I know where she came from.

"Hey, I know where Rain Catcher is," I say to the driver. "That's where I'm going too. I'll give you the heads-up."

"Thanks," he says, looking at me gratefully. The girl turns her flinty, slightly bloodshot eyes at me.

"Cool. I'm Crystal. You going up to be a trimmer?"

"What? No, I grew up there. I'm going home."

"Oh," she says. "I hear they've got this huge new crop of weed up there. My boyfriend told me about it. They just planted last month. There's enough work for a bunch of kids to do pretty well."

"I don't know about that," I say, uncomfortable. "I mean, mostly it's produce at Rain Catcher. Organic kale and stuff."

She shrugs. "Whatever."

We get on the bus. She follows me to the back, not noticing the yelps of the white-haired ladies she hits with her backpack. She plops down beside me. "So what were you doing in Frisco?"

Again, I wince. My mother hated it when people used that name for San Francisco. "I was just away for a while, visiting my grandmother. But I'm back now. My boyfriend's here and everything." It feels so good to say it. *Boyfriend*. Surely I can call him that now, can't I?

"Nice," the girl says, stretching out in the seat beside me. "Well, I'm psyched to smoke up and crash for a few weeks. Haven't seen my boyfriend in a while. We sort of had a fight, and he took off. Can you say *make-up sex*, Batman? I just hope they won't make me do too much crap."

I frown. This girl is exactly the kind of worker Big Jon hates—a freeloader. "Everyone does their share," Big Jon always says. "That's community." I hope the people at the RC won't think I brought her with me.

As we get closer, I become a little fidgety. I'm going to see Reggie today! It feels like it's been years. My stomach flops over like a caught fish as I wonder if Reggie will want to take me camping right away. Probably. The kids used to go camping together all the time, but the last night Reggie took just me. That was the surprise he'd arranged for my birthday. As usual, he wouldn't let me tell anyone we were going off together. We had to leave at midnight.

When we got there, we put on our headlamps and played cards in the tent, and then Reggie pulled out a huge bottle of wine.

"I know you hate beer," he explained with his easy grin.

Honestly, I wasn't that into this wine either. It tasted a lot like vinegar. But he kept pouring me more and more, until I started to seriously suck at cards and feel the uncontrollable need to lie down.

"Is that stuff stronger than usual?" I asked. But he just laughed and lay down beside me on his old, smelly sleeping bag. Then he reached over and kissed me. We'd made out a ton by then, of course, but this was more intense. In fact, he was so serious that, of course, I burst out laughing.

"Quit it, dork," he said, pinning my arms. So I tried my hardest not to laugh while he licked my neck—which, honestly, was kind of gross. Then he was breathing really hard and putting his hand under my shirt. He'd never done that before, but because he was so serious, I tried to get into it, even though he kept slobbering on my chest and face.

But then he tried to go further, fumbling at the waistband of my jeans . . . and even though I had done what my mom told me to do—I'd found someone "special"—it just didn't feel right. He hadn't told me he loved me. Also, why go all the way and then take off the next day?

"Stop, Reggie."

"Don't be such a tease," he said, pushing me down again.

"Reggie, no."

"Are you serious?" he asked, sitting up in frustration. "I mean, come on, Pudge. You're leaving. When else are we going to do this?"

"Soon," I promised. "I think we'd better be a couple first. You know... out in the open."

Reggie groaned. "Are labels really *that* important to you?" he asked. "I mean, you know what I've been through. This is really hard for me, Pudge."

"I know," I said. "I'm sorry." I *did* know. After all, I still woke up with a cold pit of sadness in my belly every day over my mom. Still, I wasn't ready.

I passed out after that—we both did. When you're not that used to drinking wine, a whole bottle is a lot. In the morning, Reggie was himself again, funny and goofy, throwing me in the water. But even now I can't help remembering how weird he was that last night.

Well, I decide, I *will* go camping tonight if he asks. I'm so excited to see him, I'll do anything. Anyway, I *want* to go all the way. At least, I think I do.

"Where the hell is this place?" the hippie girl says, waking me up from my daydream.

"It's remote," I say. "That's kind of the point."

"I heard it was out there, but how the hell are we supposed to get to San Francisco for parties? I mean, this is ridiculous."

I shrug. The girl digs in her bag, fishes out a pack of Juicy Fruit, and throws me a piece. I can't help smiling as I think of Madison's disdain for my Bubble Yum.

"So's your boyfriend hot?"

Again, I shrug. "I don't know. Sure. I mean, he's cool. He's, like, my best friend. My mom died last year, and he helped me pick up the pieces, you know?"

"Heavy," she says, popping a huge, slightly veiny bubble. I notice that she has green under her toenails. I look away. What has happened to me? Why do I care about these things?

A few windy, truly nauseating miles later, we finally make it to the turnoff to the RC. My body sings as we round the last bend.

"Right here!" I call. The driver nods, obviously relieved to be rid of us. With a chorus of squeaking brakes, the bus comes to a stop. I can feel the curious and disapproving eyes of the other passengers as we make our way to the front. We hop off, and Crystal whoops as the bus rolls away.

"See ya, suckers!" she yells, flipping off the passengers.

So much for taking *that* bus again.

"It's just a mile up this road," I say.

"A mile?" She heaves her pack on. "That blows. Can't you call your boyfriend and tell him to come get us?"

I shake my head and start walking. It's annoying that I'm showing up with this girl. What if Big Jon thinks she's with me? And what's a trimmer, anyway? Still, I'm so happy to be here. The smell of eucalyptus cuts through the air, and the chill from the ocean is definitely refreshing after the swampy Savannah weather. As we trudge up the dirt road, she tells me about the shows she's been to (127), the drugs she's taken (I haven't even heard of half of them), and the guys she's "done" (twelve before her current boyfriend). By the time we reach the Main, I'm truly exhausted by her adventures.

"This is it," I say, my voice shaking with excitement. I point her toward the kitchen, where the intakes happen, and run inside to find Big Jon.

The sense of familiarity is overwhelming. The smells of baking bread and moldy wood, the sound of trippy music pouring from the meeting room upstairs.

The first person I run into is Wendy, who comes stomping out, heavy braids swinging from side to side.

"Alex!" she cries out. "What an awesome surprise!"

I breathe a sigh of relief. Good. So my grandmother hasn't called ahead for me yet.

"Hey!" I say, accepting her bone-crushing hug. "Is Big Jon here?"

"Oh, sure," she says, fluffing my dreads. "On the phone, I think. Give him a minute. Look at you! Still our healthy girl. Everything okay? Thought you were living in Georgia now."

"I'm on vacation," I say, not yet ready to tell her the whole story.

"Alex!" Big Jon's voice booms from his office. "Hey!"

"Hey! I'm back!"

"I can see that. Savannah treating you well?"

"I don't know. I don't love it. And I figured you guys really needed me here, so...I convinced my grandmother to let me come back."

"Huh," Big Jon says.

"Has everything been going okay without me?"

"Sure, sure. It's been tough, of course."

"Is the Sanctuary doing okay?"

"Oh, you know. We've made a few adjustments. I'll tell you about them later."

"Maybe I'll just go see—"

"Who's this?" he asks quickly, nodding to the girl who has sidled up next to me.

"Crystal," she says. "Here for the trimming round."

"Oh, right," he says, avoiding my eyes. "Wendy, can you take Crystal to the bunks? And Alex...why don't you just chill while we see what's up with your old cabin."

"Is Reggie around?" I ask a bit too eagerly.

"Oh, I think so. Here, how about hanging in the kitchen while I send someone to tell him you're here."

"Well, can I just go see...the other kids first?"

Big Jon laughs. "I know you're psyched to see the dudes, sweetie, but I think they could use help on soup duty. You know the drill. Community!"

"Okay," I say. He pats my back, and I head down the dim, wood-floored hallway. And I really am going to help out. Seriously. But I figure a quick bike ride around the place before I cut carrots for an hour won't hurt anything. I mean, forcing me to do KP without even seeing my friends first? That's just pure torture—one of the issues Big Jon is always having us write letters to the White House about.

Quietly, I head out and grab a rickety community mountain bike off the rack, and then I take off down the path before anyone can call me back. I close my eyes briefly as I coast. It feels so good to be here! I bank right and do a quick tour of my favorite hill path, churning the pedals in the red dust of the south side of the valley. Beyond the green stretch of the main lawn, the Pacific Ocean crashes against the rocks of the RC beach. From the top of the hill, I have a great view of the whole place—the mismatched buildings, the gardens (other than my mother's root garden, which is tucked away behind a thicket of trees), and the worn playing field, where some kids are playing a lazy game of soccer. I squint my eyes at them, looking for—who else?—Reggie. Yup, there he is, his gangly body knocking around like a rag doll's as he runs after the ball.

My heart leaps into my mouth—I swear, I can taste it. I need to calm down before we talk. I take a couple of yoga breaths, the way my mom taught me, but that doesn't really work. I'm dying to talk to Reggie, but if I go sit in the Sanctuary for a while, I'll calm down enough not to make a total ass of myself. That's definitely what Mom would say to do. I turn the bike around and bomb down the path, riding as fast as I can through the trees and over the fields, finally skidding to a stop outside the gate, causing a small rainstorm of gravel and dust.

Even through the thick slats of the fence, I can see that something is wrong. It's too sunny in there. Too bare. The Sanctuary was designed to be a lush sylvan oasis. Where are the trees? And the tall plants and vines? I drop my bike and, after a moment's hesitation, push open the gate. It gives a foreboding creaking sound that I've never noticed before.

It's gone. The Sanctuary is gone. All the plants, the flowers, the vines my mother spent so many days and years tending. Instead, only mounds of fresh dirt are here, as if someone has planted rows of bodies.

I take a couple of breaths, trying to get a hold of myself. Pathetic as a dog who can't find its owner, I do a couple of careful laps, searching for any sign of my mom's plants. There are a few old seedlings of lavender and valerian, which I carefully put into my pocket. But other than that, every trace of my lovely mother's presence has been eradicated.

What could have happened? Try as I might, I can't imagine why Big Jon would want to get rid of my mother's sacred place. There's only one thing to do now: ask Reggie, the only person who will understand how devastating this is for me. Wiping the tears away, I bust out of the gate and run to the bike, then pedal back down the hill to the soccer field, riding so wildly that I lose control and fall into a pile of red mud. Billy, who is the first to see me, lets out a yelp of laughter.

"Pudgy Pudge!" he cries. "You're back!"

I pick myself up, wiping off as much of the dirt as I can. Then I look over to the field to witness the worst scenario I could ever imagine.

It's Reggie, with his arms around another girl. And it's not just any girl. It's Crystal, the girl from the bus. He's kissing her in front of everyone. I watch as his hands move down her back, then lower.

My boyfriend told me about it. Boyfriend? That's what she said.

The hair on my arms is standing on end. I feel like I'm going to throw up. What can I do? I should probably say something, but what is there to say? *Hey, Reggie, flew about three thousand miles to visit you, but looks like you're busy!* Or, *Wow, congrats! Guess you got over your girlfriend's death enough to kiss someone in public. Too bad it wasn't me!*

The coolest thing to do right now, I suppose, would be to leave. But unfortunately, I'm never very cool in this kind of situation. So I get off the bike and walk to where Billy and the other kids are hanging out, so Reggie'll see me. When he does, his eyes widen, and he drops his hands away from Crystal. At least he has the decency to do that.

"Alex?" he says, looking nervously from side to side. Hesitantly, he walks toward me. "What are you doing here? You should have told me you were coming."

I stare at him, at a total loss for words to say. Crystal sidles up to us now, looking at Reggie questioningly.

"Pudge, I want you to meet Crystal. She's…my girlfriend."

"Your…*girlfriend*?"

"Yeah," she says, snaking her arm around Reggie's. "This is the guy I was telling you about. We've been going out since eleventh grade. Haven't seen him for a while, but it's *on*, man. On like Donkey Kong!" She glances around, obviously looking for the boyfriend I stupidly mentioned on the bus.

"Crystie, give me a minute, okay?" Reggie says. He puts his arm on my shoulder and leads me aside. "Listen," he whispers, "that was—you know—a little fib I told you about losing my girlfriend and everything. I just felt so bad for you, and, you know, wanted you to feel better, about your mom and all. I felt sorry for you, you know?"

I look at him incredulously. "You mean the plane crash was a lie?"

"Not a lie, exactly. A story. For you."

It takes me a moment to respond. "For *me*?"

"I wanted you to know I understood."

"But you *don't* understand," I say. "You just wanted

me to feel sorry for you. God. Did you lie about the other stuff too? Running supplies to Burma? Helping the orphans in Ghana? Are you even *from* Bolinas?"

Reggie looks nervously at Crystal, who is obviously straining to hear us.

"I'm from New Jersey, Pudge," he whispers. "Cherry Hill. And, listen—I might not have done all of those things, but I *did* go to Mexico on a surf trip."

"I can't believe I came all the way back to see you," I say, suddenly numb inside. "I was actually going to ask if you wanted to go camping tonight."

"Camping?" And then, for just a moment, he treats me to that easy grin of his, and I think everything will be okay. "Oh, Pudge, come on. That was never a great idea to begin with."

"But...why?"

Reggie looks uncomfortable. "You're just not...I mean, you're funny and all. But it was just a fling."

My face is burning. "Is that why you wanted to keep us a secret?" I say in a small voice. "Because I'm not pretty enough?"

Reggie doesn't answer, but his face definitely does.

"And what would Crystal think of your 'fling'?"

"She won't know."

"What if I tell her?"

Reggie smiles sympathetically. "The thing is, I never told anyone about you. So why would she believe the pudgy hippie girl's story?"

Just like that, the world opens up and swallows my heart whole. Suddenly, I hate his smile. I hate it more than anything I've ever seen.

"Reg," Crystal calls over from where the kids have stopped the game to sit in a circle and smoke. "What's up?"

"Nothing. Pudge just had to tell me something."

She looks at me suspiciously. "Okay. Cool." She winks at him in a way that makes my stomach turn. "Hey, I hear that Big Jon guy has a new hot tub and a sauna in his house. Want to check it out?"

On like Donkey Kong.

"Sure," he says. "See you, Pudge."

"My name's Alex, actually," I say. "Alexandria Lee. Like the famous Confederate general."

Reggie looks confused. "Okay. Whatever."

"Wait, I came to tell you something else," I say. Reggie turns and looks at me tiredly, as if I'm as annoying as a fly.

"What?"

"I don't live in Florida."

"Huh?"

"You e-mailed to say *have fun in Florida.*"

Crystal frowns and cocks her head.

"Okay, I—"

"I told you where I was going that last night we spent together. Remember? When you tried to get me to have sex, even though I didn't want to?"

175

Crystal drops Reggie's hand.

"Yeah, well. It's Georgia. I live in Savannah, Georgia."

Then I turn and ride away from them as fast as I possibly can.

The truth, which Wendy lets me in on, is that they cleared and burned the Sanctuary the week after I left.

First, the powers that be debated it for a little while, she assures me. There was some kind of committee meeting. But apparently my grandmother's lawyer made good on his promise to get the Drug Enforcement Administration to skip inspecting the RC for ten years in exchange for my going to Savannah. And marijuana, it seems, is a lot more profitable than herbal tinctures. So in the end, urged on by Reggie, Big Jon decided to scrap the remedies my mother had used to make Rain Catcher Farms legitimate and famous, in order to use the space to grow pot.

"We had to use the Sanctuary," Wendy explains. "It's the most remote spot on the RC."

"But that's not what this place has ever been about," I say. "I thought our mission was to be a community and to grow organic. We were never about money."

She looks at me sadly. "I'm sorry, baby. Even Utopia has to pay taxes to the Man."

I shake my head. "I need to talk to Big Jon. Is he in there?"

She nods. "Sure, hang on, I'll just tell him."

"I'm going in," I say, shouldering past her and pushing the door open. Big Jon looks up from his desk, which is really an old door balanced on two sawhorses. The doorknob is still jutting up from the surface.

"Hey, Alex," Big Jon says with an uneasy grin. "So, I guess you found out about your ma's garden. Don't get into a fuss, okay? We really needed to make some changes around here."

"I guess I'm just really disappointed," I say. "I thought this place was something different."

Big Jon runs his big hands through his wild mass of gray hair. "It is, honey. And you helped make it special, and so did your mom. But time moves on. Reggie's always been... knowledgeable about this kind of thing. And for the first time in thirty years, we've got extra money. Hell, I can actually send funds to stop those bastards from destroying the rain forests!"

"Well, *have* you sent any money to charities? World Wildlife Fund, maybe? Greenpeace?"

Big Jon turns red. "Alex..."

"You're really loving that new hot tub, though. Am I right?"

I look out the window at the lush green valley and shake my head. I thought this place was a real community. A family. But it turns out we were all just working to make money for Big Jon. "So, you know, thanks—really—for selling me out within five minutes of my leaving."

"Alex, she paid us a lot of money to let you go, okay? I've got to uphold my end of the bargain."

"What do you think my mother would have said?"

"You've got your grandmother, kid," he says grimly. "We all love you, but the lady is rich as a sultan, and she seemed to be hell-bent on keeping you. Although, that might not be true anymore. I just talked to her a few minutes ago, and she told me it's up to you whether you want to go back or not. You're welcome to stay here if you'd like."

"Really?" I say, surprised. I'm a little taken aback. She *doesn't* want me after all?

"It's up to you, okay? But if you stay, you're going to have to fall into the new program. In other words, no complaining about the new business. And you'll have to learn to trim."

"What does that even mean?"

"The pot leaves have to be trimmed when they're dried. With tiny scissors. Pounds and pounds of leaves. It takes days."

I try to picture doing this mind-numbing work. My mom and I spent our afternoons in the Sanctuary performing complicated cross-pollination and botany. Now I'd be doing this new job? And Reggie would oversee the whole thing, no doubt with Crystal draped around his neck.

"I don't know. It doesn't sound very rewarding."

"I'm afraid it's all we've got."

"Okay," I say. "I get it. No grudges. But can I just ask for one last thing?"

"I'll give it if I have it."

"How about a couple of quarters?" I say. "I just really need to use the phone."

My grandmother picks up on the second ring. She pauses for a moment before answering my question. But when she does, I have to say, it's the happiest I've ever heard her sound.

"Of course we'd love to have you back, dear," she says. "Believe it or not, this is your home. All right. I'll call Sybil directly. Use that credit card of yours and get yourself to San Francisco. No time for the bus — hire a car, darling. I'll have her send Senator McPhillips's plane today."

18

Although I've been completely dreading my return—as well as my grandmother's disapproval and the lecture I'm sure to receive—I feel a sense of relief when I finally see the house again. My body's so weary that all I can think about is dropping onto my bed and falling asleep for a few hundred hours.

"Alex!" Josie says, pulling me to her chest. "What you did was evil and foolish, but bless your heart, we *knew* you'd come back." She releases me and wrests my backpack out of my hands.

"Is she mad at me?"

"Your grandmother is just happy you're not dead in a ditch somewhere," Josie says, ushering me into the front hall. "Now go on in, because you've got company."

"No way," I say. But she's not kidding. I can hear Madison's unmistakable laugh bouncing off the black-and-white marble floor of the hallway.

"Surprise!" Hayes says brightly when I enter the living room. And there they all are: my grandmother, Madison, Hayes... and Thaddeus.

"Oh, my precious sweetheart. Look at you," my grandmother says, rising and planting a regal kiss on my cheek.

"Hey," I say. It's about all I have the energy for.

"I should be furious with you, absolutely furious, but I cannot expend the energy. To be honest, it's too hot to be angry, and it's bad for my skin. I *will* say that I am glad you are safe. This country is full of serial killers and Internet predators and all sorts of trash who would just love to get their hands on a sixteen-year-old girl and leave her dead in a ditch."

What is this obsession with death and ditches?

"Have a little sweet tea," she says, pouring me a syrupy glassful. "Now, you're just going to have to sit down and tell us every awful detail."

"I'm not really in the mood."

"Well, I suggest you *get* in the mood, because your friends are here and they were worried sick about you. It was extremely inconsiderate of you to just up and run off like that with no thought as to how it would make everyone else feel. So think of this as an intervention—but an informal one that doesn't end with you being packed off to a ladies' farm in New Mexico."

"To be honest," I reply, "it sucked. Reggie, my boyfriend—"

"Miss Lee," Madison says suddenly, "I just remembered. My mother wanted to borrow that brooch from you. Is it upstairs?"

"Yes," Miss Lee says, appearing unfazed by the interruption. "Just go on up. It's on my dresser. And when you give it to your mother, tell her that I would absolutely love it if she'd have it cleaned before sending it back. I've been meaning to do so myself, but as you can see, I have my hands full trying to raise a problem teenager. Your mother wouldn't understand, because you are an absolute angel, but it is a burden."

"What happened with Reggie?" Hayes says kindly as Madison exits. I look nervously at Thaddeus, but he's studying a book on my grandmother's coffee table.

Right. How could I think he would care?

"Um, he's with someone else. And it turns out they've destroyed Mom's root-and-herb garden to make space to grow pot."

"Well," my grandmother says, growing noticeably paler at the mention of my mother, "that is the world we live in. Everyone is addicted to drugs, and no one has any respect for the past. Are you on this Facebook? I heard on the news that two out of every ten teenagers on Facebook wind up either murdered or pregnant or both. I do not like to live in fear, but those are sobering statistics."

I pray someone will change the subject.

"How was the weather?" Thaddeus asks.

"Nice and cool," I say gratefully. "Thanks for asking." He nods but doesn't catch my eye.

"So, Alex," my grandmother says, "you look like something the cat dragged in and the dog dragged back out again. You are positively *dripping* stress. Hayes, don't you think she's just about on the verge of a nervous episode?"

"I think she's been under a *lot* of pressure," Hayes says.

"Which can lead to a nervous episode. So I believe it's time."

"Time for what?" I ask, not liking the way this conversation is going.

"Time for these girls to take you out somewhere wonderful so you can relax and forget about Reggie and California and...all those other things. Hayes, what's next on the social calendar?"

"Well," Hayes says, carefully, "there's a bonfire out at the Field tomorrow night."

"There you go," my grandmother says. "A bonfire at the Field, whatever that is. Exactly what you need, Alex."

It's exactly what I *don't* need, but I don't have the energy to say so.

"Madison," my grandmother calls out, "I have a mission of mercy for you two girls. Come on down here, honey."

I look pleadingly at Hayes, but she just smiles. "We're going to have so much fun," she says.

I want to die.

~←↞

The next morning, the MGs pick me up for school. Hayes insisted, and I was too tired to argue. They look perfect, of course; Hayes is wearing a fitted navy top and little plaid skirt, and Madison is in a mustard-colored dress that only she could pull off. I wait for Madison to start in on me about my look—the standard T-shirt and my new jeans. But if she notices, she doesn't say a thing.

The kids also seem nicer today. No one stares or says anything rude; I don't get called a fat hippie; no one shoves me in the hall. Even Gilroy keeps his distance. My grandmother—or someone—seems to have called ahead about my homework, because there are no demands for assignments I missed.

But then I go to Constance's class, and suddenly she's looming over my desk.

"Alex," she says, "are you ready to take your summer-reading test today?"

Fully aware of the eyes of my classmates boring into my head, I nod.

"I'll have you know there are no favored students in this classroom," she says. "I don't care what society you—or your grandmother—belong to."

I shrug. "Okay."

She narrows her eyes. "If you fail this test, you can't take it over."

"It's fine. I read the books. I'll take it now."

She nods and drops the test on my desk. I take it while the rest of the class continues. As I fill in the answers, I shake my head. Why exactly is she so friggin' angry?

At lunchtime, Hayes finds me in the bathroom.

"How's it feel to be back?"

"Everyone's been cool, except in Miss Taylor's class. She's all mad at me or something."

"We call her C.T.," Madison says, joining us in front of the mirror. "But I think we're two letters short. She gave me a bunch of crap when I tried to get you out of that test."

"You tried to what?"

"We went around to the teachers to get you out of last week's work. Said you were doing emergency charity work for the Magnolia League."

"And that would be a legitimate excuse?"

"Because everyone knows that being an MG is important," Madison says. "We cut school all the time for 'emergency Magnolia events.' The only one who gives us any flak about it is C.T., who clearly has something lodged up some unmentionable body part."

"It didn't matter. I read the books."

"Of course you did," Madison says. "Nerd."

"Shall we hit the bench?" Hayes says. "I'm starved."

"Uh...I was actually going to eat with Dex."

"Bring him," Hayes says cheerfully. "He's totally invited."

"He is?" Madison asks. "When did we start doing outreach work with losers?"

"Dex is not a loser," I snap. "If you could just get over your whole MG thing, you'd realize he's one of the funniest, coolest people in school."

"See? Alex likes him," Hayes says, her tone full of warning. "So obviously he's okay."

Madison rolls her eyes.

"Come on," Hayes says. "You're the only runaway we know. I want to hear all the details you couldn't spill in front of your grandmother. And we'd love to have Dexter join us."

"Okay, I'll ask him."

Dex, however, is not as thrilled.

"Are you serious? Those girls are the worst. I'd rather drive spikes into my eyes."

"Come on, dude. For me? I just got screwed over by my boyfriend. I could use the support."

"Thaddeus dumped you?"

"What?" I bite my lip, realizing that I shrieked. Dex gives me a weird look. "Are you high?" I whisper. "Who said I'm going out with Thaddeus?"

"Twitter? Facebook? It's just...out there, you know?"

"No, I *don't.*"

"Okay, so then it's not true. Got it."

I don't even know how to process this right now. "Just come eat with us," I say. "You can have all my deviled eggs."

"Okay, fine. I'll come. But I fully expect it to be horrible and awkward, and I'm only doing it for you."

We walk across the lawn to the MGs' bench. With my dreads and ratty Birks, I look a lot more normal alongside Dex, in his all-black punk gear, than I look with the MGs.

Madison's nose wrinkles slightly as we approach. "Guess it's bring-your-weirdo-to-lunch day."

"Madison," Hayes says, "don't judge. Everyone has something to offer."

Madison sighs and opens her lunch basket, which is full of fried chicken, Twinkies, and Ho Hos. "I suppose every team needs a mascot."

"Oh yeah?" Dex says, reaching into her basket. Madison recoils in horror. "And what's this team fighting for? Stronger mascara wands?"

"So, Alex," Hayes says pointedly, biting into a huge, gooey roast-beef-and-Cheddar-cheese sandwich. "What happened?"

"I bolted," I say. "Bought a plane ticket and took off. With my grandmother's credit card."

"Solid," Dex says.

"But when I got there—I don't know, everything had changed. They wrecked my mom's garden to plant marijuana. Plus, it turns out my boyfriend wasn't my boyfriend. He lied to me and was making out with some...some..."

"Skank?" Dex says.

"Whore?" Madison offers, a mere split second later.

They look at each other and share a cautious smile.

"She *was* a little slutty. Yeah."

"Don't sweat it," Dex says. "It's nothing against you. I'm sure he likes you a lot. But, you know, he's a dude. We're all vulnerable to sluts. They're like our kryptonite." He offers me a piece of Madison's chicken, but I shake my head. One piece of that chicken would up my jeans size by two.

"That may be true," I say, "but I feel like I've been run over by a truck."

Hayes and Madison exchange glances.

"You'll feel a lot better after tonight," Hayes says.

"I don't know if I even want to go."

"Come on," Madison says. "You can do some slutting around of your own. See how the other half lives."

"Are you going?" I ask Dex.

"He's not invited," Madison says. "Besides, I would imagine that he's got a full schedule tonight, what with peeping in windows and posting his video suicide note on YouTube."

"Whatever," Dex says. "Sounds lame, anyway."

Madison turns to whisper something to Hayes, and Dex hurls a Twinkie at the back of her head. I wince, but without even turning around, Madison throws up her perfectly manicured hand and catches it.

"Nice catch," Dex says, clearly impressed.

Madison slowly turns and, to my surprise, treats Dex to a big, pretty smile. Then she unwraps the Twinkie and stuffs the whole thing into her mouth.

19

Now, I'd rather sip a battery-acid cocktail than go out to that friggin' field again, but by the time Hayes rings the doorbell, I'm ready to get the hell out of this house. For the past two hours, my grandmother has been fussing over me as if I were some kind of virgin sacrifice.

"No, Alex," she says when she sees my first outfit. "Red is acceptable for elementary-school teachers on Valentine's Day and for prostitutes, maybe, but not for a young lady who hopes to get married one day."

I don't have the energy anymore. I go back and change into a green shirt and a denim skirt.

"And what is *that* getup?" she says. "An outfit is fine, a costume is acceptable, but you are not walking out my front door in a getup."

"There's nothing good about a getup," Josie chimes in.

"What do you want me to put on?"

"Whatever makes you the most comfortable," my grandmother says. "Far be it from *me* to tell you what to wear."

(And then she tells me exactly what to wear.)

When I come out the front door in a white top and chinos, Hayes laughs. "Triplets!" she says, gesturing at her sparkly, snowy Michael Stars minidress. "Madison's wearing white too."

"Interesting choice for a party in a dust bowl," I grumble. I trudge along behind her and then stop when I see what she's driving: It's the SUV again.

"What happened to the Prius?" I ask, getting in.

"We need a real car tonight, sweetheart," Madison says from the backseat. "Not the eco-can."

It turns out that she's right. Hayes takes us flying out of town, north up Route 17, and then down some rural route I haven't been on before—it's so old, it makes the truck vibrate. The sun set twenty minutes before, and still we keep bumping into the gloom, with the windows open and the hot air blowing in our faces.

"Sorry, y'all," Hayes says. "The air-conditioning's broken."

I never thought Hayes and Madison would tolerate having their hair messed up like this.

"Is there any water?" I ask, my mouth dry.

Madison hands me a bottle of Vitaminwater from her purse. Besides being way too sweet for my palate, it tastes weird.

"I guess we're slumming it tonight," she says when she sees me make a face. "Drink up. There's no place to get anything out here."

Suddenly, Hayes brakes hard and turns off the two-lane blacktop into a field.

"Where's the road?" I cry.

The two of them burst out laughing as the truck lurches and bounces across the dirt. The sugar water is sloshing around inside me; I feel sick. The only thing keeping me from throwing up is the fresh air coming in the window. A horsefly blows in and whacks me in the face. *Great.*

We blast through some scrub and out onto a sandy logging road in the boonies. It's pitch-dark, and there's barely any moonlight. Hayes doesn't even pause; she just points the SUV straight ahead and steps on the gas.

Suddenly, she stands up on the brakes, and the truck slides to a stop.

"My aviators!" she cries, feeling her hair.

"Your what?" I ask.

"My Marc Jacobs sunglasses. They blew out the window."

"Boo-hoo," Madison says.

"They cost a hundred and sixty dollars!"

That's weird, I think. *When did the MGs start keeping track of their cash?*

"Well, I'm not going to get them," Madison declares loudly. "Get them yourself."

Hayes looks at me pleadingly.

"Okay, I'll do it." I pop open the door, grateful to get out into the fresh air. It's humid outside, and I feel as if I'm breathing through a wet blanket. Crickets are screeching in the woods. As I trot along the dirt road, I can feel a storm building. The air is electric.

Just as I spot Hayes's sunglasses, it suddenly becomes really dark. I look up in time to see *the truck driving away.*

Is this a joke? No, because there it goes, bouncing around a bend in the road. I race after the SUV — dreads flopping, legs cramping. But it's no use. Hayes and Madison are gone.

I stand, panting and sweating, and feel tears sting my eyes. Well. Looks like our "friendship" was a way of getting me to lower my guard, and now this is the punch line. *Is everyone out to get me? And how am I going to get home?*

I begin to plod up the road. My legs feel like lead, but I keep putting one foot in front of the other. Pick 'em up, put 'em down. Pick 'em up, put 'em down. And that's when I hear a car behind me.

It's about fifty yards down the road, creeping along at a couple of miles per hour. The headlights are off, and when I stop, it stops. To my left I spot a ditch at the side of the road—probably the one in which my grandmother and Josie will find me dead. No, no, I'm sure I'm overreacting. More likely than not, this is just a bunch of other kids on their way to the Field. This must be a shortcut or something. I walk toward the dark car and raise one hand.

"Hey!" I shout. "Do you—"

But then the headlights flick on, shooting straight out and pinning me in the middle of the road. I hear the doors open on either side.

Okay, I don't care what kind of fool I look like. I've seen *The Silence of the Lambs*. I jump the ditch and run.

But the headlights ruined my night vision, and I smack face-first into a tree. I fall on my butt and taste blood. Behind me the serial killers, or whoever they are (Gilroy?), are getting closer, so I scramble up, put out my arms, and run like the devil. I hit a tree with my shoulder, jam my fingers on another, and smash my knee into a third, but I don't stop. Tiny branches whip my face, but I don't care.

I stop crashing through the brush and crouch down to listen. I can't hear anything except the screaming cicadas and my blood pounding in my ears. I can't tell what direction I came from. I can't breathe normally. Heat lightning flickers gently in the sky. I stand up and start to walk.

Every branch I step on causes me to cringe. *Something* is in the woods with me, and whatever it is can hear me and see me blundering in the dark. At any minute, I'll see the shape of a man step out from behind a tree, and it will all be over.

Suddenly, a shape looms before me. I let out a noise and fall backward. It's massive, with its arms outstretched to grab me. I scrabble backward in the dry leaves and realize that the figure isn't moving. I freeze.

Wait, it's a . . . *statue?*

Fifteen feet tall, the sculpture is rough and primitive. When I finally get up the nerve to touch it, I discover it's made of concrete. Its arms are stretched out as if the statue is going to hug me — twenty-five feet from fingertip to fingertip. I can feel it watching me, and while in the daytime I would laugh at myself for being so stupid, at night, alone in the woods, I only want to get away. I know it's just a statue and that it's not really alive . . . but what if I'm wrong?

I creep past it and keep moving, feeling as though I'm being watched. I keep waiting to hear the statue lift itself out of the ground and shamble after me. And then I trip over the TV. I've tripped over a TV before (don't ask), and there's no mistaking the noise it makes or where it clips me in the shins. My hands hit the dirt, knocking over a broken plastic pitcher, and all around me on the ground I see light-colored shapes scattered everywhere: broken plates, toaster ovens, microwaves — it's a graveyard for smashed junk.

Then I notice the headstones and realize it's an *actual* graveyard. The stones are worn and old, leaning to the side, split in half, sinking into the mulch. I think about the dead bodies directly beneath me: how their coffins have probably rotted away, and the dirt has subsided, and their hands are just inches away from breaking through the mulch and twining around my fingers. I'm up and running again.

I pass a tree with white ribbons hanging from its branches, then another tree, this one with nothing but hubcaps dangling from chains. I swear I see white candles burning, far away, but when I turn toward them, they flicker and go out. Two massive rocks have been chopped and shaped until they look like the heads of African kings. I run between them. The trees are getting thicker. The woods are getting darker. . . . I'm lost.

Wait — I smell salt water and the sweet smell of thyme. Then the scent of cloves, cinnamon, and lemongrass. I hear the tinkling of a wind chime up ahead, and I burst into a clearing. Then I recognize it . . . Buzzard's Roost.

All the lights are out except at the Buzzard Social Club, where it's bright and loud. Music is playing. People are probably watching something on the stupid satellite dish. Suddenly, something as mundane as television seems tremendously comforting to me.

The music gets louder, and it sounds alive. *Maybe they're having a party?* Just being around people right now, having a beer or even a Coke, something processed and artificial that was made in a factory and sold in a supermarket—even that sounds reassuringly normal to me now. I burst into the social club.

"Hey, guys!" I shout. "Remember—" And then I stop cold.

The room is packed with people, and they're all staring at me. Three drummers with their hands frozen over their drums. Dozens of black people I've never seen before. Old white ladies. My grandmother. Josie. And right across from me, those two backstabbers, Hayes and Madison.

Doc Buzzard, the man I saw in the garden shed, steps out of the crowd. He's dressed in white.

"Hello, Alex," he says, as if we're talking about the weather. "We've been waiting for you."

He claps his hands, and the drummers begin to play. The noise confuses me, and everyone begins to sing something that sounds like a hymn. Is this one of those weird Christian intervention things?

I open my mouth to tell him I just want to go home, but he's shaking my hands, first my left and then my right, and then he hugs me, pressing me to one shoulder and then the other, and I'm passed along, and now I'm shaking hands and hugging someone else, and on around the circle, spinning and shaking and hugging. I want to tell them that I just want to go home, but there's a sound like a gong and then a million angry bees, and a ripple goes through the room. I stand stock-still. I'm facing Madison. She's shaking her car keys and singing a hymn. I grab her by the shoulders and give her my killer face.

"Did you drug me?" I ask.

"*Jon-ta-conku-er. Jon-ta-conku-er*," she murmurs.

But there's no way to ask her what she's talking about, because my legs go out from under me, and hundreds of hands are catching me, laying me on the floor, floating me down to it light as a feather, and draping an enormous piece of pink silk over my body.

The circle of people is moving around me counterclockwise, singing, drumming, stomping. They have their house keys in their hands, and they're shaking them like a million metal maracas, and they're stomping on the wooden floor that's vibrating like a drum now, and I can feel it all through my body.

I roll my head to one side and see that the floor is covered with cakes. Pink cakes, yellow cakes, white cakes, wedding cake, birthday cake, all covered in sugar flowers and icing and sitting on bone-china plates. Something wet splashes my face, and I breathe it in and start to choke. It's sweet and sticky, and I realize that someone has just emptied a bottle of champagne over my head.

"What the hell?"

I want to say something else, and then I realize that it's Hayes and Madison, and they're drinking from bottles of champagne and pouring the rest on my face. I can't breathe. My face feels like thick rubber, and then something happens to me. I've never taken acid before, not even mushrooms, but suddenly a vision comes together out of the noise, the drumming, the jangling keys, the stomping, and the singing.

I see myself three times. One of me is wrapped in a woman's arms, a woman who feels like my mother. I'm cuddled up like a kitten, and she's stroking my hair and whispering to me and telling me everything's going to be okay.

The second me is some kind of snake, slithering in the dust. I'm molting my skin and becoming something better. Different.

The third me, though, this one stops my heart. The third me is beautiful. My hair is glowing. I'm holding my body differently: My shoulders are back, my hips are tipped back, my legs are strong, my posture is straight. I'm not Pudge. I'm not Alex. I'm Alexandria. I've left a little girl behind me, like that snake shedding its skin, and I'm curvy and voluptuous and beautiful.

I see Doc Buzzard watching me with his yellow eyes, and I walk up to him and stare at him, daring him to say something to me. Then I whirl and begin to dance. I step into the circle, and I'm singing the songs and I know the words, and then I'm in the middle of the circle, and the candlelight is soft and beautiful. I see my grandmother, and in her I see my mother and I see myself. Someone hands me a piece of cake, and I eat it, and it's the most delicious thing I've ever tasted. I want more.

I drink from a bottle of champagne. Someone hands me a cigar, and the smoke turns my lungs into rich mahogany wood. People take my hands on either side, and we float outdoors, and it's as bright as day. Candles are lit all over the yard, and sixteen women are sweeping the dirt, back and forth, like they're dancing. In front of me the swept yard leads down to the river and the dark rush of water, and everyone is moving that way while the ladies sweep and the candles sparkle. I drink another bottle of champagne, and it tastes better than the first. It feels good on my face and running down the front of my shirt.

We reach the river. The tide must be out. Between the bank and the water is pluff mud, soft and black and warm. We walk through it and reach the water, and then the singing starts again. I look back at the riverbank, and everyone's watching. Someone's leaning me backward into the rushing water, and I go under, and everything gets washed away. Here in the cool and dark at the bottom of the river, I feel the water moving through me. It pulls out images that pass in front of my eyes:

There I am as a kid, climbing up the moon path above the RC beach, alone.

There we are, Billy and I, throwing rocks in the pond. There we are playing mud ball on the beach.

The beach! I'm older now, and Reggie's kissing me.

And now we're behind the Main, and he's giving me a joint. I push it away, but he roughly puts it to my lips again.... *I understand*, he whispers. *I'm the only one who does.*

Now he's planting the first crop at the RC. There he is, with a spade; it's Reggie, ripping up my mother's precious plants.

And finally, he is with Crystal, standing where the Sanctuary used to be. He's holding her the same way he did in the soccer field, and she's laughing. But for some reason, I don't care when I see them this time. It's like watching two strangers. He looks so ugly to me, with his scrawny body and his liar's eyes. I let the water pull him away.

I stand up, gasping for breath. Someone hands me a bottle of champagne, but it tastes flat and boring. I let it drop into the water. My salty tears fall into the brackish water, and that's the last thing I remember: crying into the Vernon River because of all the ways this world has disappointed me, while in the distance the heat lightning flickers out at sea.

20

When I wake up, the angle of the sun streaming in the window suggests late morning. I sit up, gasping, and put my hands to my face.

All right, things are looking up: I'm alive and okay and not burned or possessed or in some freaky forest. In fact, I'm very comfy in my four-poster bed, and from what I can see through the window, the sky looks nice and blue.

Man. That was one trippy dream.

I wonder how long I've been asleep. Oddly, instead of being groggy, I feel completely energized, as if I've just had a massive amount of Italian espresso injected into my veins.

Okay, obviously the MGs drugged me with something. I'm not one to use profanity lightly but . . . those *bitches*! Why would they do that? To haze me or something?

I shoot out of bed, looking around the room. I'm wearing the same clothes I had on last night. No weird robes or markings.

My mom used to say dreams were really important to reading your inner self. She'd write them down as soon as she woke up so that she wouldn't forget them. Maybe if I quickly scrawl down what I remember . . . I grab a notebook and sit at my desk.

Hayes.

Madison.

Sunglasses?

Sam. Sina. My grandmother . . .

Jonta.

What a minute. Isn't that what Madison was chanting that night at the party?

Jon-ta-conku-er.

I scrawl down the syllables and flip open my laptop. A Google search immediately suggests some person called John the Conqueror. As my skin prickles, I click on the first Web page:

John the Conqueror is a central figure from African-American folklore. Sometimes known as High John the Conqueror or John de Conquer, he is associated with the John the Conqueror root, or John the Conqueroo, which is believed to contain magical powers. John the Conqueror root is central to the hoodoo tradition of folk magic.

Hoodoo? What the hell is that?

I scrawl the name and fly down the stairs and outside, then jog across the street to the Georgia Historical Society building, conveniently located kitty-corner to the grandma-mansion. The librarian, a formidable-looking lady with a halo of white hair as wispy as dandelion petals, raises her eyebrows when I burst in, breathless.

"Excuse me," I say, my face turning red. "I'm looking for information on African folklore. But American. Rituals and stuff. The kind that might be around here. In a field in the country, maybe. With cakes and champagne."

She blinks at me.

"Sorry. Let me try again. Okay. Is there a person in Georgia history called John the Conqueror?"

"Not a real person," she says. "That is the name of a folk hero. A hoodoo myth."

"Hoodoo! Right! What?"

The librarian sighs. "Just a moment." She disappears into the stacks and then returns with a book. "Here. You could have gone to the library, or E. Shaver's, for that matter, if you were wise enough to support your independent bookstore. But you may borrow this."

"Do I need a card?"

"I know where to find you, Miss Lee. Over there, in the ostentatious mansion on the corner. Or at one of your grandmother's elitist Magnolia League gatherings. I'd make you join the historical society, but the League practically owns us. *So*."

Hmm. Obviously this lady is not a huge Mag League fan.

"Okay. Thanks," I say, smiling meekly. I take the book and hurry to the far end of the park. Taking a quick look around to make sure no one is near my bench, I open the book.

Hoodoo Spells and Conjures, the title page reads. I flip the page and begin to read:

"Hoodoo" is a spiritual and healing practice derived from African folklore. Direct cultural links have been found to several West African countries, including Angola, Congo, and Gambia. Like "Gullah" language and culture, hoodoo is not derived from a single source but is the result of the African diaspora. Mostly,

the hoodoo practice can be found in the American South.

Hoodoo should not be confused with voodoo. Voodoo is a religion; hoodoo is the practice of magic—although many who practice hoodoo have altars in their homes. Hoodoo practitioners often practice a religion such as Christianity in conjunction with magic.

The hoodoo tradition places emphasis on magic and personal power. The practice includes rituals, the use of roots and herbs, spells, and chanting. The hoodoo practitioner is often called a "root doctor." A "root," or "mojo," is a powerful charm that, when worn, is said to affect one's fate. A "root" may also be an evil spell—or a hex.

The goal of hoodoo is to allow people access to supernatural forces to improve their daily lives by gaining power in many areas of life, including money, beauty, love, revenge, health, employment, and communing with the dead. Teachings and rituals are handed down from one practitioner to another.

Although most adherents are black, contrary to popular opinion, hoodoo has always been practiced by both whites and blacks in America. Most practice hoodoo in secret out of fear of persecution, so there is no data on

how many people in America study hoodoo or how
effective the rituals might be.

Okay, well. A lot of that sounds like my dream last night. So I had a hoodoo dream? All right. Not the weirdest thing in the world, I guess. Maybe the Buzzards practice hoodoo.... That would make sense, given that altar thing in the shed, and the huge root garden. Maybe my subconscious picked that up or something.

I close the book and stand. Well, this visit was educational, at least. Outside, the city has cooled off this afternoon to a nice, balmy temperature. It feels great, actually. So great that I break into a sprint, running along the park's avenue of oaks.

"Hi!" I yell, bursting in the door of my grandmother's house.

"Alex," she says, appearing with—what else—a cocktail. "We must get your phone working. It's only polite to let someone know whether or not you'll be home for lunch."

"Sorry."

"Well. I suppose that's all right, then. Josie left you a bacon burger in the warmer."

"Great!" I go to the kitchen and eat half a burger while standing up at the counter. Then I throw my plate in the sink and head upstairs to hop in the tub. It takes ten minutes of a bath in my mom's Spiritual Cleansing

bath salts and several stanzas of "Sugar Magnolia"—
my favorite Grateful Dead tune—for me to realize the
truly weird aspect of what's going on right now.

I haven't thought about Reggie since I woke up.

Not once.

And now that I am thinking about him, *I don't feel a
thing.*

"What?" I whisper, stepping out of the bathtub
and wrapping myself in a towel. I'm over Reggie, the
first guy I ever loved, after *one day?* What is happening
to me?

I find my cell phone under the bed. There are a
couple of annoyed messages from Miss Lee, just testing
it out to see whether I ever answer. And there are three
messages from Reggie:

*Pudge, that wasn't cool, what you said in front of Crys-
tal ... but call me.*

*Pudge—I mean, Alex ... Come on. Call me back. Crys-
tal broke up with me. I really need to talk to you.*

Alex ... call me, okay? Just call me.

At one time, I would have flipped over these messages. But today I really don't care at all. And that definitely is not normal.

Without pausing to wonder any more about what
could be happening, I call Hayes.

"How are you feeling, sleepyhead?"

"I don't know why I'm calling you at all, with the
crap you pulled last night."

208

"Oh, Alex. Have a sense of humor."

"Whatever, you crazy wench. I get it—you and Madison get off on weird joyrides. But I need you to tell the truth about something."

On the other side of the phone, there is an uneasy pause.

"Okay," Hayes finally says.

"What was *in* that Vitaminwater?"

"Just some herbs," she says.

"Herbs?" I reply. "Hayes, I know all about herbs. I'm practically a licensed herbalist. Those were no herbs that I've ever heard of."

"Roots," she says.

"What roots? Specifically?"

"Why are you asking me this?"

"Because whatever you gave me not only knocked me out and gave me crazy-ass dreams, but it altered the way I *feel*. Like, I don't care about Reggie even a little anymore. Crush officially crushed."

"Well, so, that's great," she says brightly. "We've got lots of guys for you to hang with as soon as we get your hair fixed. Why ask questions?"

"Hayes. You guys—y'all—*drugged* me. Don't you think I deserve to know what's going on?"

"Hang on for a minute." She holds the phone away, and I can hear the rise and fall of Madison's voice in the background. "Okay. Tell your grandmother we're coming over."

"Why should my grandmother care if you come by?"

"Just tell her," Hayes says, a little impatiently. "Actually, what you need to tell her is that I said it's time."

Within minutes, the MGs are at my grandmother's house. What follows is a story so crazy, it's hard to retell it without questioning my sanity. But the craziest part? I'm not surprised at all. Somehow, in my very core, I know that every single word is true.

The four of us—me, Hayes, Madison, and my grandmother—gather around my grandmother's long, candlelit dining room table. She has forgone the champagne tonight for a decanter of brandy, offering each of us a glass. (My grandmother definitely has no qualms about underage drinking.)

"What did you give her last night?" Miss Lee asks.

"A potion Sam gave me," Madison says.

"Hmm." My grandmother opens a large, old book that she has brought down from her suite. It's the same one Sam had at his house: *Lady Brown's Book of Conjure and Spells.*

"Probably gunpowder, wasp nests, blood—"

"What?" I yell.

"Cayenne pepper, sassafras, bluestone...it's a won-

210

der he had enough bluestone at this time of year. You know, I think I might almost have this one down. Did he instruct you to get drops of the boy's sweat?"

"Yes. I strained the drink through a piece of his shirt," Madison says. "Got it from her room."

Reggie's shirt? My favorite vintage rock tee! So that's why the cloth in Madison's hand looked so familiar.

"You went through my stuff?"

Madison shrugs. "Had to."

"You cut up my favorite shirt and then fed me pepper and God knows what other crap? Are you insane?"

"She's not insane, darling," my grandmother says. "She was following Doc Buzzard's orders."

"What orders?"

"On how to properly conduct this spell."

"Okay." I stand up from the table, backing away from them. "It's time for you all to tell me what the hell is going on here."

"We are about to, Alexandria. Right now, actually." My grandmother pours me a tiny bit more brandy. "All right, Alex. Tell me what you know about magic."

"Magic?" I say, trying not to laugh. "What, like wizards and wands?"

Madison, Hayes, and my grandmother all give me unmistakably annoyed looks.

"Wizards? Don't be ridiculous." Miss Lee settles into her velvet chair and looks at her diamond rings. "Let me begin again. Did your mother ever talk about spells?"

"No spells."

"Curses?"

"Definitely not."

"Conjuring? The evil eye? Shadow magic? Soothsaying?"

"Okay, you've seriously lost me. Can you please bring my grandmother back now? The one who was worried about whether I cross my legs in public?"

My grandmother smiles patiently.

"Well, it seems Louisa really did keep you in the dark." She stands and paces the dining room. "Let me start at the beginning. You'll have to reach way back. Nineteen fifty-seven. At the time I, like you, was sixteen years old."

I cock my head, trying to do the math. Nineteen fifty-seven. Would that make her now, like, seventy? But how could that be? She looks forty, tops.

"I was engaged to be married," she says. "And then I found out he was going with another girl. You see, Alexandria? I know how you must be feeling about this Reggie character. After all, the entire Magnolia League started because a boy double-crossed me."

My grandmother refills our drinks and walks around turning off certain lights and turning on others, until the luxurious, fragrant room is set exactly to her liking. Then she settles down into the deep cushions of her striped silk couch.

"Things were different then. I know we older ladies always say that to you, and therefore it's a statement you likely find very boring, but down here it really was different. The debutante balls were just that—for coming out into society. I came out on Christmas Eve, 1957. A week later, Thomas Warren was at my house with a ring."

I frown, trying to imagine being engaged at this age.

"I was thrilled. Thomas was twenty, and the best-looking boy in Savannah. He was the best dancer in town and an absolutely wonderful tennis player. There was something so deliciously *aloof* about him. Also, his father was building those big hotels on the coast. All of the other debutantes—your grandmothers included, girls—were seething with jealousy at the news.

"However, I was never convinced that he was in love with me. I never told the other girls this, but whenever we talked, he seemed very distracted. He wanted to marry me, of course, or he wouldn't have asked. But it was as if he wanted to marry what I was...not *who* I was.

"I told myself I was imagining things. As you might guess, I've never had a self-esteem problem, and frankly I couldn't imagine why he wouldn't be infatuated with me. All of the other boys were. Then one day Hayes's grandmother Sybil and I were at the beach on Tybee

Island. The end of the beach was a deserted stretch back then, so we'd decided to work on our tans...alfresco, if you know what I mean. Well, we looked down the beach and there was Thomas, in an extremely compromising position with another girl. I recognized her too. A *waitress*, no less."

"What a jerk," I said, angrily picturing Reggie with Crystal again.

"Exactly," my grandmother said. "Sybil, rash as she is, wanted to run up to them and dump a bucket of water over their heads. I said no—we'd think of something better. But then something strange happened. Before I could hatch a truly great plan, Thomas's father fell horribly ill.

"It was the most frightening illness I've ever seen. I went over to be with Thomas—he didn't know at the time that I knew he was a rat—and heard Mr. Warren screaming in his bed. His eyes were wild and yellow, and foam was coming out of his mouth.

"At one point during the evening, I was alone with the patient. Everyone had left the room, presumably to have a drink or a quick bath. I was sitting near Thomas's father, horrified but too ashamed to leave him by himself. I'd always liked him. He was inappropriate at times—a grabber, if you know what I mean—but he was charming and loved spending money. I felt bad about his pain. He turned to me, his eyes desperate, his mouth dripping.

"'Dorothy, I've been hexed,' he whispered.

"'What?' I asked. 'What did you say?'

"'Doc Buzzard,' he said. 'Out on the island. The hotel property...hexed.'

"'We're taking you to the hospital,' I said in what I hoped was a kind voice.

"'It won't work,' he said desperately. *'Hexed.'*

"Then he fainted.

"The Warrens came in after that and took him to the hospital, but the doctors couldn't discover what was wrong with him. I didn't tell anyone what Mr. Warren had said to me. By the next day, he was dead."

Miss Lee pauses to drain her brandy. Then she looks each of us in the eye.

"Before I go on, I should tell you girls that I never wanted Thomas hurt. That was never my intention, even as I grew more curious about Doc Buzzard, even as I began to gently inquire where such a man might live. I *was* interested in a hex, however. My motivation — keep in mind, I was young and foolish! — was to afflict Thomas with the same illness his father had, but then I would offer a cure, thereby both scaring him and saving the day. If I managed to save him, I reasoned, he would afford me the respect I deserved and forget about the trashy tramp on the beach.

"It wasn't easy finding Doc Buzzard. No one in Savannah seemed to know him. I began with indirect inquiries, both of my friends and of Savannah's stranger

215

types. Finally Josie, who had just begun working for my family, took me aside."

"Wait," I say. "Josie worked for you back then?"

"She was twenty."

I furrow my brow, trying to figure this out. "So Josie was twenty, and you were sixteen . . . but she looks *ancient* now. I don't get it."

My grandmother shoots me a hard look and goes on with her story. "So Josie took me aside. 'What's this about Doc Buzzard?' she whispered.

"'Why?' I said. 'Do you know him?'

"She seemed to turn a few shades paler. 'Of course,' she said. 'He's the hoodoo man.'

"'Hoodoo?' I repeated. I didn't think she could be serious. I had heard of hoodoo happening on the coast, but those were silly ghost stories. Still, Josie was deadly serious. Serious enough for me to realize that I had to go see this man.

"I went out to his house on a hot afternoon in May. I remember that the sky was white and flat. It was so bright I could barely keep my eyes open. I was scared. My father had just given me this wonderful convertible, so I was as low-profile as a drunk polar bear. I borrowed a pistol from the hunting closet and took two hundred dollars from my father's safe. The road was full of holes, and I drove slowly so as not to blow a tire.

"When I got to the shack where the locals had told me the Buzzards lived, I almost turned back. It was nothing like the place is now—just a clapboard shack, evil-smelling, with stray dogs lolling about in the yard. I stayed in my car for a few minutes, hoping someone would come out, but nothing happened. Finally I walked to the door and knocked.

"When the door opened, I was surprised to see the man standing before me. His handsomeness seemed out of place with his surroundings. He was tall, with yellow eyes and smooth skin and long fingers. He smiled at me curiously and asked what I wanted."

"Wait," I interrupt. "This was Sam?"

"Sam's father," my grandmother says, and then goes back to her story.

"'I want to put a hex on my fiancé,' I said. 'The same one you used on Mr. Warren.'

"Doc Buzzard looked at me carefully. Then he invited me inside. He motioned for me to sit and then boiled me a cup of what I thought was tea. I wasn't in the mood for tea. It was ninety-eight degrees outside, after all. But he slid the cup in front of me, almost like a dare. It smelled awful, but I didn't want to be rude, so I took a sip. My insides cooled instantly, and I could suddenly think much more clearly. It was, of course, my first cup of Swamp Brew.

"'A hex,' I repeated. 'I'll pay you. I'm somewhat wealthy. I can pay whatever you want.'

"Doc Buzzard stared at me, amused. 'How do you know about hexes?'

"'Mr. Warren told me. He said that you hexed him. Then he died.'

"'Huh,' Doc said. 'I was hoping he'd die before he said that.'

"'So you did kill him?'

"'I didn't kill anyone,' Doc growled.

"'I don't think the police would see it that way.'

"'No more hexes,' he said. 'That was my only one.'

"'But—'

"'Too risky,' he said. 'No.'

"As you girls know, I have never taken kindly to being told no. Back then I was even more stubborn. Immediately, I pitched a fit.

"'You need to help me,' I said in a shaking voice. 'My fiancé is making a fool of me. I need to get him to forget this other . . . harlot and be obsessed with me.'

"Doc Buzzard took a deep breath. 'You mean you want a love potion.'

"'Yes,' I said. 'I suppose so.'

"'Well, sugar,' he said, 'you're in luck. Because that is just the sort of thing I do best.'

"And so we hatched a deal. I was never to mention hexes again. I was to keep Doc's secret about killing the hotel developer. And I was to pay him a great deal of money."

"For what?" I ask. I look at Hayes and Madison, who remain silent. Madison's on her second brandy, and they're both draped on pillows on the floor.

"Spells," my grandmother says.

"Can we just stop for a minute?" I ask. "I don't know if you've noticed, but we've sort of ventured into crazy land here. First of all, voodoo is practiced in Haiti, right? Well, I don't see anyone looking remotely Haitian in this picture. Or African, really. We're in Georgia."

"You're right, Alexandria," my grandmother says patiently. "I'm actually very proud that you're so knowledgeable about these subjects. This is not voodoo. It's *hoodoo*, and it's a very serious tradition. Primarily, the rituals are healing traditions that involve roots, herbs, plants, magnets, and salt combined with chants and objects of power. Also, hoodoo is not a religion per se—it's a practice. We don't put our fate in the hands of a god...we take control of our own fate and power. You can be a Christian and practice hoodoo—which is why it works so well for us Episcopalians and the African Methodists out there at Buzzard's Roost."

I look at the other girls again, who, as before, don't even flinch. If this is some kind of hoax, they're really playing along well.

"I'm sorry, but it's just not adding up," I say. "This is a debutante society. You aren't African."

"That doesn't mean we can't respect and use the power of African rituals," my grandmother says. "And they *are* powerful. Every Low Country native knows that. Every old family has a hoodoo story. I was simply wise enough to take it seriously. You see, Doc Buzzard offered to mix me up a spell. A potion, if you will, to win Thomas's affections."

"What was in it?"

"If we knew that, genius, we'd make our own," Madison says.

"I can't remember the steps directly. When I got to his shack, he was chanting over a red cloth laid out with herbs, what looked like a tooth, and several oils. He had written my name and Thomas's name at strange angles on a slip of paper. He gathered all of these things and sewed them into a tiny red bag. Then he pinned it to my slip. He said it was a mojo bag—"

I can't help but crack up. "Come on. Like in *Austin Powers*?"

"Don't be insulting, darling. A mojo, or a gris-gris, is a powerful amulet. It's a tiny bag one sews into clothing to shape one's fate. We always have one. In fact, I insist that each Magnolia change hers weekly to keep it fresh." My grandmother opens her blouse and reveals a tiny blue silk bag pinned to her slip. "I have the silk ordered from Turkey for mine. We request the herb combination ourselves."

I look questioningly at the MGs, who open their shirts and show me identical bags sewn to their bras. Hayes's is fuchsia; Madison's, dark gray.

"Anyhow, that mojo bag contained a pair of lode-stones, some magnetic sand, and some Love Me Oil—

Doc's secret recipe. It was a fairly simple gris-gris, compared to what Sina cooks up now."

"And it worked?"

"Not to be too punny . . . but, yes, like magic. I went back to Savannah and invited Thomas to dinner at my house, and a transformation took place over the next few days. It was wonderful at first; he was as attentive and adoring as a fiancé should be. But then Thomas started to appear at the house at all hours. Last thing at night and first thing in the morning, I'd see him standing on the lawn under the window of my room. He was acting a little desperate, honestly. He wanted to skip the wedding and elope immediately.

"I wouldn't hear of it, of course. No one was going to deprive me of that party. I reported to Doc that things were going well—very well. So well that I wanted to know what other services he could provide. But when I showed up at his door again, he wasn't thrilled.

"'I gave you your gris-gris,' he said impatiently. 'Now go back to your fancy balls.'

"But as you girls know, Dorothy Lee is not to be dissuaded. I persisted.

"'What do you want?' he asked.

"'I want to know what else you can do,' I said. 'And then I want to hire you to do it.'

"Lucky for me, Doc was in debt. And it turns out

that hoodoo spells can be incredibly useful to a young debutante on the rise. There were the love spells, of course. Doc has the ability to make a man or a woman fall in love. And—even more useful—he can make one fall *out* of love as well."

"That's the spell we used on you the other night," Madison says. "Crush Killer."

"So, let me get this straight: None of this was a dream?"

"Sorry," Hayes says.

"Well, what else do you guys use the spells for?"

My grandmother smiles. "Let's see. Love, beauty... oh! Youth. Each Magnolia is able to conjure herself once at an age that she'll stay until she dies. So I'll be thirty-eight right up until my funeral."

"Oh." Now, that explains a lot.

"And money spells," my grandmother continues. "I don't know if you've noticed, but none of the Magnolia women are in want of funds."

"I did notice. I thought you were just rich people who happened to hang together."

"Oh no," my grandmother says. "We are rich *because* we—how do you put it—'hang together.' Many of the Magnolias' families were ruined during the Depression. Doc's spells put an end to that."

"The Depression?" I say. "Miss Lee, I just can't believe you're old enough to remember the Depression."

"Let's just say hoodoo keeps me looking much younger than my years," my grandmother says.

"Well, if the doctor's so great at spells, why was he living in a shack? Why didn't he use the magic to make some cash for himself?"

"Hoodoo doctors almost never use spells for their own purposes," Hayes says. "Their business is to sell the spells to other people. The Buzzards have strict rules about using the magic for themselves."

"Why?"

"People don't go looking for magic if they're happy," Madison says. "I think the theory is, with all of that power at their disposal, the dark side can take over."

"The Buzzards have plenty of money now, though," my grandmother adds. "The Magnolias pay them well to provide us with the spells we need."

Suddenly, my head starts spinning. *Hang on!* I want to yell. But it's all literally just too crazy for words. I get up and walk to the tall window, which is draped with velvet curtains. "I'm sorry," I say. "This is just a lot to take in."

"It's nuts," Hayes says. "I know. But once you digest a little, I think you'll realize that it's also pretty awesome. I mean, Alex, pretty much any problem you have—hoodoo can fix it. We'll never run out of money. We'll always be pretty. And we can get any guy we want."

"What about bigger problems? World peace? The environmental crisis?"

"Those you'll have to work on yourself, Gandhi," Madison says. "The Buzzards can't do everything."

"I don't know. It sounds too easy," I say, looking out the window. "The Magnolias pay the Buzzards money, and they give us spells?"

"That's the basic arrangement," my grandmother says.

"Maybe I'll call Sam tomorrow. I don't think I'm getting all of this. He's so cool. He can help explain—"

"Absolutely not," my grandmother states, her voice slicing through the air. "You are not to fraternize with the Buzzards."

"Why? *You* did. Isn't that how this whole thing started in the first place?"

"All spells purchased go through me," my grandmother says. "That way things don't get out of control."

"Out of control? Meaning..."

"Alex, let's call it a day, shall we?" my grandmother says. "We don't want you to break out into unsightly hives." She rises. "Girls?"

The MGs gather their bags.

"See you tomorrow, Alex," Hayes says.

"Just wait, Alex," Madison whispers before she goes. "I know this is all a lot to take in, but you'll see. Before you know it, everything is going to change."

21

After they go, I fall asleep so deeply that a fire engine parked and blaring in my room couldn't wake me. No one gets me up for dinner, and I sleep through the night, rising confused and cotton-mouthed at four a.m.

The daze lasts for the next couple of weeks. I figure it's the result of that hoodoo drink—it's like there's a film over my entire existence. However, as for the magic itself...again I'm beginning to think I dreamed the entire thing. Whenever I try to bring it up, the MGs switch the subject. Really, they're just conducting business as usual, existing in their popular, pretty, self-involved, and slightly bitchy orbit. I thought Madison would broach the topic privately sometime, but all she does is shoulder chuck me and say, "Alex, remind me to introduce you to the wondrous world of conditioner later."

The only person who notices anything different about me is Dex. At one of our lunches, Dex comments that I've been acting really weird.

"What's up?" he asks, rooting through my backpack. (Josie's been getting crazy with my lunches lately—doughnuts, fried pork, hush puppies—and Dex has been majorly benefiting.) "For a while now, you've been totally spaced. Someone slip some poison into your morning coffee?"

"Um..." I look at Dex. What if I were to fill him in on what my grandmother told me?

Well, Dex, I'm a little out of it because a couple of weeks ago I was kidnapped and forced to participate in a hoodoo ritual that cleansed my soul. Apparently, my family has a legacy of black magic. Like, curses and love potions. Oh, and guess what? The Maggots are in on it too!

No, that wouldn't really fly. I mean, he's cool and all, but I don't know anyone who would listen to my story and then *not* send me directly to an insane asylum. Besides, Dex is the closest thing I have to a normal friend here.... I don't know if I'm up for losing him yet.

"I'm just tired," I say. "I've been having nightmares lately. That's all."

My grandmother hasn't mentioned the big revelation either. I spend the next couple of weeks watching her closely, trying to figure out exactly how this new, strange information figures into the absorbing puzzle that is my grandmother's existence. For instance, if her husband was so infatuated with her, where did he go? And could she really be almost seventy years old? And the main question in my mind: If being a Magnolia Leaguer is so wonderful, why did my mother run away?

My mother. That's a whole other door to open. Supposedly, she knew all about this hoodoo arrangement...meaning she'd used the spells herself. But as much as I try to wrap my mind around this, I can't remember her saying anything that would have indicated that she'd grown up privy to any sort of supernatural powers. Sure, she was obsessed with horticulture and tinctures, and I guess that fits in...but it seemed normal for an herbalist.

My only memory that seems to support this new insight into her past is from her thirtieth birthday. I was eleven years old. We had planned this huge party for her at the Main, with fire dancers and banjo players. Big Jon never said so, but I think he was a little in love with my mom, so this particular birthday got special treatment.

I remember I came into our cabin with a handful of flowers I'd picked from the Sanctuary. She was wearing a beautiful dress I had never seen before. It was green and silky and dipped down low in the back—much fancier than anything I'd ever seen. She had on long green gloves to match. When I came into the room, I stopped in surprise. She had lit candles everywhere and was burning some unfamiliar sweet incense. She was standing in front of the mirror, turning from side to side.

"Mom?" I said, a little scared. She seemed in a trance, almost. It took her a full minute to answer.

"Hi, honey," she said, still staring at herself.

"You look pretty."

"Thanks, sweetie." Her eyes were a little bloodshot. I couldn't help wondering if she'd been crying.

"What's wrong?"

"My first wrinkle."

"What?" She was being ridiculous. Her face was as smooth as polished stone. "No way."

"Way," she replied, smiling. She pointed to a barely discernible line between her eyebrows.

"Mom," I said, "that's not a wrinkle. It's, like, a cat hair or something."

"My mother never got even one," she said. "She went to the Doctor first."

"The doctor? Like the boob doctor?" We all used to laugh about the boob doctor. Once, a girl with boobs as round and firm as beach balls had come to the RC. In a particularly unwise moment, she told Billy she'd gone to the boob doctor. He also stretched out ladies' faces and sucked fat off their bodies with a hose, she said. After she told us that, we'd go up to her and poke her boobs with our fingers. She left a week or so later.

"Not exactly," my mother said. She stared some more. "If I had done what my mother said, I'd never have any wrinkles."

"What, like use sunscreen?" My mom was always slathering me in thick, smelly sunblock. It was a drag.

"Sort of," she said. She ran her finger over her face and then thoughtfully stroked the pendant around her neck. "I'd never have to age at all," she said. I stared at her. She was definitely being weird. "Well, I guess there's no turning back now."

"Mom," I said, "I don't know what you're talking about. You look awesome."

She turned around, smiling. "This dress is a little overkill, though, huh?"

"Maybe."

She motioned for me to unzip her. "It's something I had from a long time ago."

I waited for her to explain, but she had that forbidding look on her face that warned me not to ask any more. She hung up the dress and put on her jeans and a tie-dyed top. Then we went to the party together.

Remembering all of it—my mother's life and death—puts me in a sad mood. In fact, during the entire first two weeks of October, I'm in a bit of a funk. Finally, after passing the locked door to her room for the thousandth time, I decide to try once more to break in.

This time I move a lot more quickly—I don't want anyone catching me. I hop over the railing and leap to the balcony without a moment's hesitation. From my back pocket I take the file I'd nabbed for my previous attempt, and I jimmy the window in a matter of seconds. Pretty impressive, actually. You'd think I was a professional cat burglar or something.

I somersault through the window, landing on the floor with a loud thump. Dust rises around me in a soft cloud, which then dissipates. The room is completely dark. Cautiously, I crack open the curtains of one window. As light fills the room, I sit down with a soft gasp.

She's here. My mother, I mean. Not literally, of course. But her presence is everywhere. The room smells like cloves and baby powder. A cold feeling begins to well up in my throat. I forgot about how much she loved baby powder. If I hadn't come in here, that memory would be gone. What else of her am I losing? What else have I forgotten?

My grandmother, apparently, hasn't touched a thing since my mother left. It makes me even sadder: We share this horrible loss, but we're never able to break down the wall between us enough to talk about it. For one thing, I should thank her for leaving this room so intact. Because Louisa Lee is everywhere—the place is like a museum to her life. The room smells like the dried flowers she used to love; the bed is covered in a simple cotton coverlet that she must have picked out; the dresser is draped in an Indian tapestry, the same kind she used to throw over old furniture in our cabin. The room is painted the same shade of blue as the Buzzards' walls and gates—haint blue.

I creep over to her bookshelf and stare at the framed photos of my mom when she was younger. In one picture, she is wearing the white dress my grandmother showed me. In another, she's on the beach, in cutoff jeans and a bathing-suit top, her arm around another girl. When I lean in closer, I see that her friend is Constance Taylor, who looks pretty tough even as a teen.

Weird. They were friends?

Suddenly I hear a sound. "Mom?" I whisper. "Mom, are you here?"

My heart hammers in my chest. It would be so amazing if she were here. I close my eyes, wishing with everything I have that when I open them, she'll be here, smiling at me. But when I look around, I'm still alone.

I tiptoe to my mom's closet. It's spilling over with old sundresses, jeans, and ratty sandals. I run my fingers through the clothes, gritting my teeth at the acute feeling of loss. There are pieces of my mother here— strands of her hair, traces of the vanilla oil she put on her wrists. But *she* is gone forever. And that's the part no one understands: this tidal wave of sadness I face every morning when I wake up knowing I'll never see her again. Just when I think I'm doing okay, I'm faced with another wall of sorrow.

Wiping away my tears, I reach for the glittering object I see at the back of the closet. It's her white debutante gown. My grandmother must have returned it to its rightful place, in my mother's closet. I hold up the gown, then lay it carefully on the bed. Without even thinking, I start to strip off my clothes.

The dress is supertight, of course. My mom was way skinnier than I am. I've never been into clothes, but this dress is exquisite. It comes in tight at the waist and then flows in a column to the floor. I don't look great in it, of course . . . nothing like the way my mother looked, or how Hayes would. Still, it's the girliest I've looked in a very long time.

Suddenly, Josie's voice jolts me into reality. "Alex!" she calls. "Where are you?"

Crap.

"Alex!" I can hear her footsteps coming up the stairs. No way do I have time to change. I grab my clothes, hitch up the dress, and climb out the window. Once I'm safely in the hallway again, I hurry to the top of the stairs. To my surprise, I spot someone looking up at me. The blond figure is outlined against the black-and-white marble squares of the grand hallway floor.

"Thaddeus?" I blurt.

Crap. Why am I wearing this stupid dress? Do I have time to change? I step backward, but my foot lands squarely on Jezebel's paw.

"Yeeeeeooooow!"

Crap, crap, crap.

"Hi," Thaddeus says, his face a mixture of amusement and annoyance. Reluctantly, I shuffle back into his line of vision and head down the stairs.

"Nice dress." He's leaning against the banister.

"It was my mom's," I say. "I know, I look stupid."

"No, you don't," he says. "I mean, you look okay. It's just that the hair doesn't really match the outfit."

We look at each other for a moment.

"You want to go for a walk?" he says.

"Yeah, okay. Hang on—I'll change."

I bolt to my room, shed the dress, and throw on my normal uniform—jeans and a vintage tee. I look briefly in the mirror. A bit of dirt from the windowsill is on my hands and cheek.

I rub it off furiously and run downstairs, trying my hardest to look like I don't care at all that the hottest guy in school has randomly dropped by to visit me.

"Better," he says. "Shall we?"

He opens the door and steps into the sunlight, leaving me nothing to do but follow.

22

You know the only thing more uncomfortable than talking to a seriously snobby guy?

Talking to a snobby guy when you sort of have a huge crush on him.

We walk in silence across the street and into the park, which is alive with early-evening activity. A few people stand in the dog run, drinking beer and watching their spaniels nip at one another. Meanwhile, hordes of shrieking kids are jumping into the jets of the public fountain, gleefully ignoring the *Keep Out of Fountain* sign. A gaggle of students from the art college are Hula-Hooping in the grass. When Thaddeus gazes admiringly at their bare, toned midriffs, I can't help gritting my teeth in misery.

"Oh, man. All the hippies used to hoop like that at the RC," I say, just to make conversation. Thaddeus doesn't say anything. Does he think they're sexy? Probably. He looks pretty amazing himself, as usual. Jeans with just the perfect amount of bagginess, and a faded logoless T-shirt. As we continue to stroll along, I grow more and more uncomfortable at the disparity between us—both physically and conversationally. "So...how's school going?"

Thaddeus shrugs and doesn't answer.

"Okaaaaaay," I say. "I know that's a boring question, but I'm sort of grasping at straws here. What do *you* want to talk about?"

"Sorry," he says. "School's fine."

"Are you applying to colleges?"

"Sure. Yale, Harvard, and Brown."

"Wow. I'm from the middle of nowhere, and even I've heard of those. You must get pretty good grades."

"I study hard," he says. "It doesn't come naturally to me, the way it does to Hayes. I don't know if you've noticed, but I'm usually doing work."

I nod. He *does* usually have a book in his hand. I

sneak a look at him, then quickly look away. He's so cute that it's hard to focus.

"I actually came over to ask you to help me with something," he says.

"The only thing I'm good at is literature. But I can give you some pointers, sure."

"Thanks, but that's not it. I don't need tutoring from a pot farmer."

I toss my dreads. "I wasn't a pot farmer, Snobbeus. I was an herbalist. But fine, whatever. Believe what you want."

Thaddeus stops walking and, to my surprise, touches my arm just below my elbow. "Hey, I'm sorry. I'm an ass."

"No, it's okay —"

He blushes. "The truth is . . . I know I can be pretty awkward."

Him? Awkward? Did he not *see* my previous outfit of ass-hugging debutante dress and Birkenstocks?

"I just get nervous sometimes. For some reason it makes me say snobby things. I know it's annoying."

His hand drops from my elbow. I look down at where he touched me, as if it had left a mark. "We all get nervous. Don't sweat it."

"Thanks for calling me on it." He looks into my eyes for a moment. *Uh-oh. I think I might be levitating.* "Most people don't."

"We'll consider it my official job," I say, reddening. "So, what did you want to see me about?"

"It's my sister," he says. "You've become pretty good friends with her, right?"

"Sort of. I guess. I mean, she's been pretty nice to me. She has to be nice, because of the Magnolia thing."

"Right. Well, sometimes I feel like she gets... distracted by something. It's hard for her to focus on things like school. I mean, she's really smart. Her grades are perfect, despite the fact that she never opens a book."

"So, what's the problem?"

"Well, she indicated to me that she's not even interested in going to college. She hasn't even registered to take the SATs. But she's so *smart*. I want her to be the first Magnolia to go somewhere. It's time to break the trend."

I nod. Sounds to me like a good one to break.

"So, if she wants to go to a good school, she needs to study and focus on the extracurricular stuff." He looks at me coolly. "What do you think? Can you influence her?"

Wow. Hot-and-Weirdly-Shy Thaddeus wants *my* help? I turn red. "Hayes just has a lot going on," I say. "Jason... her friends..."

"She doesn't have that many friends."

"She has us. And Orang-Anna... and those other girls who follow her around."

"Orang-Anna?"

"Anna. The girl who's always orange from the spray tan."

Thaddeus's lips quiver in a reluctant smile.

Score! Chunky Hippie Girl: 1 Smile Point.

"But I'll talk to her. Sure. If you want."

Thaddeus nods. "It would be great for her to get your perspective, because you're so out there."

"Out there?" I feel my cheeks getting hot with embarrassment. *Does he mean that I'm fat? Or ugly? Do I smell weird?*

Crap, crap, crap!

"You've been *out there*, I mean," Thaddeus says, looking at the hoopers again. "Living on a farm in California...that's a singular experience. Most kids in this country just hang out at the mall. It's probably why you're so comfortable with yourself."

"Oh." Now my face is totally purple for completely different reasons. "Well, that's true. I'm...not really a mall queen. Or a shopper. Or whatever."

Oh God, I'm such a dork.

"I really admire that about you." (*You do?*) "I want my sister to get out there, too, you know? She's beautiful, she's bright, and she has financial freedom. She could be spending her summers in New York. Or Europe. There's a summer program at Oxford that I know she'd love. But she seems completely uninterested."

I kick at a rock with my toe. Does he know about the MGs? It's obvious to me that Hayes doesn't want to leave Savannah because she's learning about the power of the spells. But my grandmother said the League's

238

hoodoo practice was a secret. It seems that Thaddeus is in the dark too.

"I'll talk to her. Oxford sounds pretty cool."

"Don't tell her that I told you to do this," he says. "She hates my involvement."

"Okay," I say, wishing I had a family member who cared enough about me to plot a scheme to bust *me* out of town.

We're back in front of my grandmother's house now. "I'd better get going," he says. "I don't want to run into Miss Lee."

"Okay. See you at—" I stop mid-sentence. Thaddeus is suddenly looking at me intently. He leans closer.

Oh my God. Oh my God. Is he going to—

Then his reaches out and touches my necklace.

"What is this?" he asks, rubbing it with his fingers. He's so close that I can smell his shampoo. Pert Plus, I think. Or maybe Pantene.

"Uh…" *Focus, Alex. Focus.* "A necklace. My mother's, I mean. She always wore it. But it fell off before she died."

"I see," he says, turning it over in his hand. "It's nice."

"It's supposed to be good luck or something."

"Oh." He drops the pendant. "All right. I should go now. See you."

"See you."

Thaddeus turns and heads down the street. Just

hanging out with him for twenty minutes has bred an army of butterflies in my stomach.

Alex the hippie digs Thaddeus the prepster? Interesting. Veeerrrry interesting.

As I watch his retreating back, I reach up and touch my necklace. The rock is still warm from his hand.

Of course, once I think about it, I can't seriously hope that a guy like Thaddeus would really like *me*, anyway. At school he never says anything to me but "hey." Plus, it seems like he's got other irons in the fire. A couple of days after our walk, I see him in a seriously intense talk with Madison. When they spot me biking toward them, they stop talking and walk away.

Whatever.

I manage to do what Thaddeus asked, though. And it's not just because I have a crush on him. The truth is, I'm a little curious myself as to why Hayes, with all that she has going for her, seems so utterly uninterested in any ambition other than being rich in Savannah.

"Hayes," I ask at lunch one day, "what colleges are you applying to?"

She shrugs. Madison, who is sprawled on the grass, crumples up a burger wrapper and tosses it at the trash can.

"I'm thinking of going back west," I say. "Santa Cruz,

maybe. It's supposed to be amazing. You want me to get you a brochure?"

"No, thanks," she says. "Hey, you girls want to get manicures later at See Jane? Or facials? They're so awesome there. My treat."

"So, you'd rather go up north, then?" I persist.

"I don't know, Alex," Hayes answers somewhat impatiently.

"What about this summer? You girls could go anywhere. You have the money. Maybe we should go to Europe and backpack around."

Again I get stonewalled. Hayes studies her nails while Madison pulls clumps of grass out of the ground. Later that day, I find Thaddeus at his locker.

"So, I talked to your sister. I don't know what to tell you. She's just not into leaving. I even suggested we backpack around Europe, and I got nothing. Zip."

Thaddeus treats me to one of his small, haughty smiles. "I don't think Hayes and Madison are the backpacking type."

"Still, they seem pretty determined not to leave home."

Thaddeus looks at his watch.

"I've got an hour before lacrosse. Let's go hang at the bleachers." Like a puppy, I follow him across the school lawn to the playing fields. I can feel the other kids looking at us. *What's he doing with the hippie freak?* I don't care. You know what? They can think what they want. The fall air feels good on my cheeks, and the breeze is filled with the pungent smell of freshly mowed grass.

"Ever been here before?" he asks.

"No. I haven't gone to any games yet."

"You should check one out," he says.

"I'm more into solo sports than team stuff. Mountain biking, hiking, that kind of thing."

"Cool," he says. He seems genuinely impressed. "The other MGs aren't really into that."

"I think we've established I'm not like the other MGs. If it were up to me, I wouldn't be one at all."

Thaddeus nods. "Well, that's a hard one to get out of. Trust me, I grew up in a house full of Magnolia talk. I just wish my sister could see past the importance of being socially on top. There's a whole world out there."

"What about you? Won't you miss home when you go to college next year? You're pretty popular too."

"Sure," he says. "I love it here. And yeah, it's nice that I have a lot of friends. I won't deny it—life is good here. But there's more out there. I mean, *you* know that. With your crazy background and strange upbringing."

This time, I can't help but laugh. "You really are bad at conversation, aren't you?"

He looks down. "We can't all be as funny as you all the time, Alex."

My mouth drops open. *He thinks I'm funny?*

Thaddeus hurries on, as if he knows he's said something odd. "But Hayes is so into the Magnolias thing, it's like she can't see past the borders of Savannah."

"Well, that happens sometimes, right? The popular people are so used to ruling the school that they don't see the point of going anywhere else. I was like that at the R.C. Comfortable. I'd never have left if my mom hadn't died."

"I'm so sorry. That must be pretty awful for you. Was she...the one driving?"

"Yeah. She drove off a cliff."

Just saying it out loud brings the horror alive all over again.

"Oh, shit, Alex. I can't believe I asked that. I'm sorry."

"It's okay." Suddenly, I realize that I haven't thought about my mom all day. Am I losing my memory of her? What color were her eyes? Green? Brown? God, I don't know if I know anymore.

"Are you okay?" Thaddeus asks. He looks genuinely concerned. "Alex?"

"You know, I've got to go," I mumble, turning away. *Please, please, please,* don't let him see me cry.

"Alex, I'm sorry. I didn't mean to bring up bad memories for you."

"It's all right," I say hurriedly. "I just...forgot something I need to do. Later, okay?"

"Okay," he says. I give him a peace sign and run down the bleachers, just making it to the bathroom, where I shut myself in the stall, sit on the toilet lid, and finally let myself cry.

23

The next day is Halloween. In honor of the holiday, I paint my eyes and lips black and put on a Black Sabbath shirt. Dex loves it, of course, but I know I'm in trouble when Madison and Hayes flank me at lunch.

"That's it," Madison says. "We're giving you a forcible makeover."

"Madison—"

"Seriously. Get your bag. We're cutting."

"What? How?"

"We have a note saying you have a Magnolia League community project again."

I shake my head. "I can't believe that actually *works*."

"Of course it works. Come on."

I'm hesitant, but since my only remaining classes today are Mr. Roberts's history and gym, I give in, trailing after them to the Prius. Oddly, both Madison and Hayes are wearing all white again today. Hayes is dressed in white skinny jeans that only a toothpick could wear, and Madison has on a white flowing goddess top and snowy linen pants.

"What's with the all-white look?" I ask. "Is it a Halloween thing?"

"Halloween is for amateurs," Madison scoffs. "What you're in for is way better than a costume."

"What do you mean?"

She reaches over and yanks on my longest dreadlock. "*What do you mean?*" she mimics. "Do you know how much you say that? Just go with it, Alex. Life is happening to you."

Hayes drives. At first I think we're going downtown, but then I realize we're driving to Isle of Hope, a seriously plush suburb on the Skidaway River. As usual, Madison's riding shotgun and I'm in the back. On the way, neither of them bothers to explain anything about what we're doing. In fact, no one talks at all. We just sit there listening to the music and looking out the windows. My stomach turns—there's something eerie about their silence.

Madison's house is a modern estate with a main house, a guesthouse, and a pool house. Everything is white and flat and glossy; I swear, an alarm must go off if someone spills a Coke. We all head straight back to the pool house, not bothering to call out to Madison's mom to tell her that we're here. I follow Madison and Hayes through the sliding glass door, looking around with surprise as we step inside. The shades are drawn, and the room is completely lit with candles.

"Who lit these?" I ask. As usual, I get no answer. Someone must have done this before we got here. A maid? Madison's mom? And why is it so dark in here, anyway? I look quickly toward the bar, which is lined with old brown glass bottles and jars.

"Oh no," I say. "No way am I letting you crazies guinea-pig me again."

Hayes smiles. "We're not going to 'guinea-pig' you, sweetie. You know about the spells now. We're letting you in on our intentions this time."

"Well, that's very nice of you."

"Sit down, will you?" Madison says impatiently.

"Fine. But I'm not drinking anything this time unless I know what's in it."

"Oh, come off it," Madison says. "I saw you drink some organic snot juice the other day. What could be worse than that?"

"That's kombucha," I say defensively. "It's full of antioxidants." The truth is, kombucha *is* seriously disgusting, but I've been drinking it lately to try to lose weight. My mom used to brew it for people who wanted to speed up their metabolism. So far all it's done is give me serious gas.

"Alex," Hayes says soothingly before Madison and I can start bickering again, "we think the time has come for us to give you a little makeover."

"A makeover?" I frown. "Why?"

"Here's the deal, Alex," Madison says. "You need a different look."

"I don't want a different look. I mean, sure, I'd love to have Miley bods, like you girls. Otherwise I wouldn't be downing the snot tea. But that's just not how I'm built. And I know you guys are super into expensive clothes and makeup, but I've never thought that was important. If you like who you are, then why does it matter what you look like?"

"That's very noble," Madison says. "And I'm sure the hippies at the commune would be pleased with that answer. But it's just not realistic."

"It's not like new clothes can really change any-thing. You already took me shopping, remember?"

"What if we told you we could improve other things too?" Hayes asks.

I shake my head. "You girls are bizarre-o. I do *not* like the sound of this."

"You have to admit it," Madison says. "Even *you* think your hair is gross."

I think of Thaddeus and how he said my dreads were "out there."

"Okay," I say. "I'm not that into my do anymore. Fine — the phase is over. But I'd have to shave them off. We're talking baldness, people."

"We can live with that," Hayes says.

"No way am I wearing a wig."

"Just trust us," Madison says. "We helped you get over that Reggie loser, didn't we?"

"You did," I relent.

"Okay. Then sit."

Reluctantly, I obey, wincing as I see Hayes approach with a large pair of scissors.

"You might want to close your eyes for this."

"Wait . . . I . . . okay."

I shut my eyes, trying to distract myself as I hear the snip of the scissors. I can hear my heavy locks fall away and hit the floor with loud thumps.

"Ew," Madison says. I squeeze my eyes shut tighter. But when I hear the buzz of a razor, I can't help looking.

"Oh my God!" Patches of hair stick up weirdly from all of the spots that aren't shiny and bald. "I look like some sort of radiation victim."

"Don't worry, sweetie," Hayes says.

"Something bad always happens when you call me that," I grumble. "Remember how I almost got burned to a crisp at that party?"

"Just close your eyes again." The buzz is louder now. My head tickles as she mows my scalp. Suddenly, I feel something cold and wet. When I peek, I see that one of them has turned out the lights. Madison is smearing something black and disgusting on my scalp. Hayes stands behind her, her eyes glittering.

"What are you doing?" I plead.

"Shut up and trust us," Madison growls. "I'm blind-folding you until this is over."

She ties a silk scarf around my eyes. The smell is gag-inducing. Within minutes, my entire head is itching furiously.

"Ow!" I yell, reaching up to scratch.

"Don't touch it!" Madison orders.

"What? *There's a colony of fire ants on my head!*"

One of the girls—I can't see who—grabs my wrists.

"It's just a few minutes," Hayes says. "I promise."

But the sensation is unbearable. I whistle. I stomp my feet. I sing the words of my mom's favorite Phish song, the one about mangoes that makes no sense.

"I can't take it anymore!" I finally cry, ripping off the blindfold. I look in the mirror, and—

I can't believe it. The dreads are gone. I have . . . *hair.* Thick, chestnut-colored, unbelievably shiny hair that cascades (frizz-free!) down my back and around my shoulders. Seriously, I could audition for a shampoo commercial right now and win the role, no prob.

"How did you ..."

"Magic," Hayes says, smiling. "Not kidding."

"What do you think, dorkus?" Madison asks, crossing her arms.

"Wow. It's good. Really, really good."

The MGs laugh. Hayes stands behind me, rubbing my shoulders. I touch my new hair. It's soft, and so shiny it almost sparkles in my hand. It even smells good, like a cinnamon cookie.

"Is it real?" I whisper.

"Probably," Hayes says. "We don't really know how the spell works. Sam gives us the bottles and the instructions, and we use them. But it's definitely your hair to keep."

"It *hurt*."

"No one said the spells were pain-free," Madison says. She stands back. "Okay. Much better. Now ... item number two."

"There's something else?" I ask, looking in the mirror again. *What are they going to do? Chop off my nose and grow me a better one?*

"Alex," Hayes says, her hands still on my shoulders, "if you could change one thing about yourself, what would it be?"

I bite my lip. *That's* not a hard one. After all, I've just been called out for drinking the most disgusting drink on the planet in a vain attempt to shed some pounds.

"I'd be skinny. Like you."

There's a pause as the MGs glance at each other, obviously deciding how to treat this delicate subject.

Why do I feel like I'm selling my soul?

"We thought you might say that," Hayes finally says, rising to go to the spell bar.

"So you *do* think I'm fat."

"You're not fat," Madison says. "You're just a little chubby. Healthy, you might call it."

"Right," I say, folding my arms tight against my chest. God. Does everyone talk about how fat I am? Dexter? Thaddeus?

"Alex, what if we told you that you'll never have to worry about what you eat again?" Hayes asks.

My eyes fill with tears as I think about all the times Reggie pinched the fat on my waist and called me Pudge. And how Billy would never let me ride his bike because, he said, I would flatten the tires. And how skinny Crystal looked when Reggie kissed her in front of me.

"I'd say that sounds like a pretty good deal."

"Okay. Good." Madison opens a dark wooden box on the bar, extracts something, and snaps the box shut. "Put this on your wrist," she says, handing me a piece of black silk string held together with an old silver clasp.

I take the bracelet gingerly.

"Is this going to hurt?"

"No," Hayes says reassuringly. "Not this one."

This time I refrain from asking what she means.

Instead, I snap the bracelet onto my wrist. Obviously, this is going to cause something very strange to happen. But if they could do that to my hair...well. Okay.

This spell, though, is not as instantaneous. Nothing seems to happen.

"Is it working?" I ask after a few minutes.

"Give it some time," Madison says. She walks to the bar and turns on some jazz music. Hayes sits on a stool, texting someone—Jason, no doubt. To distract myself, I start leafing through a copy of *Vogue*.

"Man, I hate these magazines," I say. "Like, I'm seriously going to ride a Ferris wheel in a Prada bikini? I mean, this girl is scuba diving in a silk—"

My thought is interrupted by rabid, uncontrollable hunger.

"Hey, Madison, do you have anything to eat?"

"Sure," she says, pulling out a plate of brownies.

"Something healthy?" I ask. "You just told me I was fat. Remember?"

"You've got your talis on. As long as you wear that, you'll never have to worry about what you're eating."

"My *what*?" I say, barely able to concentrate. *Okay, I don't care if the brownie will make me fatter. I'm ravenous! What is wrong with me?* I put one into my mouth.

"Your talis," Hayes says helpfully. "Your hoodoo bracelet."

"Hang on." I stuff in two more brownies. The hunger subsides, but only a tiny bit. "Okay," I say, swallowing. "What the hell do you mean?"

"When you were at Sam's, did you see birdcages?"

"Sure," I say. "Well, not cages. It's more like an aviary. I figured he kept the birds because their waste fertilized the flowers."

"That's one of the reasons," Hayes says. "There's also one bird for every Magnolia."

"One bird for every Magnolia?"

"Oh my God—yours has got to be a *parrot*," Madison says.

"Yeah? Well yours is a nasty—"

"Girls," Hayes interrupts sternly. "Pull it together. We're working here."

"The bird burns your food," Madison says. "Get it?"

"No."

"The expression *eat like a bird* is actually totally misleading," Hayes explains. "Our bird mates are hummingbirds—they eat at least three times their body weight a day. The specimens connected to us by our talises burn our food for us. Doc Buzzard figured out a way to conjure their metabolisms into our bodies."

"Trippy." I finger my new bracelet.

"Totally. That's why we're so skinny, even though we eat everything in sight."

I nod. It all makes sense now—the buckets of chicken, the tubs of ice cream. And here I thought it was just a regular bout of teen bulimia. Just then I'm hit with another hunger pang.

"Will I always be this ravenous?"

"You'll get used to it. The good news is, you're going to get a lot thinner, fast. In fact, you'll drop five pounds today if you don't take in more than three thousand calories."

"It's kind of a pain sometimes," Hayes admits. "It gets hard to remember to eat."

"*That* I find hard to believe," I say, sneaking another brownie.

"Listen, let's quit for the day and go see Damien," Hayes says, kindly squeezing my shoulder.

"I told you guys—I'm done with shopping."

"Come on, Alex," Madison says. "It's Halloween. Lighten up! Anyway, trust me—you'll thank me. In a couple of days, you're going to need all new clothes."

24

Well, it works. Hoodoo, voodoo, fire-ant hair spells, whatever. You know what? I don't care, really. The point is, I am finally somewhat close to hot.

Over the next couple of weeks, my appearance is totally transformed. After years of worrying about my extra pounds, I'm now inarguably skinny — as skinny as I've always wanted to be. My zits are gone, thanks to some weird yellow paste that burned like acid when

Hayes rubbed it onto my face, and my hair has kept its newfound gloss.

As awesome as this transformation is, though, the changes are getting me into some embarrassing situations. For one thing, my scalp still itches. In fact, I've been scratching so much that Constance takes me aside one morning and asks discreetly whether I need to be tested for lice. And Madison was right about the clothes. After just a couple of days, nothing fits me. My shirts are looser, and my pants gap at the waist. The jeans we got Tuesday at BleuBelle's are already huge, so I have to hitch them up all day. Then, at my locker, Dex informs me that I'm giving the entire hallway a killer view of my purple tie-dyed underwear—a lone relic from arts-and-crafts day at the RC.

"Crap," I mutter, standing and pulling up my jeans.

"Dude," Dex says later at Waffle House. In a solemn commitment to cementing our friendship, Dexter has been taking me to "Awful Waffle" once a week. Our download time on Thursdays has now become a sacred tradition. "Okay, I wasn't gonna ask you this, because I didn't want you to think I was one of those metro a-holes who sit around obsessing about hair. But, okay, it's been three weeks or whatever, and it's like you're in a silence pact about it. So, gotta know: How'd you undread the bird's nest?"

"Oh, you know. Conditioner. A brush."

"I thought you had to *shave* that shit."

"What do you think?" I reply, carefully not answering.

"Good call," he says. "It's not like I'm the fashion police or anything, but that look you were rolling with was pretty heinous."

"Why didn't you tell me?" I say. "You're supposed to be my friend."

"Are you kidding? A man must never say anything about a woman's hair. Even an asshat like me knows that. Now, what leftovers do you have for Dex?" He looks at my plate expectantly.

"I ate it all," I say, my face growing warm.

"Seriously?" he cries. "The whole thing? You ordered two smothered-and-chunked hash browns. A.L., you got a bun in the oven?"

"Not possible. Unless you're a true believer in immaculate conception."

"We Jews don't buy into such nonsense. That Virgin Mary, she definitely had a guy on the side."

"Yeah, well. I've just been really hungry lately."

"Hmm." He looks at me suspiciously. "Maybe you should go to the doctor or something. You're looking a little scrawny. You might have a tapeworm."

I'm completely tempted to tell him. It would be so great to get a sane outsider's perspective on this hoodoo pact. But Dex would think I was crazy.

"I'll eat more," I say, standing up. "Promise. Listen, I've got to—"

"Hey, loser," Madison says, literally blowing through the door. She seems to have her own personal wind tunnel; menus scatter onto the floor. The humble diners of Waffle House crane their necks to stare at her beauty. "Saw your tacky van in the lot."

"Looking for me?" Dex says. "A crush. How flattering."

Oddly, Madison reddens a bit. Did Dex actually manage to insult her?

"Not likely, Mr. Doughboy. Alex, I need you. We have only a few hours of daylight left for—"

"For what? Warding off the vampires?"

"Vampires are *so* over, Dexter. Everyone knows that. Coming, Alex?"

"It's cool," I say. "I'll bike."

"Okay. Ta, loser," she says, waggling her fingers at Dex.

"I'll call you later," I say, rising.

"Beware, friend," Dex says. "These Magnolias are toxic stuff."

I shoot him an apologetic look as I head out the door. I should just make Madison wait while Dex polishes off his hash browns, but the truth is we're finishing the last step of a three-day spell for Hayes. It's my first time as a participant (as opposed to a guinea pig/victim), so I'm pretty psyched about it. I pedal hard out of suburbia's blazing strip malls and into downtown's leafy maze, making a quick stop at my grandmother's house to throw on some smaller jeans. After a trip to the kitchen to speed-feed three pieces of meat lover's pizza, I ride over to Hayes's house on Pulaski Square and park my bike inside the gate of the large, perfectly manicured garden.

From the pretty brick courtyard, I can hear Hayes's voice floating through the open window. I can't hear what she's saying exactly, but she sounds tense. She saw Jason talking to some hot band nerd by the girls' locker room the other day, and now she's convinced that he has a wandering eye. Personally, I think she's being totally insane. How could anyone as gorgeous and nice as Hayes ever doubt that her boyfriend is into her? But no one asked me.

"*Dried cat semen?*" I hear her shriek as I enter. "How the hell am I supposed to get that?"

Right. That's the thing about a lot of these spells. They all have a million steps and call for some really random stuff. Potions have to be mixed at a certain time of day; pastes have to be applied while staring and concentrating on some old picture; the steam of teas must be waved in the direction of a certain country. Often the spells involve bodily fluids — sweat, spit, even menstrual blood. And they never, ever make sense. My grandmother is always half burying old cans of lye in the garden. (They ward off evil spirits, apparently.) After Madison cast that spell to make my hair grow, she had to put a dime from my pocket into her own shoe.

"You should thank me, dorkus," she told me later. "I had to wear the same closed-toed heels for three whole days. Everyone knows I never wear the same pair of shoes twice in one month."

I have to say, even though the whole hoodoo thing really freaked me out at first, I find it pretty rad that the town's fanciest families secretly derive their wealth and power from African rituals. And once you know the secret, you wonder how you never guessed before. Signs of hoodoo are all over Savannah—from graves decorated with cans of food and bottles of whiskey, to house doors painted haint blue, to signs around town advertising hoodoo fortune-tellers and remedies. Before, I would have just dismissed them as Southern wackiness, but now I've learned my lesson: What may seem like nonsense to one person probably makes a hell of a lot of sense to someone else.

Upstairs, Hayes is still lamenting the complexity of her spell. I take the opportunity to check out the Andersons' house. Whereas Madison's personal quarters are sleek and highly designed, Hayes has gone for more of a luxurious Barbie's Dream House look with her room. The carpet is plush and pink; the walls are papered with a pink-and-gold fleur-de-lis pattern; and all the furniture, including the king-size canopied bed, is gilded. It's the sort of place an old-fashioned courtesan would think up if she were sixteen—and loaded.

Hayes is on her knees in the middle of the room in front of two red candles in brass holders. On one candle, she's carved the name *Hayes*; on the other, *Jason*. She's busy stuffing two crude-looking cloth dolls with what looks like pine straw, hair, powder, and bottles of fluid.

"Hey," Hayes says. "Glad you're here."

"Voodoo dolls?"

"Yeah. It's not routine—you know, it's not a hoodoo thing, really. But Sina wants to try out some New Orleans tricks. She likes to be fluent in both practices."

While Sam is the official root doctor for the Magnolias, the MGs often circumvent the official channels and hire Sina on the side. Though my grandmother is usually understanding, she's been known to say no to a spell. Since Sybil's not such a fan of Jason, chances are Miss Lee neg'd a mojo to help that relationship. It's dangerous to use Sina directly, of course. When Miss Lee finds out someone's done it, she gets pissed and has been known to suspend Magnolias from any hoodoo for up to a year. It's a majorly embarrassing punishment, especially to an older Magnolia, because it means losing whatever you've conjured—your age or hair or body or whatever—and looking like your natural self. You'd think they'd be okay with looking like the selves they'd been born with, but hoodoo is like any good drug:

Once you have the magic, it's tough to get off it. Apparently Khaki Pettit's sister went into hiding when she was caught illegally using Sina to put a Love No More spell on Khaki's husband—with whom she'd been having an affair. (She was penalized on two counts: illegal spell use *and* betraying a fellow Magnolia.) She was so horrified by her natural looks that she told her friends she was traveling around the world for two years and secretly had her maid bring her food in a big straw basket to her room.

"Hayes," I ask now, eyeing a suspicious-looking jar. "Is that...*pee?*"

She nods.

"It's Jason's," Madison says.

"How did you—"

"Oh, that was nothing. But getting the nail clippings was tough." She squints at the wrinkled piece of paper. "God, it's hard to read Sina's writing. I like it much better when Sam does the spells. Okay, this says *saffron*. Damn. Alex, can you go down and see if we have any?"

"Sure," I say. On the way, I take a little tour of the upstairs. Hayes's mom—Sybil McPhillips's daughter—has done a bang-up job preserving this house. As far as I can tell, there are two kinds of house owners in the old part of the city: the ones who have given themselves over to Savannah's weather and rot, and those who fight the good fight. My grandmother's house, for example, practically crumbles in your hand. Ivy chokes the brick; the walls literally sweat with humidity, causing the wallpaper and paint to peel; weird drafts curl around the corners, slamming doors and blowing papers; odd smells waft from the pipes and vents. Hayes's house, however, is filled with gleaming, polished wood and freshly washed linens. Each piece of furniture is precious, polished to a gleam, and carefully arranged. You get the feeling that Hayes's mom spends every moment painting, upholstering, or waxing. Like, the dog's bed matches the tea towels, which match the doormat that matches the toilet paper holder, and I'm fairly certain none of that is an accident.

I wander down the blue plaid hallway into the yellow-and-red kitchen. Saffron... where would that be? Tentatively, I open a cabinet and peer inside.

"What are you looking for?" My heart leaps into my throat.

"Thaddeus!" I slam the cabinet door shut quickly. "I thought you'd be at lacrosse."

Immediately, I'm horrified. Now he'll know that I've totally memorized his schedule.

"I skipped today. I need to study for my calculus test. Unlike you girls, I actually study for things." He gazes at me quizzically. "You look different lately."

"It's nothing. I just straightened my hair."

"That's it?" He steps back and looks me up and down. I have to admit, even though I don't believe in the power of expensive clothes, I'm pretty happy to be wearing these awesome jeans right now.

"Well, I've been . . . riding my bike a lot."

"Huh. Well. Listen, about the other day . . . I'm really sorry about your mom. That's all I wanted to say. I can't imagine what that loss must feel like. My mom's a crazy Martha Stewart wannabe, but I'm glad I have her. Anyway—I'm sorry."

"Thanks," I say, my face growing red.

"Alex, hurry up," Madison snaps as she enters the kitchen. "We've only got an hour. Oh. Hi, Thaddeus."

"Hey," he says to her. He opens the fridge as if he's looking for food, then frowns. "Sorry I forgot to call you back about that thing."

What thing? They call each other?

"Sure." She looks at us. "I'm glad to see you both here, actually. There's a rumor I want to clear up."

"What?"

"Well, Thad, word on the street is you have a little crush on Alex here."

My face heats to a thousand degrees.

"Madison—"

"So, my question is, what's the holdup? If it's true, don't you think you should ask her out already?"

Thaddeus, clearly mortified, doesn't say anything.

"I mean, she looks great, doesn't she?"

"You know I can't, Madison. She's . . ."

I feel tears searing the edges of my eyes. So, I'm not good enough for Thaddeus. Just like Reggie.

I turn and leave the kitchen, heading to the porch. I know I'm supposed to help Hayes with her love spell or whatever, but now the tears are seriously coming down. I wipe them away angrily. First, I'm dumped by Reggie because I'm too fat. Now Thaddeus obviously thinks the same thing. Or something like that.

Not my type, man. Too chubby. Too weird.

I run down the porch steps to my bike, hop on, and begin pedaling away.

"Alex!"

Thaddeus is following me down to the garden.

"Alex, wait!"

He catches up to the bike and reaches for the handlebar. I swerve too quickly, falling on the drive. Crushed oyster shells bite into my hands.

"Crap!"

"Are you okay?"

"Leave me alone."

"Alex, you need to understand," Thaddeus says, holding out his hand to help me up. I brush it away, but he grabs me roughly under my armpits and yanks me up. "I promised myself I'd never date a Magnolia again."

I look at the ground. My knee is bleeding. "You didn't think I was too fat? Or too 'out there' or something?"

"No. I think you're cool. I *like* that you're different."

Wait. Whaaaat? This is a *complete* one-eighty from what I thought was happening. This guy is a total high school god, and he likes me. *Me.*

"Um...I..."

Thaddeus gently puts his hand on my shoulders, then leans closer and looks into my eyes. "Alex," he says, "you know I like talking to you. But this is the part where you shut up. Okay?"

Oh. My. God.

I nod. And I realize that, up in heaven, my mom must be cooking up a hoodoo spell of her own in my honor. Because just then—miracle of miracles—the hottest guy in school—no, on the *planet*—leans in and kisses me.

25

Okay, so. Life is now *officially* awesome.

I don't think I'm overstating even a little when I say that the past month—it's been exactly thirty days since Thaddeus first kissed me—has been the best in my existence, if not the history of the world. Just looking at the guy makes me so nervous that I want to throw up. Yup, he's *that* good-looking. And cool. I love how he just sits on the sidelines and watches what goes on instead of being all aggro about ruling the social circle, like Madison and Hayes. Not that he couldn't rule the school. He just chooses, instead, to be cool about it. Which is why everyone likes him.

But you know what else is awesome? Being the coolest-guy-in-school's *girlfriend*. People who before had no idea who I was now go out of their way to talk to me. I mean, the MGs had already put me on most people's social radar, but now it's like I'm the *most* popular MG. I've had two invitations to go to exclusive beach house parties, plus an invite (from Orang-Anna) to go to Sun Valley for winter break. On top of that, three guys have asked me out behind Thaddeus's back, including Jim, the boy in the rugby shirt who ignored me on the first day of school. He passed me a note in math class: *If you ever get sick of Thad, I'm all over it, hottie.* So much for bros before hos.

Of course, it's not like Thaddeus and I are that hot and heavy or anything. It's funny: Kids spend so much time wondering what the popular people are doing, and it turns out we're doing nothing exciting at all. Mostly, Thad and I just hang out, reading or playing chess. (He's not as good as I am, but he's catching on.) We've been going out a month, but we've kissed only twice — the first time was that day by the bike. Overall, I have to say, it's been pretty chaste, except for one afternoon last week.

We were outside my grandmother's house. We'd been walking in the park when it started pouring, so we ran to the grandma-mansion, but not before getting completely soaked. The front door was locked, and we ran to the side door in the garden. I was just yanking it open when he suddenly grabbed me and pulled me back outside.

You know what rocks? Kissing in the rain. Even though Reggie and I made out a few times, I've never kissed anyone like that before. There are all these places for the hands to go, new places to touch, and I swear I completely forgot where I was until Thaddeus stopped.

"Wow," he gasped.

"Seriously." I stared at him, scared of the bump I'd felt pressing into my hip. The last time I'd felt that, I had to fight Reggie off. Was Thaddeus going to pressure me the same way? Before I had time to worry about it too much, he kissed me again. But when things started to get really crazy—I mean, my heart was pounding so hard, I felt like I'd just biked up Shasta—Thaddeus pulled back.

"I'd better go," he said. "Homework." He took off, and I went inside to change my clothes. All I could think about was that if he'd wanted me to go all the way, I would have felt quite differently this time. It was a pretty trippy thing.

Now I just wish he'd hang out with me more at school. Everyone's noticed that he doesn't. Especially Madison, who says as much during break.

"Why don't you ask Thaddeus to have lunch with us

today?" she says, grabbing my history notebook. Hayes might not be going anywhere, but Madison's hot on a fashion internship. It requires a 3.75 GPA, so she has to actually care about her grades all of a sudden. "It would be a good move for all of us. That way everyone will know that the whole thing is normal and that there's no stickiness because he and I went out last year."

I look at her seemingly innocent face. I guess I have no reason to doubt her—after all, she stood up for me in the kitchen when she thought Thaddeus was messing with me. Still. Would she *really* want me to go out with her ex-boyfriend?

"I would ask him to have lunch," I say somewhat uncomfortably, "but he told me he doesn't like to eat with his sister."

"Really? Huh. He used to eat with us *last* year. Oh well. See you at the bench."

I watch as Madison struts toward the lawn, and then I immediately make a beeline for Thaddeus's locker.

"Hey, why don't you have lunch with us today?" I ask. "I'd love to hang out with you."

He shakes his head. "No way. A man cannot be seen having lunch with his own little sister at school."

"But you and your sister get along. You're, like, the only siblings in the universe who actually enjoy each other's company."

"True. But part of the reason is that we don't spend time together within these hallowed halls."

"Well," I can't help saying, "you used to eat with Hayes when you went out with Madison."

A cold expression passes over Thaddeus's face. I put my hand to my necklace, scared of what I've said. *Why did I bring that up? I'm such an idiot.*

"You're right," he says grimly. "But that relationship didn't turn out so well, did it?"

I shake my head, scared to say anything else.

"Listen, I don't want to get into this now, but let's drive out to Tybee Island after school today," he says gently. "I'd love to show you the beach. And, no — I never took Madison there, just in case you were wondering, okay?"

That much I know is true. Madison thinks Tybee is for rednecks. She's strictly a Hilton Head girl.

"Okay," I say, beaming. This plan is *so* much better than him coming to lunch with the MGs. In fact, as I cram down my three BLTs on the lawn later, I can't stop grinning.

"Damn, Smiley," Dex says. Despite his showdowns with Madison, he pretty much always eats at the bench now. "You back on the pipe again?"

"No...just in a good mood."

Madison rolls her eyes. "Oh my God. Everyone around me is annoying me with their perfect relationships."

"So you and Jason are okay again?" I ask Hayes.

"Yup," she says. "The gris-gris totally worked. He came over last night with, like, a thousand roses."

"I don't even want to know what a gree-whatever is," Dex says. "You girls are dirty."

Hayes smiles wickedly and takes another bite of peanut butter pie.

Oh, Dex, I think. *If only I could tell you the truth.*

"So, are we hitting the Awful later?" he says as we walk to our lockers. "Thursday tradition."

"Oh, crap. Dex, I can't."

"You're canceling? Sacrilege."

"I know. I'm sorry. I've got...a date."

Dex shakes his head. "Man. First, you say you aren't dating Hot-eus. Now you're so up in it, you're choosing him over Eggos and Country Crock. How could you?"

I grin. "I'll make it up to you."

"It's cool. Just be careful."

"What do you mean?"

"Something's up with you," he says. "It's not just the hair and the insta-skinniness—which, by the way, I totally don't trust. Diet pills went out in the eighties. Didn't you know?"

"I've just been—"

"Biking a lot. Right. Last time I checked, you weren't signed up to train for the Tour de France, Alex. And that's the only way to explain the twenty pounds you've dropped in the last month. I don't know if it's because of Thaddeus or what, but I think these girls are getting their claws into you."

"Don't be crazy," I say. "I'm my own person. If nothing else, my mom taught me that."

"Fine, but if I catch you listening to Lady Gaga, I'll seriously know you're possessed."

I laugh nervously.

"Okay," he says. "Later days. And next Thursday, Awful Waffle, three o'clock. No excuses."

I nod. "Count on it."

Dex flashes me a thumbs-up. Then he hoots and moonwalks all the way down the hall and out the door.

26

After school, Thaddeus takes me to Tybee Island in his old diesel Mercedes. There was a time when I would have lectured him about running his car on used corn oil, but right now I'm so happy just to be with him that it's hard for me to think about anything else.

"It's so pretty," I say, looking at the river.

"It is. I love it out here. My family's had this beach house for generations."

"Oh, right," I say, remembering my grandmother's

story of her long-ago trip to Tybee Island—the fateful afternoon when she saw her fiancé with another girl. "I think my grandmother and your grandmother used to come out here."

"It's crazy how far our families go back, isn't it?"

"Yeah, it is." I feel a pang as I think about the word *family*. I don't even really have one anymore. "And yet you don't really know me at all."

"Well, I know you a little," he says, throwing me a crooked smile that makes my heart skip a beat.

We drive down the causeway, which is hemmed in by marsh on both sides. The wetlands, with their yellows fading to green, are not as dazzling as the crashing waves and sharp cliffs of Mendocino, but I think I'm beginning to like this scenery almost better. It's subtler, more welcoming somehow. I stare out the window, taking in the huge live oaks draped with moss and the fall colors of the marsh.

"I want to show you something," Thaddeus says. He drives down a side road and stops in front of a stretch of marsh. We get out of the car, and he points to a lone tree.

"See it?"

I nod. The tree is decorated, roots to tip, with bright shoes, Easter grass, ribbon, and glass bottles.

"What is it?"

"That's the Tree of Life. The locals decorate it. It's a Gullah tradition."

"Cool," I say, unsure of what to reveal. How much does Thaddeus know?

Suddenly, a huge clap of thunder shakes the car. We both jump.

"Wow," Thaddeus says, pointing to a black cloud looming to the west. "I didn't see that coming." Fat drops start hitting the windshield. "I was going to take you to the beach. . . . Well, we've come all this way. Want to at least see our beach house?"

I nod giddily. "Sure."

"I should warn you: It's a dinosaur of a place. No one goes there but me."

"Sounds perfect."

He drives past the tacky beach bars and the crab shacks. According to my grandmother, Tybee used to be the ultimate Southern classy beach resort, but "ruffians" have taken over. Not to be classist, but it sort of looks as though she's right: The shore is clogged with bars sporting signs for beer and wet T-shirt contests, and stores selling bright beach toys and sunglasses. The far end of the shore is quieter. He drives us to a cluster of beach houses at the slightly wooded, peaceful area of the island and pulls up in front of an old, weathered bungalow with a wraparound screened porch that faces the ocean.

The rain is pouring down in sheets now. We run from the car to the house, screaming and laughing. He fishes a key out of his pocket and opens the door. When I look around, I love it instantly. The air smells like old books and sunscreen—sort of like the Main at the RC, minus the pot. We wander from room to room. Most of the furniture has been covered by white drop cloths, creating an effect of lazy ghosts lounging on the floor.

"We hardly come here anymore," Thaddeus says. "We're always in Hilton Head or downtown or whatever. But I'm glad it's in the family." We go back to the porch and look out at the beach. Suddenly I feel shy, even though we've been hanging out constantly.

"Sit with me," he says, touching my waist. He takes my hand and leads me to an old wicker sofa. He's dragged a blanket out of one of the closets, and together we huddle under it, legs and hips touching. He reaches over and plays with my talis bracelet. For a while we don't say anything. I wish my mom could see me. I don't think I've ever been this happy.

"So, tell me about your life," he finally says.

"Right."

He presses into my arm. "No, seriously."

I pause. Where to start? Growing up as a hippie? Life on a pot farm? Teen voodoo spells?

"You first," I say.

"You know it all. I grew up in Savannah. My mom's a Magnolia, my dad's a rich doctor. We're pretty normal. I like tennis and reading. And girls." He grins, pulling a strand of my hair.

"Can I ask—" I hesitate. "Can I ask about you and Madison?"

He shifts away ever so slightly. "I was wondering when this would come up."

"What happened?"

"I've always liked her. Even when we were little. I mean, she's gorgeous, of course."

I nod, trying not to appear as devastated as I feel.

"But we have nothing in common, so I never went there. Then something just...happened to me. Well, actually, I know what happened. She pulled a spell."

I swallow. "So you know about those?"

"Yeah," he says. "I live in a house filled with Magnolia women. They never told me, of course—they never tell anyone. But I read my sister's diary."

"Why didn't you mention anything before?"

"I keep it on the DL that I know. And I can't see that it hurts anyone, anyway. The Buzzards get dough, and the Magnolias get power or whatever. As long as they don't screw with me. Because last year, they definitely did." He rubs his neck. "Did Madison tell you?"

I shake my head.

"Well, I don't know what she slipped me, but it made me completely...*mad*, really. It came on very suddenly. These spells are extremely powerful elements. I was unhealthily obsessed. I had dreams about her, and serious urges.... I was going out of my mind."

"Right," I say, my stomach curdling at the thought of Thaddeus obsessing over Madison.

"And then..." He stops.

"What?"

"Well, I sort of lost control of myself."

"What do you mean?"

"One night she wouldn't call me back. Playing hard to get, I guess. I wanted her so badly — I guess I was scary, or annoying. Something."

I nod, thinking that I never played hard to get. *Should I have been trickier?*

"Anyway, I went to her house and was pretty much stalking her. I knew it wasn't right, but I couldn't help myself. She locked herself in that glass house and wouldn't come out. But I could still *see* her. It was hurricane season, and a tropical storm was coming. There were all these warnings, but I couldn't pull myself away."

I don't say anything. I just don't know how to respond.

"I ended up getting pneumonia... even went to the hospital."

I shake my head.

"And then it was the weirdest thing. It must have been the experience or the antibiotics or something. I had this really trippy dream about her, and then I just... wasn't into her anymore."

"Crush Killer," I say. "Probably your sister."

"Yeah, maybe. Or my mom or my grandmother. Who knows? That's why I hate the magic. *No one's* straight about anything. I got seriously jerked around. It was the worst feeling of my life."

"Is that why you got so pissed about what happened at the party? With the fire?"

He nods. "Not that I even know how you did that."

"You know what?" I grin. "I don't either."

"Look, Alex. I know it seems pretty cool, but if I were you, I'd steer clear of using the black magic."

"Well," I can't help saying, "it seemed to work for Madison."

He shakes his head. "But it didn't. With those bullshit spells, you never know if someone really likes you for *you*. That wasn't a real relationship. You know, we might have actually made it, Madison and I, if she had just let it happen naturally."

I shrug, scared that if I say anything, I'll reveal that this conversation is making me miserable. But he must sense that he's gone too far, because he puts his arm around me. It feels strong around my waist. "The way you and I are letting it happen on our own. I mean, I *know* I like you. No potions needed."

I nod, trying not to look as ecstatic as I feel. My elbow rests on his stomach. I concentrate on the rise and fall of his chest. His breath tickles my neck. He smells clean, like good soap.

"I love my sister," Thaddeus continues, "but I don't like the influence the whole Magnolia League thing has on her. You're different. You had a whole life before this, and you're your own person. But sometimes I worry about you too."

"You do?"

"Sure. I can tell that you've started dressing differently since you've been hanging out with Hayes and Madison. You straightened your hair.... I get it. You want to fit in. Just be careful, Alex. I would hate to see you getting totally wrapped up in it."

"I won't," I say. "I have other friends. Well, one other friend, anyway."

"And promise me something."

"What?"

He links his fingers with mine. "Never use a spell on me."

"Of *course.*" How could he possibly think that I would?

"If you do, that'll be the end. I seriously can't let myself get into a mess like that again."

"Absolutely," I say, squeezing his arm.

"No, seriously. You might be tempted. Just ... don't."

"I won't, Thaddeus," I say. "I promise."

He looks at me, and then away. I'm struck for the thousandth time by how beautiful he is. *How can I be so lucky?*

"You should know something," he says.

"What?" I ask blissfully.

"I lost my virginity to her," he says. "Madison. So I'll always ... care about her."

"Oh." I look at the ocean. Wow. The hair on my arm is standing on end. *They had sex.* This is heavy news.

"But, Alex, it just didn't feel natural. It was probably just the spell."

Probably?

I swallow. "Does . . . this feel natural?" I curl my toes, waiting for his answer.

"I think so." He elbows me. "What do you think?"

"Well, it's more normal than any relationship I've ever had. But then again, I grew up on a communal pot farm."

Thaddeus laughs, then suddenly turns serious. After a moment, he leans in and kisses me. Maybe it's the rain, or the old house, or the way the place smells like a good, solid library, but this kiss blows all of the other ones out of the water. The storm outside gets louder. I can hear thunder out over the water. We kiss like that for a while, our tongues sort of getting to know each other. He's got the best lips ever. I wonder whether mine are okay too. *Do I have bad breath? Am I doing this right?* I must be, because now he's tipping me backward onto the sofa — not pushing me, the way Reggie would have, but just guiding me with his hands.

"Alex, is this all right?"

I nod. Slowly, his hands move up my shirt to my back. And then *I* turn into the crazy one. I can't help myself. It's like all of my pent-up teenage hormones are suddenly released to run rampant with this beautiful guy I totally like. I start kissing him all over — his neck, his chest. He kisses back, hard, and I loop my feet around his ankles.

I feel totally safe. See, Thaddeus isn't like Reggie. He's not pulling at my pants or anything. In fact, we have all our clothes on — even our shoes. Still, I've never been this excited. I hold on tight and press myself into him through my jeans. He breathes a little harder, and — *oh my God, what am I doing?* — I feel this awesome weird burst, and a wheel of color takes over my brain.

"Sorry!" I say, rolling over in horror. "Oh my God. I'm really sorry."

I lie on my stomach and bury my face in the musty sofa cushion. I can't believe I just did that. I'm so embarrassed. Will Thaddeus think I'm a freak?

"Are you okay?"

"Sure," I say. "I'm just...sorry. I didn't mean to do that."

Thaddeus starts laughing.

"What?" I ask, my face still covered.

"Alex, don't panic. I was into it."

"You were?"

"Of course," he says, still smiling. "So the next time you call a book 'orgasmic,' I guess I can be sure you know what you're talking about."

"Oh, crap."

"You should see your face," he says. "It's totally glowing."

I put my hand on my cheek. "I feel really stupid."

"It's not stupid. It's cute."

"Well, yeah. It was...um...my first one."

"Cool," Thaddeus says, stroking my hair.

I'm seriously nervous to ask the next question. I know he'll probably dump me or think I'm a prude. But, thinking of Reggie, I ask anyway.

"Hey...do you mind if we take this slow?" I look at him fearfully. "I know I went kind of nuts just then, but I'm new at all of this, and..."

"Of course." He kisses my cheek. "That's what I want too. Especially after last year."

I sigh with relief. "You don't think I'm a prude?"

"What?"

"There was this guy in California...he thought I was a tease. And he called me fat."

"You're not a tease. And you can Skype that guy and show him how awesome you look now. He'll be sorry."

The back of my neck prickles with fear. I'm only pretty to him because of the hoodoo tricks; this isn't my real self at all. If he knew, would he dump me? And will I turn into a fat pumpkin at midnight?

Then Thaddeus kisses me again, and for now I try to push those thoughts to the back of my mind. Still, they're there, along with my nagging jealousy of Madison. I know I'm the one with Thaddeus now and, really, that's all that is important. But no matter how hard I try to put it out of my mind, I still find myself picturing Thaddeus—my boyfriend—camped under Madison's window in the rain.

27

Constance Taylor wakes up in her soaking-wet bed. She is panting, her heart is pounding, her room is too hot, and her throat is too dry. Traveling all over the world, sleeping in hundreds of different rooms in dozens of different countries, has trained her to wake up when something is wrong. Right now something is very wrong. Right now someone is in her room.

She looks at the closet: The door is closed. She looks

at the window, but she sees nothing there. She turns her head to the doorway, and there he is. The outline of a man standing in the hall, watching her. She freezes, but it's too late. He's been watching her a long time; he watched her thrashing in her sleep, he watched her wake up, and he knows she sees him.

Excited, he makes a little wet sound with his mouth and starts walking toward her. He has a doctor's bag in one hand, and he opens it and takes out something ruined and nasty. He holds it out. It's a dead cat.

Constance overcomes her paralysis and grabs for the bedside table, yanking open the drawer, going for the little lady's .22-caliber she keeps there. The surgeon covers the distance to her bed in three quick strides, and his muddy hand clamps down on her wrist. He pulls her out of bed and she falls to the floor and she...

Wakes up.

The first thing Constance does is take her gun and limp from room to room, turning on every light in the house, checking inside every closet and under every bed. When she's sure that she's really alone, she makes a cup of instant coffee and pulls out an old, tattered copy of *Aunt Sally's Policy Player's Dream Book*. The policy is an old lottery guide that was popular in the black community. Players would use *Aunt Sally's* to turn the imagery from their dreams into lucky numbers. When she and Louisa were in high school, they'd always use it to interpret their dreams. Although the topics were different then — boys, grades . . . boys.

Constance flips the pages, running her finger down the columns:

Surgeon (bad fortune coming, the arrival of an enemy) 4, 17, 28

Cat (a disease or malignancy, worse if the cat is dead) 7, 1, 2

She remembers the wet nastiness of the dead cat, and she looks up *filth.*

Filth, anything dirty (jinxing, crossing an enemy) 11, 8, 69

"Well, it certainly doesn't sound good," she says to herself, and she sits back and sips her coffee, desperately trying to remember the dream she was having before the surgeon's visit. It's all a vague rush of dim images, things she can barely remember; the harder she thinks about them, the faster they slip away. But then one image floats to the top of her mind, clear and sharp, causing her heart to crawl into her throat.

She was sitting on a grassy bank beside a highway. Down the road, a wrecked car was burning. Someone was sitting next to her, but she couldn't turn her head to see the person. Out of the corner of her eye, she could see legs and one arm, but that was all. And so she strained and she struggled, and she used every ounce of willpower she had, and finally she got a good look. It was Louisa, with blood streaming from her hair.

"You've got to help Alex," Louisa said. "They're coming for her."

And then Constance's old friend was surrounded by a flock of buzzards that hopped forward and pulled her apart.

28

Two weeks before Christmas, my grandmother summons me to her room.

"Alex, it's time to get serious about the ball," she says. "Madison and Hayes have done an excellent job with your appearance. Even I am impressed with how ladylike you look as of late. But your *manners*. They're atrocious! Every time I see you eat a meal, your elbows are on the table, and Mary Oglethorpe even said she heard you belch in public."

"Gas is natural, Miss Lee. You should just be glad I've started shaving my armpits."

My grandmother glowers at me. "Alex, Magnolias *represent* something in this town. Grace. Power. We strive to be examples of what a lady should be. These traditions are important. You go around acting like a barnyard animal and you're going to drag the whole League down."

"Okay, okay."

"Work on it, please. Study Emily Post. As for your dress — well, obviously, that's very important."

"Obviously."

"I've set up an appointment for you, Madison, and Hayes this afternoon at Damien's showroom. He should be able to take care of things. I assume Thaddeus will be your escort to the ball?"

"I guess." Because he's so weird about the Magnolias, I haven't officially asked him yet.

"That's an excellent choice," Miss Lee says. "Of course, you'll have attendants as well. I'd set that in stone soon, if you can."

"Sure," I say.

Satisfied, she waves me away, and I go back to my room to get ready to go shopping. Pausing in front of the mirror, I note that my skin has completely cleared up, morphing into the same alabaster glow that Madison and Hayes have. My hair is shiny and long. Even the color of my eyes looks somehow deeper. I open a dresser drawer and take out a photo of my mom and me that was taken two years ago. The girl in the picture looks like a different person—plump and ruddy but happy. Would my mother even recognize me now? I stare in the mirror, looking for any sign of her I can find. Nothing. Disappointed, I grab my bag and head out to my car.

I know. *I know*. But after getting bicycle grease on my new size-zero J Brand cargoes last week, I decided to let my grandmother buy me that car she's been bugging me about. Two days ago, Josie presented me the keys to a green Mini Cooper convertible. It's so new that it still smells like the cappuccino machine at the dealership. On the way to the car, I stub my toe on a half-buried can. Crouching down, I see it's a can of Red Devil lye, buried at the edge of the garden. Frowning, I start the car. *What kind of evil is my grandmother warding off now?*

Hayes and Madison are waiting for me in Damien's private fitting room. Madison, who designed her own dress, is bent over, sewing the trim. Hayes is standing in front of the mirror in her underwear, talking on her phone.

"Jason, *no*. We already spent the last four days together. I need some time to get ready for the ball." She pauses, listening. "No, you can't come here right now. Because

I'm busy. And listen—no more flowers. I'm developing a serious allergy, and there's no more damned surface area in the house to put 'em on, anyway! Look, I gotta go." Shaking her head, she flips the phone closed.

"Gris-gris a bit too strong?" Madison asks.

"He's driving me crazy. Seriously. Must have got the blood-pee-verbena ratio confused, or maybe I mixed it wrong."

"It'll wear off," Madison says. "Take his sock out from under your bed. That's probably overkill." Sensing yet another question forming, she cuts me off before I can ask. "On top of the rite, she filled his sock with the hummingbird mixture and put it under her mattress. It's an old New Orleans trick."

"Is that what you did to Thaddeus last year?" I ask.

Madison looks up from her work. Hayes shifts uncomfortably.

"Thaddeus knows I'm sorry for what I did. It was a mistake."

"But was that the trick?"

"Yeah. Among other things."

"My grandmother okayed it?"

"No," Hayes says. "She went straight to Sina. Now, come on, are we going to try on dresses, or what?"

Case closed, I guess. BleuBelle's has a killer formal department, and Damien has hung up a small but exquisite selection of white dresses for Hayes and me. A year ago, I never dreamed I'd be into this but, I have to say, trying on couture is pretty fun. We turn side to side, trading gowns.

"Too tight!" Madison barks as we stand in front of her. "Too cheesy!" After an hour, Hayes has settled on a Marchesa gown with crystal trim, but nothing looks right on me.

"I can't believe it," Damien moans. "You don't like *anything*?"

"It's not that we don't like anything," Madison says somewhat impatiently. "It's that nothing's *perfect*."

She crosses her arms and looks at me, pursing her pink lips. My face turns red as the old insecurities come back. Is she thinking that I'm too fat for these dresses? Too dumpy? For a moment I can't help hating her long legs and round doll's cheeks.

I lost my virginity to her . . . so I'll always care about her.

"It's supposed to be our major spotlight moment," she continues. "Look how far she's come. It's not about covering anymore. This is about fucking *celebrating*."

Damien nods. "You know, you really do have a designer's eye," he says admiringly.

"Wait! I think I know the dress," I say, suddenly remembering the gown my mother wore. "It was my mom's."

Damien clasps his hands together. "I *sold* her that dress! Back in the day. It's a beaded Chanel."

"Probably too eighties," Madison comments.

"No, it's a classic," Damien assures her. "I remember it perfectly. Well, it does have those puffed sleeves. . . ."

"I can work with that," she says, granting me a brief, rare smile. "Come on, Moonbeam. Let's go dig it up."

While Hayes stays to get some final touches on the gown she's selected, Madison and I go to my grandmother's house. As usual, we ride in silence, listening to the music. The house is empty when we enter. Then I remember—the dress is in my mother's locked room.

"Wait here," I say. I run upstairs, scaling the outside of the porch. The window is still unlocked from last time. I climb in, noticing that the room is much cooler than the warm fall air outside. We spent such a long time at Damien's that it's just about sunset by now— and the room is almost dark.

Suddenly, I see what looks like a black shadow dart into the corner behind the bed.

"Hello?"

Nothing. Nervously, I take the dress from the closet. As soon as I hold it in my hands, I forget about being spooked. The material is so *awesome*. Once Madison removes the muttonchop sleeves. . . I hold the dress up in front of the mirror, blinking as I see how much I resemble my mother now. In fact, if I didn't know better, I'd say *she* was staring back at me from the mirror.

"Alex!" Madison calls. "Dorkus! Let's see it." I dart out of the room and down the hall to my own room, where she's waiting for me. "Where were you?"

"My mother's room. My grandmother keeps it locked."

"Why?"

I shrug. "I have to sneak in. It's like a museum in there."

"Well, at least you know boo hags can't get in."

"What?" I say, stripping off my clothes and stepping into the dress.

"The Escher on the door. Boo hags and plat-eyes are obsessed with mathematics. Did Sina tell you about those? I've never seen one, but if you pay the Buzzards enough, you can use them to scare the hell out of anyone you want. I used one on Orang-Anna when she was getting out of line last year. I'm pretty sure Sybil McPhillips uses them to intimidate her husband's political opponents. Anyway, a hag would hover for hours outside that door, trying to figure out the puzzle; by daybreak, it would be too late." She steps back and looks at me critically. "Okay, yes. This is good."

"You think so?" I turn from side to side.

"Absolutely. Guess we've pretty much pared your bod down to your mother's size exactly. I don't have to let in or take out anything. Although...those sleeves are going to be a bitch. Give it to me, and I'll fix it."

"Thanks." I change back into my semi-ruined cargo

pants and a tank and hand over the dress. Madison puts it in a shopping bag. Just then her phone rings, and she glances at it.

"Oh," she says. "It's Thaddeus." She shrugs her shoulders and answers. "Hello?"

I try not to look as annoyed as I feel. How often do they talk? And why does he still feel the need to be friends with her? I watch her toss her hair and play with a silver earring. She *is* gorgeous—probably the prettiest of the MGs. Is it possible he's not over her?

"She's right here," Madison says, interrupting my thoughts. She hands me the phone.

"Hi," he says. "Did you buy a dress?"

"No, but I found one."

"I just want to say the only reason I'm going to the damned thing is to watch the world's unlikeliest debutante come out to society."

"*And* to watch your sister."

"Right, that. Hey, can I talk to Madison again?"

"Sure." I hand over the phone.

"Hello?" Madison cocks her head and laughs. "Sure. See you later." She hangs up.

"What did he say?"

"What?" Madison tosses off an infuriating shrug. "Oh, nothing. Okay, I'm taking this. See you later."

As I hear her descend the stairs and head out the door, I can't help seething. I walk over to my chest, looking at the ingredients I've gathered over the last few weeks: a vial of baby tears, goofer dirt, four jars of John the Conqueror root. It should be enough—at least, I hope it is.

I know it's the wrong thing to do. I promised Thaddeus I wouldn't. After all, he's with me now. But there's a voice in my head that says *maybe he's not*, and it's making me crazy—seriously crazy. The only way to make it shut up is to get in my new car and drive through the deepening dusk out to Buzzard's Roost.

29

When I arrive at Buzzard's Roost to find Sina, the first person I run into is Sam. I try to duck behind one of the houses, but he's too quick for me.

"Alex!" he calls. "What are you doing out here?"

"Um..." I clear my throat. "Getting something from Sina for Miss Lee."

"Really?" he asks, clearly suspicious. He seems to be dressed for a night out; he's wearing dress pants and a beautiful linen shirt. I swear, the guy could be in *GQ*.

He steps back and looks at me proudly. "I'm not sure what they've done with you, exactly, but these days you look just like your mother." His eyes mist over for a moment.

"Sam, how well did you know my mother?"

"Oh, we were tight," he says. "There's no one I miss more than her." He shakes his head. "She was so warm and funny. Man. I'd do anything to see her again."

"Me too," I say. "Anything."

"Baby Magnolia!" Sina calls from her house. "You here to see me?"

"Gotta go," I say. Sam kisses my cheek, and I hurry to Sina's cottage.

"Should've known you'd be out here before too long," she says when I enter. She hands me a cup of Swamp Brew. She must always keep some on the stove.

"Why?"

"New boyfriend, lots of history. You're not the first Magnolia to darken my door over Thaddeus's ass. Still, I thought you were different."

"I *am* different!" I say. But she's already walked inside.

I follow her into the dark room. It smells like cloves, cinnamon, lemon, and basil.

"Making a love spell for yourself, Sina?" I say, trying to get a rise out of her.

"Getting a jump on things," she purrs in the dark. "The Christmas Ball is coming up. I know some

Magnolia who can't hold on to her man will be visiting me soon enough."

"Working on anyone in particular yet?" I ask, trying to sound casual.

"Never conjure and tell."

"Has someone been coming to you about Thaddeus?" I can't help it. I have to know.

She laughs.

My face turns red. "Don't laugh at me!"

"Listen, Baby Magnolia," she says, suddenly serious. "I know every girl wants to be the only girl, but trust me when I say to you that no one is chasing him right now. Not with my help."

I'm relieved.

"So, you sure you want to do this?"

"I wouldn't have come if I wasn't sure," I say.

She cocks her head while she spreads a red cloth over the table. She studies me. "I can't read you," she says. "I've seen Magnolias come and I've seen them go, but you're a strange little cricket. You talk about being different and doing things different, and then you come out here like all the rest, begging for things that you should be doing for yourself."

"Look, if you think I'm like the rest of them, then you must be blind."

"No, Baby Magnolia. You're sitting right there saying the same things to me that those Magnolias have been saying to me for a long, long time."

"How long, exactly?" I look around the room for any sign of what generation she might belong to.

"I was in your mother's class," she replies. "I dropped out."

"So you're thirty-six."

"Thirty-six, sixteen, seventy, one hundred and eleven. See, unlike you precious Magnolias, I get to choose more than once. I can be whatever age I want."

"Then why sixteen?"

"Sixteen's pretty good, don't you think?" Sina says, frowning as she measures a bit of oil into her dropper. "Gravity hasn't raped your face yet. You still got a lot of energy and a fairly positive outlook. Seems to me all people want to do past sixteen is get back there. You heard the songs? The only thing you *don't* have is money. But thanks to you tired old things, I have more than enough of that."

"If you hate us so much, then why do you keep doing it? All that whining and complaining certainly doesn't keep you from cashing our checks."

"Listen to you," she says with a sneer. "Who's this *us*, anyway? You a Magnolia in your heart already?"

She leans over and sniffs me, then sits back, her eyes glowing yellow in the candlelight. "You know, I really liked your ma."

"So, you knew her?"

"Of course. She was always here, hangin' on my brother. All the girls were, but she was the only one who came out here from time to time. She was a whole basket of fun. Smart. You? Oh, you're rotten through and through, ain'tcha?"

"I am not." It drives me crazy that Sina knew my mother. *What does she know?*

"When you first came out here, you were going to change things. You wanted to make a difference. And now just smell yourself."

"I *do* want to change things," I say. "I do want to make a difference. I *will* make a difference. It's just that . . . I want this first."

She doesn't even dignify this excuse with a response. Instead, she hands me the paper and pen. I write Thaddeus's name nine times, then my own name over it five times.

"My poor brother," she finally mutters. "He always trusts you whores. Never listens to me."

"At that party at the Field," I say, handing the paper back, "you said you were onto me. What did you mean?"

"I figured you were here to sit at the right hand of Miss Lee," she says. "You would take over the League, the way she wants you to. Then I found out you had the rock, and I thought I had you wrong. Maybe you were here to kick up some dust, change things around. Or maybe you were just going to up and leave. Now I see you sitting here across the table from me like a greedy little fat girl in a skinny girl's body, and I think that maybe you're here to sit at your grandma's right hand after all."

"What is it about the necklace?" I ask.

She looks over her shoulder and then leans closer to me.

"It's a powerful charm," she whispers. "My daddy calls it a Fear Not to Walk Over Evil."

"What does it do?"

"Sina!" a man's voice barks from the door.

I jump in my chair and turn to see Doc Buzzard standing there, eyes blazing behind his blue sunglasses.

"Wrap up that girl's things and get her home," he says. "And not a word more."

"What's wrong?" I ask.

"That necklace is the last thing you have of your mother's," he says. "Treat it with respect. It's not some object for old ladies to gossip and buzz about."

He looks pointedly at Sina when he says this. She wraps up the potion and hands it to me. "Remember, three drops. No more, no less."

"How much do I owe you?"

"We'll put it on the Magnolias' tab," Doc Buzzard snaps. "Now get on home, little girl. You've got no place being here without your grandmother. Trust me. Your own time will come."

30

The night of the Christmas Ball is clear and cool. Through the window, I can smell the sharp scent of wood smoke. Josie must have lit a fire downstairs. I can hear my grandmother clicking around down below, getting ready to depart for the party. Before getting Sina to cook up the root for me, I was planning on taking a ritual bath with a little love attraction charm (archangel herb, lovers' incense, and spearmint) mixed in. But now that the agenda has changed, I switch to a hyssop cleanse (four teaspoons of dried hyssop brewed to a dark tea and then poured into the bathwater) to neutralize any competing energy. I light candles (red and white for love) all around the bathroom and bedroom and then soak for a while, chanting:

"Holy hyssop,
cleanse me to the core,
and drive all evil
from my door."

Later, I get out of the tub and look at myself in the mirror. What would my mom think if she knew I was about to use a spell on someone? Especially when I specifically promised that person that I wouldn't? It doesn't matter, though, does it? Because my mom's not here. She left me and is gone forever. The fact is, I'll never see her again.

I put on my robe and pour myself a cup of Swamp Brew. Although Sina gave me the gris-gris to slip into Thaddeus's drink, there's a lot of prep work to do. I've set up my altar exactly the way Sina instructed: I snipped a piece of Thaddeus's shirt, put out a cup of wine, and placed the piece of paper with his name on it. I chant:

"Although you are free,
belong to me—"

"Um, Alex?"

I whip around. Thaddeus is standing in the doorway

holding a bottle of champagne. His face is the color of blank paper. "What are you doing?"

"Uh..." I stand up, knocking over the altar. The wine spills over the candles, causing them to hiss and die out.

"Is that a picture of me?"

"I know this looks really bad."

"Yeah. It does. It looks extremely, extremely bad."

I fully expect this to be the moment he tells me I'm a psycho and then runs out. After all, he's just walked in on me praying to a hoodoo altar with his image on it. That would scare off most guys immediately. To my surprise, though, instead of getting angry or freaked, he just sighs and sits on the bed.

"I was afraid this would happen," Thaddeus says.

"What?" I say, still stalling. "This is nothing. Not a big deal. I was just fooling around."

"Here's the thing, Alex. I said before I couldn't be with a Magnolia. Then I went ahead and went out with you because you were so cool. I took the risk. I mean, that episode with Madison really messed me up. It's beyond horrible not knowing whether your feelings are real or not."

"Is this about Madison?" I ask. "About how you're still into her?"

"I like *you*, Alex."

"Sure," I say, my eyes filling with tears. "Now that I've had a Magnolia makeover."

"Actually, I'm not even into the new look. I like the old Alex. The weird hippie girl with the great sense of humor, who totally says the wrong thing sometimes. The girl with the beautiful smile."

I look at my closet, stuffed with expensive new clothes. "You're not into the new . . . me?"

"Come on—you look great. Really great. That's not the point. The Magnolia League is changing you. That's what it does, Alex, and that's why I wanted you to help me get Hayes out of it. But it looks like you've drunk the Kool-Aid."

"What about Madison?"

"What about her?"

"Why do you talk to her so much? You guys are always off whispering and talking to each other on the phone. If you're so over her, what's the deal?"

Thaddeus sighs. "Look, I wish I could tell you, but I can't. I promised I wouldn't."

"Convenient."

"I can tell you that it's not what you think, though— whatever the hell you're thinking. Because if you knew, you wouldn't be jealous at all. Not that that's even the point."

"And what *is* the point?"

"You promised me you wouldn't do this. And then you turned around and did exactly what I asked you not to. How am I supposed to trust you again?"

He picks up the John the Conqueror root from the floor.

"It's just that I got really burned by my last relationship, Thaddeus. I mean, Reggie *cheated* on me."

"I know." He shakes his head.

"I wasn't thinking straight. I'm sorry, Thaddeus."

"I am too."

"What are *you* apologizing for?" I ask, putting my head on his shoulder.

Thaddeus shakes me off and stands. "Because I can't go to the ball with you."

"What?"

"I can't trust you, Alex."

"Thaddeus, I said I was sor—"

He shakes his head. "It's too late."

My stomach starts to curdle as I feel the cold fingers of panic set in. "Come on."

"Look, I feel really bad about this. I never should have gotten involved with you in the first place. I knew this magic bullshit would get in the way eventually. That's the thing about it, isn't it? If you can have anything, how do you know what's real?"

"How we feel about each other *is* real."

"Is it?" Thaddeus asks, exasperated. "Or did you just slip some love potion into my sweet tea?"

"Thaddeus—"

"I'll see you around."

And with that, the guy of my dreams puts the champagne on the bureau and exits, leaving me alone with my mother's beautiful dress and the unused spell that ruined everything.

31

Well, my grandmother was right. It's the Magnolia League Christmas Ball, and everyone in Savannah is here.

Josie drives me to the Oglethorpe-Williams House, where the ball is always held. I look out the window, trying to stay far enough behind the tinted glass so that the crowd filing in won't see me as we cruise past the front porch. I was supposed to arrive with Hayes and Madison, but after Thaddeus ditched me, I texted them to say I'd rather get ready solo. Josie parks at the back of the house, near the kitchen entrance. Magnolia girls who are being presented go in through the back so no one will see them before they make their entrance down the grand staircase in the front hall. For months my grandmother has been telling me, "In through the kitchen, out through the hall," as if it's some kind of magic charm.

"Going in?" Josie asks.

"I guess."

"You look very pretty," she says kindly.

I shrug.

There's a loud pop, and I jump at the sound. Josie hands me the warm bottle of champagne that I was supposed to enjoy with Thaddeus.

"It's not cold, but it'll do," she says. "Drink yourself some liquid courage."

I take it from her and slug back a gulp.

"I heard you and your boyfriend talking about that root magic," she says. "He's right. It's no good for love. You got to do love on your own."

"Okay."

"Okay? What does *okay* mean? Miss Alex, you listen to me. The Buzzards never use their own magic — other than some beauty tricks. What does that say to you? They sell their mojos and their roots all day and all night, but they don't ever bite off any for themselves."

"So what?"

"You ask yourself, who's stronger? The Buzzards or

the Magnolias? One knows the spells; the other can't get along without them. The cleverest ladies I know, they'll use a little pinch here and there, but they make sure those pinches are spread out. Like your grandmother. She knows how to conjure, but she thinks twice before doing it."

"Well, thanks for the too-late advice," I say, handing the half-empty bottle to Josie. "Okay. Here I go." I open the car door and lurch onto the sidewalk, my head spinning. I don't mean to be rude to Josie, but shouldn't she have told me all this a few months ago?

No one's supposed to see my dress yet, but the wannabe girls, like Orang-Anna, wait around the kitchen entrance to get in a final bit of ass-kissing before the main event.

"You look so awesome!" Anna squeaks, running over to me. "This is so cool. It's the first year I've been allowed to come. Thanks so much for the invitation."

"Yeah, sure. No problem." Because I'm me and had to do something at this ball to annoy my grandmother just a little, I've invited the entire junior class — nerds, jocks, potheads, and all. Apparently, they actually care about this crap. Idiots.

"I *love* your dress. Where'd you get it?"

"It was my mother's." The mention of my mom brings the shame rushing in. What would she say if she knew how easily I'd been taken in by the very thing she'd run so far away from? I want so badly to talk to her that I feel a sharp pain in my chest. "She wore it in 1989."

"Well, it's still awesome, even if it *is* super old."

"Thanks."

I push past Orang-Anna and hike through the kitchen. Two waiters in black tie show me to the cramped back staircase.

"This way to the Pretty Room, miss," one of them says with a little bow. I notice that most of the kitchen staff are black. One of them looks familiar to me, but I'm not sure why. Then I place her: the night of my initiation. She catches my eye and stares at me like I'm something in a zoo. I blush and hurry up the staircase.

At the top, another tuxedo-clad waiter ushers me down the hall to the Pretty Room, where the debutantes are stored like pieces of meat before being introduced to Savannah's richest white people at the Small Ball upstairs. Hayes and Madison and the other three girls who are making their debuts are already inside. Since this is the South, there's plenty of champagne and not a thing to eat.

"Alex!" Hayes whoops as she links arms with me. "We thought you were getting cold feet. Did you see Thaddeus? You haven't seen my brother until you've seen him rocking a tux. And I'm so glad you're here, because I am about to officially explode. Do you know who Madison's secret date is? You won't—"

"Uh . . . Thaddeus isn't coming," I say.

"What?" She whips out her BlackBerry. "What the *f*? Did he fall asleep or something? Let me call him. I'll tear him up one side and down the other."

"No, don't. It's totally my fault. I screwed up."

Hayes's voice drops when she sees the tears in my eyes. "What did you do?"

I want to tell her so badly. I want to tell her and cry and have her hug me, and then she'll fix my makeup and tell me that everything is going to be okay. I want her to take me under her wing and protect me from all these awful people and, more important, I want her to protect me from myself. I want her to fix everything that I've ruined. But how can I tell Hayes that I put a love spell on her brother? Just as Madison did, but worse, because I knew what might happen to him, and I ignored it. I can't disappoint her like that.

"I got jealous of him and Madison. And I did something stupid."

"What did you do?" she asks quietly.

"I didn't... nothing like that, Hayes," I lie. "I freaked out on him. He came by the house and I freaked out and screamed at him like a crazy person and accused him of cheating on me with her and told him I never wanted to see him again."

Hayes's eyes are laughing. "Do you want to know who Madison's escort is?" she asks.

"Who?"

Just then, Madison comes out of the carefully

313

concealed door that leads to the powder room (God forbid anyone in Savannah actually say "bathroom" out loud), and Hayes waves her over.

"Madison, you have to tell Alex!"

"Calm down, for Christ's sake," Madison says, rolling her eyes. "It's no big thing."

"Spill!" Hayes can hardly contain herself.

"It's Dexter, okay," Madison says. "My escort is Dexter. And he's wearing a powder-blue tuxedo, which is probably the most embarrassing thing to ever happen to me in my life."

But she looks kind of proud of him too.

"But I thought you and Thaddeus—"

"What?" she says.

"You aren't..."

"Nope!" Hayes squeals, and she actually claps her hands.

"OMG," Madison says, realizing what I meant. "I'm a bitch, but not that kind of bitch. Thaddeus likes *you*. He's been coaching me on how to clean up Dex and make him behave himself, that's all. If you want that kind of man stealer for a friend, then head back to Cali. The MGs don't roll that way. Okay?"

"Okay," I say weakly.

Hayes waves for the champagne, and I take two glasses. She and Madison are acting as though this is the funniest thing they've ever heard.

"Relax, Alex," Hayes says. "Thaddeus will be here. Our mom will actually commit murder if he doesn't show up. I'll talk to him, cool him down. He'll be fine."

"Oh no, look who's here," Madison says, staring over my shoulder.

We turn and there's Constance Taylor, standing awkwardly in the door, wearing a loose denim dress.

"A jean dress?" Madison mutters. "She's actually wearing a *jess*? To a ball?"

My heart plummets even lower when she spots me and walks over.

"You all look . . ." She searches for the word. "Very appropriate. Alex, I need to speak with you privately."

"She's got a full schedule tonight," Madison says.

"It's okay," I tell her, and I let Constance lead me to the powder room.

The powder room has a love seat, vanity tables, makeup mirrors—anything to hide the fact that this is a room where a woman might actually hitch up her dress and pee. Carson, that little monster who got the snakebite out at the Field, is leaning out the window smoking a cigarette. When she sees Constance and me, she stubs out her butt and swishes from the room.

"I work so hard to educate you kids," Constance says. "And yet you all insist on doing the same dumb things over and over again."

"Just because one of us smokes, it doesn't mean the rest of us do," I say. "Is this what you have to tell me? Smoking causes cancer?"

"I'm talking about the Magnolia League. You have to get out now."

"Constance—I can call you Constance off campus, right?"

She nods.

"I hear you, okay? The Magnolia League is elitist and privileged, and it's totally not fair that we have the advantages that we do. It's like hogging the carpool lane of life, and it sucks for everyone else. I get that. But it's really important to my grandmother that I be in it, and my friends are here, and it's not as stuffy as it seems. And there's some other stuff—"

"The hoodoo," she says.

I'm too surprised to lie. "Who told you?"

"You all think you're so unique and special. The Magnolia League has been around for more than fifty years. You kids are not the first to discover hoodoo and think you've found the solution to all of life's problems."

"Why do you even care?" I ask.

"How deeply are you involved?"

"Not too deeply," I say. "Well, we did this big ritual to cleanse me of my ex-boyfriend."

"At the Roost?"

"Yeah."

"Anything else?"

"Some hair spells. And . . ." I'm hesitant to tell her. I don't want to be fat again.

"What?"

"I've got a bird doppelgänger that eats all my food."

She exhales with relief. "Those are relatively harmless."

"What are you afraid of?"

"Listen, Alex. You're the star of the show tonight, so we don't have much time. Have you heard of a Blue Root?"

I shake my head.

"It's a hex on someone to bring that person harm. If a Blue Root is on you, then you *will* die; the only question is *how*. There's a Blue Root on the entire League. That's the bargain they made: They can be queens of Savannah, but only Savannah. Your friends, Hayes and Madison? If they leave Savannah, they die."

"But . . . my *mother* left."

"She had this," she says. "This is your ticket out of here."

It takes me a second to realize she's pointing to my necklace.

"*This* fugly thing?" I say. "Come on."

"That fugly thing is more powerful than you can imagine. It protects the wearer from all harm."

I want to laugh in her face, and then I remember what Sina said. "A Fear Not to Walk Over Evil," I say.

"Who told you that?" she asks.

"Sina mentioned it."

"You need to go. This place is poison. You're a bright, intelligent girl, Alex. You can write your own ticket. I'm begging you: Walk out that door and go. Now. Tonight. Before it's too late and you're trapped here for the rest of your life."

"But if I have the necklace, why should I worry?"

"How do you think your mother died?"

I shake my head, speechless. What could Constance possibly be talking about?

"*She* had the necklace. Then someone conjured it off her. I don't know how she was deceived or manipulated, but she lost that buzzard's rock, and the Blue Root took her. Someone meant her harm and it happened, necklace or not. And... I've been having a dream."

I can't help laughing.

Constance grips my chin with one hand. "Don't you dare laugh at a dream," she says. "Not after what you've seen. Dreams are where the dead travel. Your mother has been coming to me every night for weeks. She says that the one who harmed her wants to harm you. Your life is in danger, Alex. The necklace didn't stop the Blue Root when they came for your mother, and it won't stop them when they come for you."

"If she's been coming into your dreams for weeks, then why are you only telling me now?"

Constance bites her lip. "I was scared."

"Of what? The Magnolias?"

"Back when your mother and I were in school together, I thought the League was exploiting the Buzzards. I did a big school paper article on hoodoo, and I told Miss Lee that I'd expose the Magnolia League's secrets. If no one believed me, I'd keep talking until I found someone who did. I made a big scene about it—I was like someone else I know, full of big world-saving ideas.

"Then one day, a snake came up out of the drain while I was in the shower. It bit me once, and while I lay there paralyzed, it struck me in the leg again and again. There was so much tissue damage, the surgeons thought they were going to have to amputate. When I got out of the hospital, this was waiting for me."

She hands me a worn envelope made of heavy yellow paper. I take out a card, an ivory square embossed with a navy outline of a magnolia bearing only six handwritten words:

Next time, it'll be an alligator.

My fingers feel numb.

"I'm sorry I let them intimidate me," she says. "Your mother was my friend. I should have watched over you more carefully."

I throw the card back at her. "I don't want to listen to this!"

"Alex, I know this is hard, but you need to deal with it."

She hands me another, flimsier envelope. "It's only five hundred dollars. It's all I could get out of the ATM tonight. I'd mail you a check, but it's better if you don't tell me where you're going. They might get it from me."

My eyes fill up with tears. I haven't cried in a long time. Mostly, I've just felt numb. "I'll pay you back," I say, then hug her.

She stiffens. "Be careful. Go out and pretend to socialize for a bit. Then run." She turns to the door.

"Constance, wait," I say. "Who conjured the Blue Root?"

"The Buzzards," she says, not turning around.

"They don't conjure for free," I say. "Who *asked* them to conjure the Blue Root?"

One of her hands is on the doorknob. She lowers her head as if she's suddenly very tired. This is how I'll always remember her—the way she looked right before she told me.

"Your grandmother," she says. And then she opens the door and is gone.

I sit, trying to take in everything that Constance has told me, but my mind just keeps replaying the last thing she said.

Your grandmother. Your grandmother. Your grandmother.

I walk out into the Pretty Room and, like a bad joke, my grandmother is standing there waiting for me.

"Magnolias!" she trills from the doorway. "It's time!" She looks at us, as if counting her chicks. "Alex, Hayes,

Madison. Carson, Mary Michael, and…" She pauses for a minute. "And that other one. It's time to meet your guests, girls."

Madison and Hayes are full of energy.

"I can't believe Dex is wearing that thing," Madison moans. "Do you think he wants to embarrass me to death?"

"At least it's vintage." Hayes giggles and then turns to me. "What did Constance want?"

"Nothing. Just apologizing for being such a pain all year."

"I'm surprised it didn't take her longer, then," Madison says.

"Come on," Hayes says. "Society awaits."

In a way, all this fake formality helps. Once the Christmas Ball commences, it keeps rolling from one silly tradition to another with no time in between. First there's the receiving line, where all six of us young Magnolias stand with our families and get introduced to every important person in Savannah, from the mayor to the head of the historical society.

"This is my daughter, Madison Telfair."

"Pleased to meet you."

Smile, handshake, curtsy.

Then we strip off our white gloves (made grimy by

all the handshaking), take a new pair of kid gloves from a silver tray, and "walk the stairs." The house has a grand, curving staircase that descends to the front hall, and each debutante's father escorts his daughter down the stairs as her name is announced. At the bottom of the stairs is the real party: food, booze, guests, escorts, the band. The only thing left to do after you walk the stairs is give your dad the first dance.

There's only one problem: I don't have a dad. No mom either. My grandmother took care of that. So I am to be presented by the queen of the Magnolia League herself, Miss Dorothy Lee. Just looking at her makes me want to scream. I have to get away from her. I have to go somewhere quiet so I can think and figure everything out, because as long as I'm near her, my brain is like a roaring river full of nothing but hate. But at the moment I have to stand at her side in the receiving line.

"Dr. and Mrs. Jonathan Bailey, this is my granddaughter, Alexandria Lee."

"Pleased to meet you," I say automatically.

They give me limp handshakes and move down the line.

"Are you on drugs?" my grandmother hisses out of the side of her mouth.

"Yes," I whisper.

"Don't vex me. You are being obnoxiously vague tonight."

"Okay, then. Here's the deal: I want to go to college."

"Mr. and Mrs. William Cox, allow me to present my granddaughter, Alexandria Lee."

"Pleased to meet you."

Handshakes. They move on.

"You *are* going to college," my grandmother whispers.

"No, Grandma," I say, and I relish at how she stiffens when I use the G-word. "I want to go to NYU or Brown. Or Reed. Somewhere out of state."

"Out of the question. We will be far too busy to send you to some godforsaken Yankee school."

"Also," I say, "the Blue Root would kill me, wouldn't it? I mean, my car might careen off a cliff or something."

To her credit, my grandmonster doesn't even flinch as the next guests approach.

"Mr. and Mrs. Spencer Bradshaw, allow me to introduce you to my granddaughter, Alexandria Lee."

"Hello," I say.

"She looks just like you," Kate Bradshaw says, beaming, and then moves down the line.

"This is neither the time nor the place," my grandmother hisses. "Whatever that Sina told you is sheer lies and manipulation. Only a child would believe anything she says."

Sina? Why would she think Sina told me anything?

"Oh, Buck, Hattie. How special to see you. Mr. and Mrs. Buck Getty, meet my granddaughter, Alexandria Lee."

"She looks just like her mother," Mrs. Getty says.

"I bet she's as curious and as smart as her mother too," Buck adds.

"Well, I always try to remind her of what curiosity did to the cat," my grandmother says under her breath.

The Buck Gettys move on.

"So tell me the truth yourself," I hiss.

"Khaki Pettit ran off to New York thirty years ago," she says. "She's always been a blabbermouth, and she told her new society friends there about our secret. People started asking questions—someone even sent a reporter down. God forbid! We had to go *collect* her and end her engagement to a horrid man she'd met."

"How nice of you."

"She would have been *miserable,* and she would have ruined everything." My grandmother smiles at a passerby. "After that, we all realized that there needed to be an incentive to stay in Savannah. There needed to be limits. So I did what was necessary to restore some security and order. I put Khaki in a local Betty Ford for a while so that no one up north would find her credible, and I had the Buzzards set some boundaries."

"So if I leave Savannah, I die?"

"A Magnolia may not leave once she's had her initiation ritual," my grandmother says, pausing and looking at me somewhat sadly. "Which you have."

"So I'm stuck here?"

"All Magnolias return eventually."

"And what about Mom?" I ask quietly. "She'd had her initiation too. Didn't you think about that?"

To my surprise, my grandmother's flinty eyes fill with tears.

A red-nosed penguin waddles up to her. "I hope it's not the company," he bellows.

"Eddie Reauchauer! You rascal! Mr. and Mrs. Eddie Reauchauer, please meet the light of my life, my granddaughter, Alexandria Lee."

They shake my hand. They move on down the line.

My grandmother pauses before she speaks.

"I thought she was dead," she says quietly. "It had been almost twenty years. I didn't know."

"That's no excuse. You've still got her blood on your hands."

"Don't you judge me," my grandmother says. "I lost my daughter, only to learn years later that I had lost her a second time. Even Christ was crucified only once."

"Spare me."

The line slows down.

"Ladies," Khaki Pettit calls from the end of the room. "Exchange your gloves, please."

"Ugh," Madison calls over to me, peeling off her opera gloves. "These are disgusting. I want to go swimming in a big pool full of Purell."

A waiter with a silver tray of fresh gloves and a basket moves down the line. He reaches me, and automatically I drop my damp gloves in the basket and take a clean pair from his tray.

"And now, if y'all will take your place to walk the stairs," Khaki calls.

All the mothers race to the back stairs so they can go down to the front hall and witness their daughters' moment of glory. All the fathers take their daughters by the hand and proceed to the head of the grand staircase. My grandmother tries to take my hand, but I keep it clenched. She grabs it and attempts to pry my fingers open. I'm shocked by her strength, but I'm stronger. I yank my hand away.

"Do not disgrace me right now," she whispers fiercely. "This is not the time to give in to petty personal issues."

I hear Khaki Pettit on the microphone downstairs in the grand hall.

"Making her debut tonight, and presented by her father, Mr. Michael Shaw, the Cotillion presents to Savannah—Miss Mary Michael Shaw."

Applause, some weak wolf whistles, flashbulbs popping. A bigger roar when she does her St. James bow on the landing. Then a giant cheer—probably her dad kissing her on the cheek.

"Petty personal issues?" I snap. "You killed my mother."

"You don't have all the facts," my grandmother says, drawing herself up. "I have been a victim in this more than anyone else, and unlike you I don't have the luxury of throwing a tantrum. I have fed you and clothed you. I have welcomed you into my house and let you sleep under my roof. I have indulged you past the point of reason. And I will be damned if I let you humiliate me tonight of all nights. You will walk the stairs with me, Alexandria, and you will smile and be gracious, and you will have your first dance with a young man of my choosing if your escort cannot be found, and you will stop acting like a brat and comport yourself like a Magnolia right this minute."

"Grandmother," I say, "screw you."

I walk to the head of the stairs, leaving my stunned grandmother in my wake. For once she's speechless.

"Where's your grandmother?" Hayes hisses as I approach the waiting area. Down the stairs we can hear shouts and cheers as Carson Moore is presented. Apparently her St. James bow is something else, because the yells practically tear the roof off the place.

"She won't be joining us," I say. "I'm walking the stairs alone."

Hayes gapes at me. "But you can't... you can't walk *alone!*"

"You're up, Alex," Madison calls from up ahead. "Where's Dorothy?"

"I'm going alone."

"What?" She trots back to me. "What the—say *what?*"

"Alexandria," I hear my grandmother call. "I'm coming."

"If you were ever my friends, don't let that woman near me," I say. And then I take a deep breath and walk to the top of the staircase. I stand in the shadows, waiting for Carson's applause to die down, just as we've practiced. Behind me, I hear the daddies doing double takes as they realize I don't have an escort.

I look over my shoulder. Madison is blocking my grandmother's way—not so obviously that you can tell that the maneuver is intentional, but firmly enough so that Miss Lee can't get past her. I hear the silence. Khaki takes a breath, made audible by the microphone. I prepare for my public humiliation.

"And now," she says, "making her debut tonight, and presented by her grandmother, Mrs. Dorothy Lee, the Magnolia League presents to Savannah—Miss Alexandria Lee."

I feel a gloved hand grip mine. I turn and see Hayes grinning at me. "Hos before bros," she says.

Another glove grips my other hand. I turn. It's

Madison. "Don't ever doubt that we've got your back," she says.

And hand in hand, the three of us walk the stairs.

There is silence for a moment as everyone gapes. Madison and Hayes are very obviously not my grandmother. The flashbulbs stop. The room goes so silent I can hear our dresses brushing the carpet as we walk. Even Khaki is staring up at us, her mouth open like a fish's. But breeding trumps all, and while she might like her white zin a bit more than the next lady, let it never be said that Khaki Pettit doesn't have breeding.

"I'm sorry, it must be too much celebrating, and I plain forgot. In the newest tradition of the Magnolia League, tonight our three youngest members are presented without their fathers. Savannah, please welcome Miss Madison Telfair, Miss Hayes Anderson, and Miss Alexandria Lee."

The applause feels like an earthquake. The flashbulbs are like lightning. The only way I know we've reached the landing is because the floor is suddenly flat.

"Now," Hayes whispers. "All together, St. James bow."

The three of us sink gracefully to the floor, bow our heads, and then rise. Somewhere in the crowd, Dexter lets out an enormous "Boo-yah!"

"So embarrassing," Madison mutters, but she's loving it.

Hayes squeezes my hand. "One more flight, and then we can all have about twenty drinks," she says under her breath.

We continue descending the stairs, and I feel like everyone in the world is cheering for us. Tonight is too much. I'm being pulled in too many different directions. I don't know how to feel about any of it. And then, suddenly, I *do* know. Looking up at me, standing by the open front door, is Thaddeus.

"Didn't I tell you?" Hayes says. "Go."

I shove my way through the crowd and find him by the shrimp tower. "So, you came after all."

"I'm leaving Savannah for winter break," he says. "Backpacking somewhere. Costa Rica, maybe. Or Spain. The point is, I want you to come with me."

This is one turn too many. I think my face goes slack. "What?" I manage to stammer. "But... you hate me."

"I hate what you're becoming," he says. "And I'm going to hate whatever the Magnolias turn you into if you don't get away from this place. And most of all, I'd hate myself if I just walked away and let it happen. But I don't hate you."

"I know I messed up," I say. "I'm sorry. I was scared, and I did something stupid. It's this place, I think."

"Which is why we need to leave for a while. Now. Tonight."

I grab him hard and don't let go. I can't talk and look him in the eye at the same time. Not after what I did.

"Okay—yes! Backpacking sounds rad."

"You have to be sure about giving all this up before we go," he says.

"I'm sure. Seriously. Very, very sure."

He looks at me doubtfully. "Look, I know I really messed up and that you don't trust me," I tell him. "But I think—"

Oh God. Can I say this? Thaddeus folds his arms, waiting.

"I think this thing between us is *real*, Thaddeus. I don't want to just give up on that."

He doesn't say anything—but he does kiss me. I'm so happy I want to die. Right here, right now.

"You can't tell my sister. We've got to just go."

"Well, it has to be tonight—or else I'll never get out of here."

He nods toward the buffet table, where Hayes, Madison, and Dex are huddled together.

"All right," he says. "I'll get my stuff and pick you up in an hour. We'll have to buy our tickets by Black-Berry in the car."

"Okay," I say, thinking of the five hundred dollars Constance gave me. It was a nice gesture, of course, but let's face it: Five hundred bucks isn't going to get me much farther than Raleigh-Durham. Still, that's the only money I have — I can't use Miss Lee's credit card, or she'll find me. Speaking of which...

"Listen, don't come to the house. My grandmother or Josie might see the car. Park off Drayton instead, and meet me at the fountain in Forsyth Park."

"Fine."

I look up at him, smiling like the hugest dork in the world. "Thaddeus, I'm really happy right now. I just... I've never... liked someone as much as I like you."

God, can I be more of an imbecile?

"Me too," he says.

I pat the top of my head quickly to make sure my brain hasn't exploded with joy.

"But this is your only chance, Alex," he says. "If we're leaving, we're leaving now."

I nod. I want to say it, but I can't. *Just say it, loser!* my brain screams. Give him the L-bomb! But then I see Hayes and Madison heading toward us.

"One hour," he says, ducking out before they flank me.

"What was that all about?" Madison says. "Did you work things out?"

I look at Thaddeus's retreating back. I really want to spill our plan, but I can't afford to screw up our getaway. It's too dangerous.

"No," I say, trying my best to look devastated. "I said I was sorry, but he really was done."

332

"Well." Madison looks at me sympathetically. "This party rocks anyway. Just try your best to forget him, honey."

"Yeah. My brother can be a stubborn ass," Hayes says. "Come on. I can't believe we did that. Your grandmother is ready to skin you alive, but Khaki seems happy for some reason."

"I think she's drunk," Madison says.

"I'll be right there," I say, glancing around to see if anyone's near enough to the door to see me slip out. My heart is pounding. *Am I really going to do this?*

"Okay, but don't be too long," Hayes says.

"Yeah, this booze isn't going to drink itself." Madison laughs, wrapping an arm around Dex's waist.

But I'm not listening anymore. I don't have to. I feel sorry for my friends, that they have to be trapped here. But I've got the key to freedom — the necklace.

I dive back into the party, then dart to the ladies' lounge. I've already scoped out the window I'll use to get the hell out of this place.

32

The Oglethorpe-Williams mansion is only a few blocks away from my grandmother's house, and I run all the way, with my long beaded gown hitched up to my thighs. I tossed off my silver Miu Mius outside the hall, hoping they'll be found by someone with a shoe fetish and size-nine feet. I figure I have about a half hour before everyone realizes I'm not at the ball—just enough time to stuff some clothes into my backpack and get out of here.

I assume that once I cross the Savannah border, all the magic will wear off. I'll be back to my medium-to-large self and sporting the old dreads again — or, worse yet, bald. I guess I'm okay with that, especially since Thaddeus said he liked me better the old way. But it also presents a packing quandary: Do I pack my old clothes, which I pretty much swim in now, or the new stuff? If my old body returns, I won't be able to get even one leg into those size-zero pants. I settle for a mix of both old and new clothes, plus a couple of the most expensive pieces, because maybe I can sell those for extra cash.

The money is the trickiest part. Without my grandmother's ridiculously generous allowance and her gold card, I have almost nothing. My mom left only her personal effects; and though her collection of crystals has a lot of sentimental value, it won't bring much at a pawnshop. Of course, this house is full of expensive stuff, but even though I detest my grandmother and what she did to my family, I can't bring myself to steal from her. The most valuable thing I own is my buzzard's rock — a piece that wouldn't even go for a dollar at a regular store. I touch it with my fingers, thanking my mother for the key to my freedom.

But then I remember all of those pearls and rings in my mom's room. Technically, I inherited everything. She'd want me to have them. So, after changing from the ball gown into my cutoffs, I head out to the porch one last time to break into my mother's room.

As soon as I do my signature awkward flip and hit the floor, I can feel that something is different. I've never been in here in the dark before. At those other times, I could feel my mother's presence, but tonight it's stronger.

In spite of myself, I'm spooked. I make a beeline to her dresser to look through the jewelry. Just as I remembered, there are a couple of strands of pearls with jeweled clasps, a delicate silver watch, and an opal ring. I guess my mom didn't think she'd need them when she left Savannah.

Then I freeze. *There is someone behind me.* A woman. I can see her silhouette against the dim blue light from the window. And even though I might be crazy, I know exactly who it is.

"Mom?" I whisper.

She steps forward.

"*The night they drove old Dixie Down...*" she sings.

"Mom?"

It's definitely her. She's pale, and her eyes are darker than I remember, but it's my mom. I reach out and touch her arm. Her skin is icy and clammy. I draw away.

"Are you alive?"

"Is Constance coming over?" she asks.

"Constance? Mom, are you okay?"

"We're all going to the concert, right?" She looks around then back at me again. "Are you from school?"

"Mom. It's Alex. Your daughter."

"Sam?" my mother cries. "Sam?" She looks at me and screams.

"Mom! Stop!"

"Who are you? What are you doing in my room?" She backs against the wall. "Why is everyone so late? The concert was *years* ago...."

My mom begins to sob. My mom. Here. Right now. I can touch her. She must be hurt, though. Some kind of head trauma. I race out of the room, heading for the phone in the front hall.

Heart pounding, I pick up the receiver, and my fingers are numb as they press the numbers 9-1-1.

The call disconnects. "I wouldn't do that if I were you," a voice says.

I scream. Then I recognize the voice. "Sina!" I yell. "This isn't the time to fool with me. My mother is alive!"

I hear Sina's voice again. "She's not. She looks alive, but she's definitely not."

"Where are you?" I shout into the darkness.

"Over here," she says calmly.

I see a fuzzy shape crouched halfway up the wall. A shadow darker than the shadows around it.

"I don't understand." My words come out as a whine.

"If I want, I can be a boo hag," she says. "I can slip my skin whenever I want. Tonight I decided I wanted to watch y'all at the fancy ball. Then I saw someone come out the window and run hell-bent for leather. 'Who could that be?' I said to myself. 'Why, self,' I said, 'that appears to be Miss Dorothy Lee's one and only granddaughter and the future of the Magnolia League. Now, what on earth is she doing running away from her big old soiree?' So I followed you here, and I can't say it hasn't been interesting."

"It's *not* interesting, okay? My mom is really hurt! She needs help."

"Your mother is dead."

"But I just *saw* her."

"You saw her spirit. Looks like your grandmother got between Louisa and her second burial, managed to trap her spirit somehow. She's dead, but she can't leave. No spirit could get out of that room. Not with those walls. We use haint blue to keep spirits out— looks like your grandmother uses it to do the opposite. Your grandmama may be mean, but she is smart."

"What's wrong with my mom?" I ask Sina. "She's acting crazy."

"That's death. It messes you all up. You don't have any sense of time. She thinks she's your age again—and she's terrified."

"Sina, can you help me?"

"What are you offering?"

"I don't know." I feel frantic. I look at my watch. I have to meet Thaddeus in forty minutes. "What do you want?"

"I want something simple," Sina replies. "I want an

end to this bargain between the Magnolias and the Buzzards. I got other agendas. The problem is that only my daddy, Doc Buzzard, has the power to stand against your grandmama, and he would never do that."

"So what do you want me to do?"

"You're the next in line for the mantle—your grandmother is grooming you to be next in command. Once you have it, you can shut down the League for good. So I'll make you a deal: You cozy up to your grandmother and take over the League as soon as possible. I'll learn how to free your mother."

"How long will it take for you to figure it out?"

"Could be weeks, could be months. No more than a year. Maybe two. I'll need to do some studying, some learning, some prying. In the meantime, I need you to burrow into the Magnolia League like a tick. And when the time comes, I'll send your mother to her second burial, and you'll take apart this League."

"How do I know you'll hold up *your* end?"

"Here," she says, and a little purple bag, the size of my thumb, drops to the floor. "I made this out of the goofer dirt you brought me. Pin this to your mama's shirt. It'll bring her a little bit of comfort and let her get some rest."

I pick it up warily and go upstairs. Inside the room, my mom cowers in the corner.

"Mom, it's okay." I rush to her side and put my hand on her shoulder. Her skin feels doughy.

"Get away!" she screams. My body hits the wall with a slap.

"Mom, quit it! *Please!*"

She growls like a dog.

Then I remember the book from the historical society. *Okay, what the hell. I can try it.*

"John the Conqueror," I whisper.

> *"John the Conqueror,*
> *John the Conqueror."*

I keep murmuring the words, moving slowly toward her. She watches me but doesn't scream this time. It's like talking to a wild animal.

> *"John the Conqueror,*
> *John the Conqueror."*

I get about a foot away, then leap on her. My mom screams and scratches at me, but I wrestle her down and pin the mojo on her sleeve. She pushes me away again. This time, my head hits the corner of the bed. It hurts so much that I see a white flash.

"Mom..."

The last thing I see is her lying on the bed.

I open my eyes after what feels like a few days, but when I look at my mom's silver watch, I see that only half an hour has passed. I'm supposed to meet Thaddeus in six minutes! My mom is asleep on the bed, the mojo pinned to her sleeve. She finally looks peaceful, the way I remember her, and I know in my heart that I won't be meeting Thaddeus anytime soon.

I creep back downstairs. "Sina?"

"She sleeping?" Sina's voice comes from my right. I look over—she's taken her normal form again. But she doesn't look sixteen anymore. Her face is as weathered as an old boat shoe.

"You've got a deal," I say.

"If you promise, then I need a blood shake. Hold still." She leans forward and cuts a small slice in my wrist with a knife.

"Ow!"

Sina hisses at me, and then I feel her hot breath on my wrist as she takes the blood into a vial. "Go back on this bargain," she says, "and you'll hurt in ways you never thought possible."

"I'm not walking away, Sina," I say. "I'm here until this is finished."

There's silence.

"Sina?"

She's gone. I don't hear anyone in the house. I go upstairs and carefully place the watch and the pearls back in my mother's dresser. Then I slip out of the room. I have to get back to the ball. I put on my dress again— it still looks okay. My hair is mussed, but I can pass that off as the result of a night of partying. I wrap a piece of silk around the oozing cut on my wrist, slide my feet into my old flip-flops, and run downstairs.

Out on the street, I look toward Forsyth Park. Thaddeus is certainly already there, waiting for me. I could go and explain but, really, what am I going to say to him? I can't betray him twice in one night and still expect him to forgive me.

"I love you, Thaddeus," I say out loud. It's true too. I really do. But he can't hear me and, besides, I've made my choice. I love my mother more.

~~✒~~

"I love you," Sybil says, hugging Hayes.

"I love you too," Hayes says, hugging her grandmother back. Sybil had pulled Hayes into an upstairs powder room, and Hayes had a sneaking suspicion that she was about to be given the keys to a boat, or maybe the beach house. Except her dad wasn't there, and he was always there whenever money was being spent. So what was it?

"I am so proud of you tonight," Sybil says. "And that's why it is so hard to talk to you about this matter, but you need to know. Honey, your friend Alex has crossed you."

"Grandmother, it was my idea to walk the stairs like that," Hayes says.

Sybil reaches out her hand and cups her granddaughter's cheek. Such a trusting girl, always sticking up for her friends. The kind of girl who always winds up in trouble.

"Sweetness, this isn't about walking the stairs. Have you ever told Alex about the troubles with Madison last year?"

"Of course."

"We all know that Madison didn't mean anything by it; she was just a silly little girl making poor choices. But Alex has put a love spell on your brother. And not just one, but *two*. He could die, Hayes."

"Alex wouldn't do that," Hayes says. "She knows what happened the last time. She knows how dangerous it is."

"You know I worry, and I keep track of your things," Sybil says. "Thaddeus has been missing socks recently, and last week he was missing a shirt. I wasn't going to kick up a fuss, but then I found this under his mattress." She pulls out a piece of brown paper. On it, unmistakably in Alex's handwriting, is Alex's name written five times over Thaddeus's name. "You know what that is," Sybil says.

"But they're breaking up. He tried to break up with her...."

"Maybe that's what you thought," Sybil says. "But her hold on him is strong."

Just then Hayes's phone buzzes. She fishes it out of her clutch and sees the missed call from Thaddeus. She listens to the voice mail: *"Hayes, I don't want to leave things like this with you, but Alex and I have to get out of Savannah. We need to clear our heads, and we can't do it here. I can't tell Mom, because she'll be angry, so will you? I hate to ask you, but if I talk to her, she'll just try to stop me. I'll e-mail when I can. I know you, H, and I know you're going to blame yourself, but there's nothing you could have done. By the time you get this message, we'll already be gone. I love you."*

The message ends. Hayes plays it again, and then she looks up at her grandmother. "Why would she do this?" Hayes asks.

"I don't know, sweetness," Sybil says. "But I do know that Dorothy Lee's granddaughter is not your friend. She may act like it, but she's playing a dangerous game with your brother. I know these things can be confusing, but there is one thing you can always trust, and that's family. You hold on to your family and you'll always know which way is up."

Sybil takes her granddaughter in her arms as Hayes begins to cry.

"I hate her," Hayes says. "How could she do this?"

"Some people just aren't right," Sybil says, smoothing Hayes's hair. "Some people think they can push and push, and they don't ever expect other people to push back."

"If that's what Alex thinks," Hayes says, her tears starting to dry, "she's going to be surprised. Because I'll push back. I'll push back hard."

The ball is still in full swing when I get back.

"Where were you?" Madison demands. If I'm not mistaken, she almost seems a little suspicious.

"I took a walk. Have you seen my grandmother?"

"Um, is Orang-Anna wearing your MiuMius?"

"I gave 'em to her," I say, spotting my grandmother and making a beeline for her before my nerves fail. She is sitting on a fainting couch and talking with someone I was introduced to in the receiving line but whose name I can't remember.

"Miss Lee," I interrupt.

My grandmother looks up at me coldly. "Alexandria," she says.

"I'm sorry for the way I acted before," I say. "I'm a teenager. We're flighty and irrational."

"I see. Excuse me," she says to her companion. Then she stands up and walks toward the bar.

I follow her. "I'm ready to do this," I tell her. And it pours out of me in a rush. "I'm tired of fighting you. I'm tired of complaining about Savannah and threatening to leave. I'm not like my mother. I'm not going anywhere."

Out of the corner of my eye, I see Madison and Dexter trailing us. Hayes is coming from the other direction.

"You're a young lady now," she says. "A Magnolia debutante. The time for being 'a teenager' is over. You're expected to be a woman of quality and character. I don't think you can do that. I'm sorry, Alexandria, but you are right in one respect: You're not like your mother at all. She had iron in her spine. You're merely unhappy. She had character; you have whims. She believed in something. You're just selfish."

She asks for a vodka on the rocks. My grandmother believes that brown liquor is for men and lesbians.

"I know." I want to argue with her. I want to prove her wrong, but there's too much at stake, and so I swallow my pride. "I know. But I'm different now."

"No," she says, sipping her vodka. "You're not different. You're just wanting something. And even if you think you are serious, as soon as the wind changes direction, you'll decide you want something else and off you'll go. No, Alexandria. You've taught me not to put much stock in what you say, because tomorrow you're liable to be singing a different tune."

I didn't come this far to let it end here. But how do I prove myself to her? And then I have an idea.

I turn to where Hayes is pretending not to eavesdrop. As I walk toward her, I unfasten the Fear Not to Walk Over Evil.

"You're too smart to stay in Savannah all your life,"

I say, and I hang the chain around her neck. I thought I would feel panic when I lost my only protection, but suddenly I feel calm. I feel right. "Your brother told me about this awesome summer program at Oxford. You should do it. You're free now."

Hayes just stares at me with hard eyes. Of course she's confused. She knows what this means.

I turn back to my grandmother, who is looking at me the way she might gaze at a particularly difficult crossword puzzle.

"I know I missed the first dance," I say. "But I'd hate to let all that practice go to waste."

We stare at each other for a moment, and an understanding blooms between us.

My grandmother turns to Dr. Jonathan Bailey. "Johnny, is Owen near? I want him to meet my granddaughter. She's got a bright future with the Magnolias ahead of her."

My stomach flip-flops as Owen shuffles out from behind his parents. He's a big, shambling blond who wears too much Axe body spray. The MGs call him SlOwen.

"Take her out for a spin," his dad says with a laugh, clapping his grinning son on the shoulder.

"Shall we?" I say, and I offer him my arm. SlOwen licks his lips, and we walk out onto the dance floor.

"Moon River" is playing, and as we begin to waltz, I see everyone watching me. My grandmother is bragging about me to the Baileys. Madison and Dexter are walking onto the dance floor to provide me with some protective cover, because I'm a pretty terrible dancer—although not as bad as SlOwen. Hayes is staring at me, probably still moved by what I did. But now she's turning toward the door.

Out of the corner of my eye, I see Thaddeus push his way past the guests, his tuxedo rumpled, a backpack over his shoulder. He stops when he sees me, and his face is cold and hard.

I want to run over and tell him I'm sorry, that it's all a lie. *I love you, Thaddeus. Seriously.* But I can't—not if I want to free my mother. And by the look on his face, I can tell it's too late.

"I'm sorry," SlOwen mumbles as he steps on my toes for the third time.

So am I.

Across the floor, Hayes is trying to talk to Thaddeus, but he's already walking out the door and out of my life.

"Moon River" is over now. It fades seamlessly into a truly stellar version of "That Old Black Magic." SlOwen's hanging on tighter now—his grip is so tight that it's hard for me to breathe. All I want to do is curl up in a ball and cry. Instead, I draw my shoulders back like a lady and smile sweetly at my grandmother. She beams proudly, knowing nothing of the storm that's brewing.

Hang on, Mom—I'll get you out of there. I promise.

The White Glove War has begun.

EXCERPTS FROM

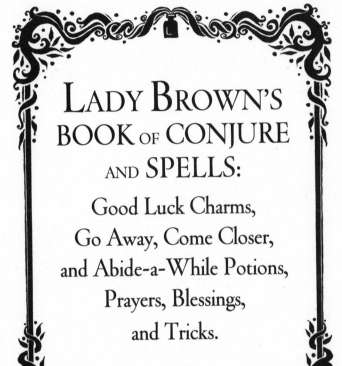

LADY BROWN'S
BOOK OF CONJURE
AND SPELLS:

Good Luck Charms,
Go Away, Come Closer,
and Abide-a-While Potions,
Prayers, Blessings,
and Tricks.

CONJURE UP A NEW LOVE

To find yourself a new love, you must be clean and pure. Cleanse yourself, avoid alcohol and tobacco for three days, avoid eating meats or sweets for the same period of time. Wear only white, red, or pink clothes, including underclothes. Avoid the colors black, blue, and brown. Make sure one piece of your clothing stays the same for all days of this ritual.

On a night with a waxing moon, place six pins in three white candles, and six pins in three red candles. Burn them down; then bury the wax leavings in the dirt by any fruit-bearing tree. Go inside and sleep.

For the next four nights, come out and stand on the spot where you buried the wax, and recite Psalm 111:4, six times each night.

On the sixth night, dig up the wax and melt it down over a burning white candle. When the wax is like water, pour in six drops of honey and six drops of salted wine. Place in the wax six apple seeds and six rose petals.

Cut a square from the clothes you have been wearing for the six days, and wrap the wax in the square. Make sure its neck is tightly sealed. Place it in your hand, and walk around the hole where you buried the wax six times while saying Psalm 111:4.

When that's all done, sleep with the conjure bag underneath your pillow, and carry it with you for six days and nights. Then bury it again. At the end of this time, you will find a new love. When you grow weary of the new love, dig up the gris-gris bag and burn it quickly, and your new love will grow a wandering eye.

DRIVE-AWAY HEX

A distracting type of woman comes between your heart and the heart of your lover. The only way to deal with this type of aggravating person is with foot-track magic.

Find this person's footsteps, and take the dirt from one of them with a spoon. Wrap up a button from her clothes in a bag with your spit and your blood wiped on it. On Wednesday, bury that bag on the north side of her house for two nights. Every night before bed, say the following prayer:

> *I put stones in your crossway.*
> *I put stones in your yard.*
> *Stones go down on Wednesday.*
> *Now your track is barred.*

Dig back up that gris–gris bag, and find where your enemy will walk. Over that place you will lay down a trick. Take a piece of chalk and draw your cross-marks on that path. The exact pattern of your cross-marks will have come to you in a dream: a pattern of X marks or wavy lines, or a circle or series of small circles. Place the button and scatter the foot-track dirt all over the cross-marks to activate them. When your enemy walks over those cross-marks, she will soon wander from your lover and he will come back to you.

To avoid foot-track hexes crossing your path, put black pepper in your shoes.

COME WITH ME, BOY

Your lover sometimes will not stay happy with you but will become discontent and disheartened. To make your lover's heart stay true, you must have one of his socks or a shirt— some piece of clothing full up of his sweat. It can be old sweat or new sweat, but it must smell of his skin.

Then take a piece of white paper and cut it into a circle. Using a red pencil, write the name of your lover nine times; turn the paper ninety degrees and cross his name with your name written nine times over it. When you do this, imagine your lover at home, sitting next to you, and happy and content.

Fold the paper nine times, and then place this paper underneath your lover's bed.

After nine days, take back the paper and wrap it in the sweat-soaked clothing of your lover. Burn this. Place the ashes underneath your own bed for one night. Then burn them again and scatter them. After twenty-seven days, there should be some result. If there is no result, repeat the ritual as needed. If your lover still does not return to you, consult the spell "Conjure Up a New Love."

MONEY BLESSING TO RETURN HUNDREDFOLD

Take a dollar bill and write this blessing on it: *Call down money, Moses. Blessings to you and your family.*

Go out into the world and hide these dollar bills. No one should see you do this. Leave the bills in newspapers. Leave them near the milk in the supermarket. Leave them in the tax forms at the post office. Do not watch your dollars. Every bill that is found will return wealth to you one hundred times.

DRAWING MONEY UP OUT OF THE WELL

Place three shiny dimes in a saucer of your bathwater. Each dime should have a leap-year date on it. Place the saucer in the moonlight on the night of a full moon. When you first awake the next morning, drink the water from the saucer. Then tie up the dimes in a piece of green cloth, and wear it in your right shoe. That day money will come to you threefold.

BRINGING MONEY IN THROUGH THE DOOR

Bury nine ten-penny nails and nine straight pins under your front door. They will capture money coming in and will trap it inside your house. Work this trick on Friday for best results.

MONEY, STAY WITH ME

For this spell to work, you must trap a piece of a no-good spirit in your wallet. Find the grave of the most miserly, no-good sonofabitch you know, and at midnight on a full-moon night, spoon up a pocketful of dirt from over the person's heart. This is goofer dirt, and to keep it happy and to keep its power full charged, you need to close it up in a jar and feed it sugared rum and drops of turpentine. Put a chicken neck in the jar with the dirt, too, to make the spirit fat and happy.

After three days, take the dirt out of the jar and rub it on your wallet while reciting Psalm 119:17–24. Then say, "Listen, *(name of buried person)*. You were a miserly, selfish, poor-hearted soul when you were alive. And now that you're dead, you're going to do your work for me. This here wallet is your home, and as long as I feed you, you best keep it full, or I'll pour you out in the yard and not spare you another drop of rum."

Catch the goofer dirt and put it back in the jar. Every night, make sure you keep your wallet near the jar of goofer dirt. Once a week, on Friday, take out the spoon you used to pick up the goofer dirt. With that spoon, put three spoonfuls of rum and three spoonfuls of sugar into the jar. As long as you feed the goofer dirt and keep it near your wallet, you will hold on to your money.

BANK VAULT OPENER

This is to relax the tight hold of a bank on your money and to direct it to you. Use this conjure when asking for a loan or an extension on mortgage payments. This should only be used once per year, and it will not work on any bank built on the south side of the nearest street. Also, it will not work on a bank with more than three pine trees built up on its land. This conjure can be performed only by those who were born under the sign Cancer or Aquarius.

One Sunday night, when the moon is either full or waxing, put on a piece of orange clothing and walk around the bank counterclockwise seven times while holding an orange candle. Don't light your candle yet.

Find someone who worked at a bank who has died, and burn the candle on the person's grave that same night. Ask him in your own words for his guidance and his hard work to assist you in whatever working you need from the bank. Take off the piece of orange clothing and, using the candle flame, light it on fire. Leave the ashes and the candle and go home. When you go to the bank to ask for help, the spirit will smooth the way and make your tasks go easy for you.

ACKNOWLEDGMENTS

I would like to thank my editor, Elizabeth Bewley, and my agent, Rob McQuilkin, for creating this possibility. Elizabeth, you are seriously brilliant. I look forward to seeing you accept your directing Oscar someday.

Thanks to Grady Hendrix for collaborating with me on this novel.

Many thanks to Phoebe's wonderful grandparents—especially Mom and Rhoda. I could never have finished this without your help. We love you all very much.

Thanks to Peter, who hates being thanked.

I would like to recognize the Penn Center in South Carolina as an invaluable resource on the fascinating Gullah culture of the Sea Islands. Much appreciation also to the ladies of Savannah who took me to tea and told me their stories.

Finally, a big thank-you to Camp Nebagamon for Boys in the north woods of Wisconsin—a wonderful place to spend the summer, and an unexpectedly fantastic place to write.